CRAZY LITTLE THING
CALLED LOVE

Tom Bromley was born in 1972 and
grew up in York. He currently lives in London,
where he works as a copywriter for a publishing house.
Crazy Little Thing Called Love is his first novel.

TOM BROMLEY

CRAZY LITTLE THING CALLED LOVE

PAN BOOKS

First published 2002 by Pan Books
an imprint of Pan Macmillan Ltd
Pan Macmillan, 20 New Wharf Road, London N1 9RR
Basingstoke and Oxford
Associated companies throughout the world
www.panmacmillan.com

ISBN 0 330 48985 2

Copyright © Tom Bromley 2002

1 3 5 7 9 8 6 4 2

A CIP catalogue record for this book is available from
the British Library.

Typeset by SetSystems Ltd, Saffron Walden, Essex
Printed and bound in Great Britain by
Mackays of Chatham plc, Chatham, Kent

FOR JOANNA

Acknowledgements

I would like to thank my mother, my father, Simon Trewin, Mari Evans, Imogen Taylor, Nicholas Royle, John Ramster, Kris Kenway, Cathy Hume, Jon Sanwell, Phil Tinline, Aoi Matsushima, Andrew Gordon, Tamsyn Berryman, Tracy Reed and Elizabeth Bromley.

You don't have to act like a great big star
You can be a hero, be who you are . . .

'Just Say No', Grange Hill Cast

1

It all started in late November 1991, the day Freddie Mercury died. It was the day I met Rich Young. It was the day my parents set off on their second honeymoon.

Honeymoon's an understatement. My parents were leaving on a six-month round-the-world trip, taking in the sights from Halkidiki to Honolulu, Palm Springs to the Pacific islands. Actually, the intricacies of their itinerary remained a mystery, for when my father started explaining where they were going, my mind was lost in the mesmeric beauty of the word 'going'. My parents were *going*. Far away. For a long period of time. When I'd first considered taking a year out before university, the prospect of living at home had been a negative rather than a plus. Now, though, my year off was most definitely *on*.

On the way back from driving my parents to Gatwick airport, I was so happy I hardly noticed that the car radio was playing nothing but Queen songs. 'Bohemian Rhapsody' followed by 'Bicycle Race' followed by 'Flash' followed by 'We Are The Champions'. Must be Freddie's birthday I decided, and sang merrily along all the way back to Brighton. It was only when I arrived at Melanie's party that I discovered what had happened.

'Have you heard the news?' Melanie asked when she answered the door. 'About Freddie?' Melanie was as short and curvy as I was tall and thin, her hair as blonde and curly as mine was black, straight and greasy. Mel and I were mates from sixth form, the only ones from our circle of friends who were taking a year out before university. We were both working at Bright Ones, a supposed centre of excellence for foreign students wishing to brush up their English. The school promised qualified teachers, which was true, though not in the way the brochure implied. The only way I'd found their training course intensive was in relation to my bank balance.

'Freddie who?' I asked, cheerfully unaware. 'Freddie Starr? Freddy Krueger?'

Then Melanie burst into tears.

It was not, it would have to be said, the first time I had so spectacularly said the wrong thing. It took a lot to beat telling Stephen Mitchell that Tanya Williams' new boyfriend snorted like a pig during sex, only to discover that Stephen Mitchell *was* Tanya Williams' new boyfriend. My bad timing was about as legendary amongst friends as my punctuality at parties. As I followed Melanie into her empty house, I wondered if I would ever learn that eight on an invite meant nine, nine-thirtyish, and certainly not before.

'It's awful isn't it?' Melanie sniffled into my armpit. We'd come to a halt in her kitchen, three large bowls of punch in front of us on the table. The punch was so strong, it was giving off an alcoholic haze, like the fumes you get at petrol stations on summer days.

'It certainly makes you think,' I said.

And it did. I was shocked, stunned that all my teenage years I'd never known the truth about Freddie. All those years of playing guitar on a tennis racket to 'Tie Your Mother Down'. Those times of over-doing the operatic bits to 'Bohemian Rhapsody'. One of my earliest memories was seeing Queen on *Top of the Pops*, their freaky video with all the hands coming up through the floorboards. Indeed, for most of my formative teenage years, I'd had a poster of Freddie Mercury above my bed, one of him standing proud in his trademark white singlet. What Melanie was telling me now, what had never even crossed my mind: well, it was going to take a while to sink in.

'It changes the way you look at the world,' I said, and felt Melanie nod against my chest in agreement. She hugged me tighter, and despite everything, I couldn't help feeling a twinge of excitement at the warmth of her body. Melanie wasn't unattractive, and this was the closest I'd got to her in all the years I'd known her. Typical that it took such a huge shock to bring us so close.

'It makes me feel so stupid,' I said. 'All this time, and I never knew.'

'Hey,' Melanie looked up at me with teary eyes, stroked my face. 'It's all right, Will.'

And then she leaned up and kissed me on the cheek. I felt my face igniting with colour. I thought of the countless occasions in film and television and soap operas when bad news led to good, distress to desire. Could this be happening to me? And as we held each other's gaze, for that split second it felt that anything could have happened.

'You're taking this badly, aren't you, Will?' Melanie asked.

I nodded. 'I certainly am. I mean, can you believe it? Freddie Mercury was gay.'

There was a pause, as I felt Melanie's entire body stiffen.

'You *are* joking, right? You didn't *realise*?' Melanie pulled her head back, barked in disbelief. 'No, I'm sorry, Will. Not even you are that stupid. Why do think he had that moustache?'

Oh my God. I had the most horrible thought. Did everyone know he was gay apart from me?

'The moustache was a seventies thing, right?' I laughed, just a little nervously. 'I mean, they're hardly the most fashionable band ever. Look at Brian May and his poodle perm.'

'Why did you think they were called Queen?'

I blanched. Oh God, oh God, oh God. Everyone *did* know.

'I thought they were patriotic.'

Even as I said it, I couldn't believe how ridiculous it sounded. I felt so *foolish*. It was like the time that Stephen Mitchell told me in front of the whole class that no, Will, oral sex was nothing to do with having dirty conversations on the telephone. It was like that time at junior school, when Musical Youth's 'Pass the Dutchie' was at number one. For weeks everyone kept asking me what a dutchie was, and I'd say, 'It's a kind of saucepan. I saw them tell Simon Groom on *Blue Peter*.' It was only after years of being called 'Saucepan' that someone let me in on the joke. Dutchie is apparently slang for joint.

Melanie, meanwhile, was smiling for the first time all day. 'Oh, *Will*. What about his clothes then? The leotards? The feather boas? That video where he dressed up in drag?'

'OK. So it *sounds* obvious when you put it like that, but I still don't think it was that clear cut. Why did he sing all those songs about women? What about "Fat Bottomed Girls"?'

The doorbell went, as did any semblance of a chance of a possibility of a snog.

'*Bottoms*, Will,' Melanie sighed, and went to answer it.

*

Welcome to the not-quite-so-wonderful world of Will Harding. A world of womanising homosexuals and passing saucepans on the left-hand side. A world where freebase is the command for the bass player to strut his stuff. A world where women are more than welcome, but less than likely to hang around. I wish it didn't matter as much as it does, but it does. It does.

It's not easy being nineteen. Not when you've been legally allowed to have as much sex as you like for three empty, miserable single years. They could raise the age of consent to forty for all I cared. I still wouldn't be able to get myself arrested. I *am* dealing with it, though; I've downgraded my expectations accordingly. I'm working to a ten-year action plan – a kiss by 1993, with tongues phased in over the following twelve months, a fondle by 1995 with a handjob to be fully implemented before the end of the millennium.

What worries me is that this is meant to be my sexual peak. Girls don't know how lucky they are, having until their mid thirties to sort themselves out. I'm there already, though you'd never know it. And the really depressing thing is it's all downhill from here. I'm really not sure what it is about me. If I did, then I guess I wouldn't be moaning about it. I'm not the best-looking guy in the world, but neither am I the ugliest. I'm not the funniest guy in the world, but neither am I the freakiest. I'm what you'd call a nice bloke, plain and simple. And I guess that when it comes to women, nice blokes just come last. Or in my case, not at all.

But sex is only partly the thing. What I *really* want is to fall in love. I want to be head over heels about somebody, someone I could care and share and dare with. I want to find my match, the one who'll spark up my life and set my heart on fire. The inspiration for all those songs and poems and novels and films and plays and lyrics, I want a bit of that. I want to feel *moved* like that. I want to listen to some absolutely cheesy pile of nonsense on the radio but because I'm in love, listen to it as though it's about me and my feelings.

What would my ideal girl be like? Well, I guess she wouldn't be ideal. She'd be a bit like me; a bit of a mess, a bit awkward, a bit weird, but with the sense to laugh about it all, happy to take me as I am. I once read in a magazine that there are four people in the world who are perfectly compatible with you. Well I'm not greedy. Just meeting one of them will do.

Here's my dream. I have a vision of sitting outside, in the summer, in a park, silent save for the rustle of the wind in the trees. And I'm sitting there in the sun, back to back with my girlfriend, both of us reading, mutually leaning on each other. And I can feel the shape of her spine press against mine. And I know if I tilt my head back far enough, I can touch hers, feel the warmth of where the sun has touched her hair. And as I lean back, she does so as well. 'Tell me you love me,' she murmurs. And I do, because I do.

That's how I want to feel. I want to know what love *feels* like. I want to break free from my life, from my parents and my job, I want to forget about work and bills and dues and deadlines, about my downcoming degree in accountancy, and have it all turned upside down by a crazy little thing called love.

*

'The name's Rich. Rich Young.'

The first thing you think when you see Rich Young is just how fucking *good* he looks. Red brocade trousers, a chocolate lurex shirt, his seventies look topped by octagon-lensed sunglasses and more than a hint of cheekbone. He looked great. Compared to my sweaty jeans and 'Cool as Funk' T-shirt, he looked fantastic.

'Will Harding,' I shouted back above the noise of the party. Over the past four hours, Melanie's front room had mutated into some sort of sixth form disco, complete with tinsel hanging from the ceiling, 'Dizzy' by the Wonderstuff blaring out of the stereo, and the stench of bad punch just *everywhere*.

'Yeah,' I added, 'um, nice one.'

Nice one? That's the problem with beautiful people. Their presence reduces the rest of us to a gibbering heap, saying things we didn't mean to say. You can try to affect boredom, chew gum, whatever, but they'll always see through you. Rich was infinitely cool, whereas I looked and sounded like a moron. Before I could make amends, the conversation had moved on.

'Liked the gig,' Rich said. 'The music was sound.'

'Oh right. Thanks.'

Having a band at the party had been Melanie's idea. Not only was Melanie a friend and a fellow teacher, she was also a really good saxophonist. I was a not quite so good bass player, but Mel still managed to persuade a couple of other teachers, a keyboardist and a drummer, to join us. The plan had been to jam a number of jazz funk grooves, which we would have done had the day's events not compelled us to rewrite the set. It was a rush job, but I felt our selection of Queen classics was just the right side of tasteful. 'Bohemian Rhapsody', complete with funky frills and slap bass solo, was poignancy itself.

'You impressed me,' Rich said, 'and that's not an easy thing to do.'

'You want me to introduce you to Melanie?' I asked, trying to work out what he wanted.

Rich laughed a seventies laugh.

'The sax player? Not in my league.'

Mine neither. I was a division down, though. Rich was one above.

'Here, you can have one of my cans.'

Free beer? From a beautiful person? I don't actually like lager, my teenage taste buds having yet to graduate from cider, but I wasn't about to make a fool of myself. I opened the can, which sprayed everywhere.

'You're not a bad musician, Will. For a bass player.'

Musical compliments? Maybe he was after some gear.

'I've no stuff on me, mate. You'd have to ask Mel for that.'

Rich shrugged. 'I don't care about Mel.'

Maybe I *had* managed to pull after all. Looking at Rich, he certainly seemed to have a hell of a lot of dress sense for a heterosexual. No matter. If there was one part of sex I'd mastered, it was putting people off. I adjusted myself, then started to pick my nose.

'So, what do you think about Freddie, then?' I licked my fingertip.

'Awful,' Rich took a step back from where he'd been standing. 'Music's really going to suffer. The charts will feel the effects for years.'

'You reckon?'

'Oh yes. The cash-in compilations. Brian May's solo career. The half-finished songs, cobbled together as Freddie's last . . .'

'Hey there, Rich.'

On either side of Rich appeared two of the most gorgeous girls ever to have graced my life. The girl on his left was wearing more hair than clothes. The girl on his right, who looked as if she could've been in Abba, seemed to be thinking, This guy knows so little about fashion he probably thinks I look as if I could've been in Abba.

'Tasmin, Camilla, this is Phil.'

'Will.'

'Whatever,' said Rich. 'That was him playing bass earlier on.'

Tasmin and Camilla regarded me blankly.

'Did you enjoy it?' I asked.

'Not really,' Camilla answered, after a pause.

'Oh right. So what sort of music are you into?'

'Tech-no. Hard-core tech-no.' She pronounced each syllable as though I was four years old.

'Friends?' I asked, as Tasmin and Camilla disappeared into the kitchen.

'Very good friends. They'd drop everything for me.' Rich took a swig from his can. 'And I mean, *everything*. You got a cigarette, Will?'

'Sorry, I don't smoke.'

'I'll have to have one of my own then. Hold this.' Rich handed me his beer can, started patting his pockets for his fags. 'Talk to me, Will. What do you do?'

'Well, at the moment I'm taking a year out between school and university.'

'Good move,' Rich lit up, flicked the match into the fireplace. 'Want to sample a bit of the action? Try some new shit out?'

'Sort of.'

Not really. It had all been a bit of a balls up. I'd

messed up my A-levels, missed my first choice university by one grade. My parents, against my school's advice, lodged an appeal, and sure enough, the grade got changed. Downwards. I ended up missing my back-up choice too, and had to take the year out to reapply.

Rich took his beer can back. 'So what are you going to read at university?'

'Accountancy. At Keele.'

I don't know why, but when I say that, people always react as if someone has died.

'And at the moment?' Rich tactfully moved the conversation on.

'I'm teaching English at a language school.'

'Now that sounds more like it. What kind of students are you teaching?'

'The usual. French, Spanish, Italians . . .'

'You're a sly one, aren't you? Give them a few extra lessons, eh? Help them with their oral?'

I wished. My students might not understand my English, but they had little problem reading, and rejecting, my body language. *I'm a nineteen-year-old male*, it said. *I'm desperate for a shag. Or a handjob. A fumble, whatever, I'm not fussy you know.* I'd had no dates but my communication skills had improved no end. I now knew the words for 'touch' and 'bargepole' in a variety of European languages.

'So what about you?' I asked Rich. 'What are you up to?'

'I'm a singer,' Rich said. 'I'm getting myself a band together at the moment.'

'Oh right. What sort of stuff?'

'Cool stuff. Sixties sounding, a bit of the Beatles, the Kinks, things like that.' Rich smiled. 'You know Sound City?'

'Can't say I do. When were they around?'

'It's not a *band*. It's the annual industry showcase, where unsigned bands play in front of the music business bigwigs. It's in April next year, in Norwich,' Rich took a drag on his cigarette, 'and I've got a headline slot at one of the major venues.'

'Wow. You're going to be, like, famous.'

'Oh, I'll get a deal from it,' he continued. 'All I need are three half-decent musicians to back me up.'

'Guitar, bass, drums? The classic rock line-up?'

Rich stubbed his fag out, dropped the butt into his can.

'What else? I want a drummer like Keith Moon, someone who can give the kit a good battering, and anyone else who gets in the way. A guitarist who knows the blues, who can lick and riff with the best of them. And I want a bassist, ever reliable, to hold the thing together.'

Ever reliable? That sounded familiar.

'Will, what I'm saying is that from what I've seen tonight, I reckon you'd do. You know your music, and your bass playing is really . . .' Rich chose his compliment carefully '. . . really *solid*. What's more, you've got that extra something any great band needs.'

I had?

'What you've got is something special, something that I could never have, however much I wanted it.'

Me? Special? What could I possibly have that Rich didn't? Gullibility? Naivety? Bad breath?

'Go on,' I said, excited.

'Oh I can't tell you just like that. You might go off and join another band.' Rich flicked his hair. 'You've got to come in with me first.'

'Give me a second to think about it.' I paused. 'All right, I've thought about it.'

What do you say to an offer like that? What do you think you say? I was tempted by the money, by the celebrity, by my own paragraph in the footnotes of rock history. 'Harding', the caption beneath my photo would read. 'Solid'.

But what really swung it for me was the women. Women like Tasmin and Camilla. They'd drop everything for me, Rich had said. *Everything*. Imagine that. In Rich, I saw someone I could look up to, learn from. He had cool. He had charisma. He had sex appeal. He had sex. Maybe he could be my mating mentor. Maybe I could pick up some tips on picking up women. And maybe then, I could finally get to fall in love.

'I'm in,' I held my hand out to shake on the deal. 'Now, what's my special something?'

'Later,' Rich handed me his empty beer can. 'I believe it's your round.'

2

The day Freddie Mercury died was a big one in my life, but the day after was even more important.

It was the day I met Lauren.

I'd agreed to meet Rich at two o'clock in the gardens behind the Royal Pavilion. An off-white, elephantine structure, overloaded with tacky turrets and onion-shaped domes, it symbolised Brighton in the same way that concrete cows did Milton Keynes. I remember reading an article for my General Studies A-level which described architecture as being like 'frozen music'. If that was true, then the Royal Pavilion was the worst sort of cacophony.

With the emphasis on cack.

The gardens themselves weren't so bad, especially if you faced away from the palace. Some of the best trees had been uprooted in the hurricane of four years earlier, but there was still a pleasant, terribly English recipe of formal flower beds, with benches and grassy banks to sit on. The weather was mild for the end of November, and a cross-section of the daytime television audience were taking advantage of it: a smattering of grannies, three students discussing the finer points of *Neighbours*, and two girls with too much make-up on, emphasising the fact that they should have been at school.

Twenty minutes after Rich was meant to be there, a girl walked by. She was tall, gawky and striking looking, with unruly black hair that unravelled halfway down her battered sheepskin jacket. She had a camera bag flung over her shoulder, which made me think she might be a tourist. When she walked round the gardens for a second time, I decided she must be meeting someone, and tried to match her up with the people in the park. The girls? No, she was too old. The grannies? Too young. The students? I smiled. In their dreams.

The girl disappeared round the other side of the gardens, then came back and sat next to me, flinging her bag down on the bench between us.

'I'm guessing that you're Will,' she said with an accent I couldn't quite place. She had pale skin and soft eyes, a silvery shade of blue.

'Yeah,' I said. Wow, I thought. This girl was about as backward in coming forwards as I was forwards in coming backwards. 'And you are?'

'Lauren. Rich's partner.' She pushed her hair back behind her ears, revealing a pair of CND stud earrings.

'Oh,' I said, hiding my disappointment. 'Right. Hi.'

Lauren, I have to say, was not what I had expected Rich's girlfriend to look like. I thought she'd be some size eight model with blonde wire for hair, probably French, possibly petite, certainly perfect looking. Lauren was different. Her build could so easily have made her look clumsy and awkward, yet she had the confidence to carry it off. She was effortlessly fashionable, one of those people who casually fling on a few old clothes and still manage to look fantastic. Bastard. When I casually fling on a few old clothes, I look like I am about to do some painting.

'So you're a photographer,' I said, nodding at her bag.

'You're a sharp one, aren't you? Yeah, I'm doing a course up at the poly. I'm specialising in portrait shots, capturing what people are really like.'

'Right.' It was turning into one of those conversations where everything I said was wrong. 'And what am I like?'

'I'm not sure. You're not how Rich described you.'

'And how was that?'

'Like a trainee accountant.'

Lauren smiled, and I noticed how big her mouth was. By the time I'd worked out she'd said I *didn't* look like a trainee accountant, and perhaps this was meant as a compliment of some sort, the conversation had moved on.

'Will you look at that building,' Lauren glanced round at the Royal Pavilion. 'I can never get over how cool it is.'

'Cool? You like it?'

'Oh yes. It's so over the top. Whoever had it built knew a thing or two about kitsch.'

'George IV.'

'George IV.' Lauren grasped the front of the bench with her hands, leaned forwards. 'Now there's something you don't get often. A man with vision.'

'I don't think so.' At last. I was able to add something to the conversation without sounding stupid. 'If he had, he'd have worked out that the building would attract huge crowds of visitors. King George couldn't stand tourists, see, and it was only when Queen Victoria came to the throne . . .'

'You know,' Lauren yawned, 'for a moment there, I was beginning to like you.'

She liked me?

'Sorry,' I smiled apologetically, 'but when you've been dragged around as many times as I have, these things tend to get stuck in your mind. Were your parents as cruel?'

'You could say that. When I was five, my parents dragged me to England.'

'England?'

'I was born in New Zealand,' Lauren added helpfully.

'Wow. That must've been a bit weird, moving at that age. A new country, a new school . . .'

'Oh I didn't go to school.'

Huh?

Lauren sighed like she'd told this story a thousand times before.

'When I was five,' she explained, 'my dad got a job in Britain. He makes guns, got headhunted by some big arms manufacturer. They were offering him a lot of money, and so we decided to move. Six months later, the stupid bastard . . .' she smiled, '. . . I'm not bitter about this you'll notice, the stupid bastard shacked up with his seventeen-year-old secretary. My mum couldn't face the humiliation of going home, so we stayed on, moving round the country as she had rebound fling after rebound fling. Eventually she gave men up altogether, got into the peace movement. All very symbolic, I think, protesting against those big phallic missiles.'

'And your dad made guns.'

'Exactly. We went on marches and rallies and dem-onstrations, this was when nuclear weapons were big news. In 1981, '82, or whenever it was, the Americans brought Cruise missiles into Britain, and we moved into a tent on Greenham Common. And that's where I grew up . . . oh *there* they are.'

Lauren pointed to Rich arriving at last, mate in tow, swaggering across in a leather jacket. 'They're a good-looking pair, aren't they?' she whispered to me. 'Eminently fuckable.'

'They're not really my type,' I whispered back.

'No?' Lauren laughed. 'You're missing out.'

'Lauren, sorry I'm late.' Rich leaned forward to kiss her, winked at me. 'Will, you're looking rough.'

'I know,' I said. 'Who's your friend?'

'Oh yeah, this is Loz. Loz Green. He's another musician, sings in a band called Frug.'

Loz Green, by the look of him, came from the same gene pool as Rich, though probably from the shallow end. He had flicked-back blond hair and that same smug expression of self-importance.

'Lauren. Bill. Hi.' Loz kissed Lauren, didn't offer to shake my hand. He just pointed at me and nodded. 'Rich's told me all about you. You're the, um . . .'

'Bass player,' I said.

'Bass player. Right,' Loz sniggered. 'You look like lowlife.'

*

Do you believe in love at first sight? Can one really fall so fast and so quickly for someone? Or is it just a comforting childhood fantasy, like Father Christmas, the Easter Bunny, the belief that England really *could* win the World Cup – a fantasy that curls up and dies at the first dose of adult reality.

And if it does exist, is it necessarily the best kind of love? Is it special, more 'real' because the feeling is so spontaneous and so immediate? There must be other loves out there too apart from love at first sight – there has to be, unless God has got it in for blind people. Love at second opinion, for example. Love after getting to know someone. Love after being friends for years and years and then getting pissed at someone's wedding and finally getting it together.

The answers to my questions – for me at least – are yes, yes, I don't think so, England do have some good young players coming through, and yes. I'm not knocking those other types of love – I think there are probably different types for different people – but I can only speak from my beliefs and own experiences, and for me there is only one show in town. I'm a bit of a romantic. A dreamer. And that means love at first sight without giving the others a second glance.

How does it feel? Well it works like this. You don't sit there, and instantly think, Wow! I'm in love. You don't realise straightaway that you are in love. That realisation, that acknowledgement comes days, weeks, perhaps even as much as a month or two later. But when you do realise it, and it seems so blindingly obvious you've been in love for ages, then you try and trace the feelings back, try and work out the first time that you felt like that, try and pinpoint when it all started.

And for me and Lauren, I can trace it back to that first meeting in the park. Quite specifically, and I can still visualise the image with astonishing clarity, it was the moment she grasped the front of the bench with her hands, and leaned forwards. There was something about the way her hair swung down, the way it caught the afternoon sun, that momentarily caught me off guard. And at the time I remember my stomach feeling fleetingly odd, sort of butterflies but different, a feeling I didn't recognise. Now, though, I know different. I know exactly what that feeling is called.

*

Barney O'Blarneys was a newly renovated pub, on the edge of Brighton's renowned North Laine, a ramshackle area where cafés and bars rub noses with second-hand-clothes shops and record stores. It was the cooler end of town, and consequently somewhere I'd always felt slightly out of place. The recession had hit the area hard, like much of Brighton, and for every shop open there seemed to be one shut or with an 'everything must go' sale or with some cowboy inside who was selling 'authentic' clothes or car accessories until the police came and evicted him.

Barney O'Blarneys was 'the next big thing in booze' according to Rich. It was a trial Irish theme pub, that if successful was going to be replicated up and down the country. The place wore its cod nationality on its sleeve.

You could have any colour pint you liked, as long as it was black. The jukebox was jammed with the likes of the Pogues, the Chieftains and the Dubliners. On the walls were a gallery of Gaelic heroes – Yeats, Heaney, Collins, Dana – all taking pride of place in hand-carved frames. Well, except for the picture of Dana, anyway. That was glued to the centre of the dartboard.

'My round,' Rich pulled a twenty out of his pocket. 'Everyone want Guinness?'

'Um,' I said.

'Not sure?' The barman was burly, surly, and sounded suspiciously English for an Irish pub. 'This is the real thing, mate, not the washed-out shite you get in most places.'

'If it's all the same, I think I'll give it a miss.'

'Your loss,' shrugged Rich. 'Three pints of Guinness and a lager, then.'

'Hang on. I, er, don't actually like lager.'

Rich looked confused.

'You drank it last night when I gave you a can.'

I'd drunk a mouthful and a half in total. The rest had been consumed by a nearby potted plant.

'I was, er, being . . .' I tried to think of a word that made me sound rock and roll. I failed. '. . . polite.'

'What do you want then?' Rich asked. 'Bitter? Bourbon?'

'Could I, I have a cider?' My voice sounded small and whiny.

'Cider?' Loz snorted.

'I know.' I was really struggling by now. 'It's a, er, a West Country thing.'

There was a pause, then Lauren said, 'But I thought you grew up in Brighton.'

'Maybe I'll have an orange juice,' I said. 'I'm still feeling a bit dodgy from last night.'

'Ice?' the barman asked sarcastically. 'Lemon?'

'Straw?' Loz added, to sniggers from the others.

We sat down, sitting on a choice collection of former church pews. Everyone lit up apart from me. Lauren smoked Marlboros, Loz Silk Cut, Rich someone else's. The smoke, with its in-built non-smoker homing device, instinctively moved in my direction. Lauren slipped off her jacket, her tight green top bearing the slogan IT'LL ONLY SEEM KINKY THE FIRST TIME. The T-shirt showed off her skinny arms, her big, bony shoulders, and, as I read the slogan, the fact that she wasn't wearing a bra. I noticed Lauren noticing me noticing this. She pulled a face as if to say pur-lease, and blew smoke in my face.

After a couple of minutes the barman brought the drinks over, the Guinness having finally settled. To everyone's amusement, apart from mine, he'd put my orange juice in a cocktail glass, complete with a cherry and paper umbrella.

'I'd get a taste for Guinness if I were you,' Rich said to me. 'Cos we're going to be spending a lot of time here. You see that door over there? That leads to the back room, where we're going to play our first gig.'

'We're going to play here?' I didn't know Barneys put on live music. 'Not the Richmond? The Zap Club?'

'New sound, new venue,' Rich said grandly. Then added, 'That and the fact I'm in with the bloke here. I can get us a bigger cut than at any of those crappy indie venues.'

I wondered if that bigger cut would filter down to the rest of the band.

'But the real beauty about this place,' Rich continued, 'is that it's going to be part of a chain. Get the punters in here, and we've got guaranteed gigs in every major town across the country.'

'And as much Guinness as you can drink,' Loz said.

'Or orange juice,' Lauren added.

Rich pulled on one of Loz's fags, blew out away from me. 'So talk to me about music, Will. What's 1991 going to be remembered for?'

'Well. Um.' Rich's smoke had done a U-turn, and was heading back towards me. 'Bryan Adams I suppose . . .'

His sickly single, 'Everything I Do (Goes On And On For Fucking Ever)', had been number one for sixteen long, painful weeks.

'I was thinking more about rock music,' Rich said.

'Right. Well I think Nirvana are really good . . .'

I'd just bought their new single 'Smells Like Teen Spirit', a song which looked like giving the band their first hit. It rocked, with a riff so simple even I could play it on the guitar. The music press were all over them, reckoned that they and the so-called grunge sound could be the next big thing. The starting point of an era of American dominance.

Especially as British music was comatose. The heady days of Madchester were nothing but a fading memory. The only new scene was the not so much forward as downward-looking 'shoegazing' sound, a movement with a stage act of everyone staring at their feet, a movement with Slough as its insipid and uninspiring capital.

'. . . but overall it hasn't been a great year,' I concluded. 'Since the Stone Roses messed up, there's been nothing doing at all. It's almost as if people are waiting for the next big thing to come along.'

'Exactly,' Rich started pointing his cigarette at me, as if it were a dart and I were the dartboard. 'It's like this, Will. There's this lineage of great British bands, starting with the Beatles and the Stones, going through the Sex Pistols and the Clash to the Smiths and Stone Roses. We're overdue the next link in the chain. Well overdue. Music needs someone to kick-start a scene, like Liverpool in the sixties, Punk in the seventies, Madchester in the eighties. And you know what?' Rich tapped his ash into the ashtray. 'It's just about to go off.'

'It is? Where?'

'Here. In Brighton.'

Brighton? My immediate reaction was, sure! Like anything interesting ever happens in Brighton. I was about to argue the toss, when I had a thought. If anything exciting was going down, who'd be the last person to find out?

'I've just moved down from London,' Loz said. 'There's such a vibe here at the moment. The place, it just *hums*.'

'That'll be the sewage,' I said. 'It's meant to get pumped out to sea, but keeps on floating back in. What did you do before?'

'Music journalism. Used to do freelance stuff for the *Melody Maker, NME* . . .'

'Loz's got contacts coming out of his ears,' Lauren said.

'Whereas you've just got wax,' Rich stubbed his fag out.

'And what about you, Lauren?' I asked.

'I'm going to sort the image out.'

'Starting with yours,' Loz added.

'That and taking photos,' Lauren pushed at Loz playfully. 'I'm going to chronicle the whole thing as it happens. The movers . . .' she looked at Rich. 'The shakers . . .' she looked at Loz.

'The hangers on,' Rich winked at me.

I asked Loz what sort of music he was into.

'I'm into the same kind of stuff as Rich,' Loz said. 'A lot of classic sixties bands. The Beatles, the Kinks, the Small Faces, all that kind of English lyricism. Red telephone boxes, pints of beer, nuns cycling to church on a misty Sunday morning . . .' Loz's eye went similarly misty for a moment. '. . . very sexy, nuns you know.'

'Behave,' Lauren laughed, pushed her hair back.

An English sound in a chain of Irish theme pubs? It didn't seem quite right somehow. But what bothered me more was the age of the musical references.

'Isn't this all a bit retro?' I asked. 'I'm not saying I'm not into that sort of music, I'm a massive fan, but are people going to go for the same sort of stuff that their parents like?'

'Of course they will,' Rich said. 'We're going to have

ourselves two audiences. A young one who won't have heard it all before, and an older audience who'll be reminded of when they were that age. The record companies will love it. As well as a great new movement, there's all those classic albums they'll be able to repackage to a new generation. Even stuff that was too shit to be released the first time around, that can be flogged as anthologies of "rare out-takes" and "exclusive new versions" of favourite songs . . .'

It was very difficult not to be charmed by Rich. He sounded so certain, spoke so confidently that you couldn't but believe what he said. And I desperately wanted some of that charm and swagger to rub off on me. Rich was a person who could make things happen, I was sure of that. *Sure*, I thought to myself. See? It's beginning to happen already. A couple more weeks in his company and I might even start pulling people like his girlfriend.

I had to say, I liked Lauren so much more than I liked Loz. Loz was funny, but mainly at other people's expense, particularly mine. Lauren was sharp, too, though she wasn't so cruel with her words. When she laughed, she was laughing with you, not at you. And she wasn't bad looking either. I'd always had a thing about shoulders and hers were fantastic, an arresting, angular pair of blades about as sharp as her tongue.

'So has the scene got a name?' I asked. 'Have you thought about that?'

'Of course we have,' Rich rolled his eyes. 'First thing we did. That's why we came to Brighton to set this whole thing up.'

'We looked at other towns,' said Loz, 'but couldn't quite get the name right. The Great Rock And Roll Swindon. Rocks-ford. Leicester Sound Design . . .'

'Leicester Sound Design?' I said. 'Hang on, I don't understand that one.'

Loz sighed. 'You see, the initials stand for . . .'

'Loz, that's why we didn't go there, cos you've got to explain the name every time you use it.' Rich shook his head. 'So we thought Brighton and came up with Bright Pop . . .'

'Which almost works, but isn't quite there, somehow. Like it's a couple of letters too long or too short or something.' Loz smiled. 'And then it hit us.'

'What?' I asked.

Rich said, 'It's obvious isn't it? Brighton *Rocks*.'

3

I didn't see Lauren again until a week later, when Rich rang to say he'd found a guitarist. His name was Danny, and he worked in a music shop called Riff Raff. Rich had asked him if he could put an ad up for a guitarist, and the two of them had got talking. One session in the pub later, and Rich's smooth talking had won Danny over.

The next afternoon, after I'd finished my teaching for the day, I popped in to say hello. As I closed the door of Riff Raff behind me, I wished I could do the same with my ears. The shop thudded with the sound of third-rate guitarists playing first-rate songs on second-hand instruments. Like the metaller, mangling 'Smells Like Teen Spirit' and smelling like ... urgh. Or the sad thirty-something, desperately trying to deal with his impending baldness by proving he was still in touch with 'the kids'. The only person I had any sympathy for was the geeky bassist in the Zebedee T-shirt. Bassists have it hard in music shops: they haven't got a back catalogue of riffs to impress with. A decent bassist will therefore use the occasion to show off his knowledge of obscure-sounding jazz scales. Zebedee wasn't a decent bassist and had instead opted for hitting low notes and getting off on the vibrations. Not very musical, but at least he was enjoying himself.

I walked past the electrics, the acoustics, the acoustic electrics and the electric acoustics, and made my way to the till at the back. The bloke behind it had his trainered feet on the desk and was listening to a Walkman. He was young, about eighteen, wore a navy blue Adidas top and had a black *Rubber Soul* haircut. Cool, and yet kind of contrived. The top was too big, the fringe too long, like he hadn't yet grown into either.

Oh yes. And he was painting his nails.

'Hi,' I said, taken aback. 'I'm, er, looking for Danny.'

Painting his nails? I was crap when it came to spotting sexuality but even I could read that one. I was impressed, not like *that*, but because someone this young could be this open. If I was that way inclined, I'd have hidden my nails inside a pair of gloves. The shop assistant acknowledged me with a nod, then finished off polishing his index finger. He pushed the brush into the pot, and picked up a microphone that was lying on the desk.

'Er, yeah, you, the Nirvana fan.' He spoke softly, his voice booming around the shop. 'It's G *sharp*. And keep it down.' He put the microphone down, pulled his headphones off. 'I'm Danny,' he said, screwing the brush back in the bottle. 'You must be Rich's mate. The solid one.'

Solid! I'd rather be solid than a nail painter. I may not have been the world's most happening person, but that didn't get you singled out in the queue at the chip shop. *OI YOU! THE SOLID ONE! OUTSIDE NOW . . .*

'I'm Will,' I said, holding out a hand.

'Later, mate,' said Danny. 'Paint's not dry yet.' He blew across his nails. 'Should try it sometime.'

'I'll pass if it's all the same to you.' I tried to cough in a masculine manner, but something got stuck in my throat, and I ended up spluttering.

'Stick some on,' Danny threw me the jar. 'Changed my life.'

Just what any band needed. A TV evangelist. It'd certainly open up the merchandising opportunities. *You've seen the concert, you've heard the album, now buy the lipstick . . .*

'It's made for people like us,' Danny continued.

Did I send out the wrong signals? No wonder I never scored. Or was it Rich's doing? *'And then there's Will the bassist, a really solid player. You've got a lot in common with him, Danny. He's never had a girlfriend, if you know what I'm saying . . .'*

'So, er, have you been painting your nails for long?'

'Couple of years. I've got the whole range at home, mate. No More Breaks, One Coat Instant Strength. This one's my favourite, though.'

'Hard as Nails,' I read. 'Protects against splitting, chipping and breaking.'

I imagined our debut appearance on *Top Of The Pops*. Danny in lipstick, frilly skirt and push-up bra.

'Nothing worse than a broken nail,' said Danny. 'I can't play half as quick when I'm using a plectrum.'

I pictured him pouting, blowing kisses at the camera.

'Tell me about *your* strumming,' said Danny. 'Do you use something? Or can you get by with just your fingers?'

This was too much. If we were going to work together, this was going to have to be sorted out from the start.

'You want to know how I strum?' I said loudly. 'I'll tell you, shall I, Danny? I get a magazine, maybe a copy of *Playboy* or something, slap it open on the centrefold. Look at a great-looking woman, one who's just that second walked out the shower or is riding a horse naked or has accidentally spilt ice cream over her chest. Then I pull down my trousers, whip it out, give it fifteen to the dozen . . .'

I became aware of a silence in the room. I turned round and saw everyone staring at me.

'Mate,' Danny said quietly, clicking the microphone off. 'Think we're talking about different sorts of strumming.'

The metaller, in shock, hit the chord he'd been searching for. Then he blinked, and tried to work out what he'd just played.

*

Danny made some tea and we sat down to talk about music. I liked him. He was soft spoken and quietly unassuming, the sort of person who got where they did by dint of hard work. His thick fringe hid his eyes, which I reckoned suited him just fine. It helped him keep himself to himself. I reckoned he'd swap my company for a guitar any day, though I didn't think it was personal.

'So have you played in bands before?' I asked.

'Nope.' Danny was holding a hand exerciser, squeezing it to strengthen his guitar playing muscles.

'Really?' I took a sip of tea, put it down on the counter. 'So you've never played live?'

'Well. Did some classical concerts from the age of nine, but that doesn't really count.'

Nine?

'Just some, you know, concertos and stuff. With the county schools orchestra. Wasn't a big deal or anything, like.'

Not a big deal? When I was nine, all I could play was the descant recorder. Badly.

'Are your family fairly musical, then?'

'My mum was.'

'Was? Is she . . .'

'Yeah,' Danny squeezed the exerciser a little harder. 'A couple of years ago.'

I didn't know what to say. I said 'Oh,' which didn't come out as sympathetic as I'd intended. I added, 'Sorry,' which sounded equally unfeeling.

Danny nodded. To me, to himself, you couldn't tell with that fringe. 'What about your family, Will?'

'Oh, very musical. My mother, she sings regularly at national events . . .'

'Land Of Hope And Glory' at the Conservative Party conference.

'. . . and my father, he's a bit of an expert when it comes to hi-fis.'

Turning them down, turning them off, snipping the wires with a pair of scissors . . .

'It was their idea for you to, like, play the bass?'

'That was my father. He bought me one for my thirteenth birthday.'

I'd actually asked for a normal guitar, but that was my parents for you. *We looked at the electric guitars, William, but this one was better value. It's that little bit longer, so your money goes that little bit further.*

'How about you?' I asked. 'Why the guitar?'

'Mum was a folk singer,' Danny switched the exerciser to his other hand. 'Didn't have any hits or anything, but I think she was quite influential. Everyone knew her.'

'You'll have to play me some of her stuff.'

'Yeah. Maybe.' Danny put his exerciser down, picked up his mug of tea. 'She was cool my mum, not like a normal folkie. Used to get wild, dead drunk cos she was nervous of performing. Read this interview about her once, in this back issue of *Melody Maker*. Wouldn't believe some of the stuff she got up to.' Danny's voice had an edge of excitement to it. 'She used to hang around with lots of rock people, the really smart ones.'

'Your mum was in *Melody Maker*? She hung around with rock stars?' Wow. My mum did many things but hang around with famous rock stars she did not. The closest she got was writing letters to the *Daily Telegraph*, suggesting that rock stars should be hung.

*

Wakka. Wakka wakka wakka wakka wah wah. Wakka wakka wakka wakka wah wah. Wakka wakka wah wah wakka wakka wah wah, wah wakka wah wakka wakka wah wah. Wakka wakka wah wah wakka wakka wah wah, wah wakka wah wakka wakka wah *wow*.

On paper, Danny's idea for a riff doesn't amount to much. With Riff Raff now closed, allowing Danny to meticulously wire up every available amplifier, it steam-rollered you into submission.

'Cool,' I said, of his red-hot riff. 'Can I join in?'

I picked up a bass guitar, a Fender Jazz I could forget about ever owning, and attempted to play along. Danny was fantastic, caressing and stroking his Strat, teasing the notes out in a way that made me look like the amateur I really was.

'Keeping it simple. Smart,' said Danny.

The less I played, I figured, the less I'd get shown up.

Twenty minutes later, Danny nipped out back for a smoke. I sat there, trying to work out what key Danny had been playing in, when there was a knock on the door.

'We're not open,' I shouted.

'Men never are,' said a familiar female silhouette. 'It's me.'

'Oh right. Hang on.'

I got up, and wrestled with the out-of-date door lock.

'Today would be good,' the silhouette continued. 'I just love standing on this corner, looking like I'm soliciting.'

'You wouldn't round here,' I twisted the lock to no avail. 'You'd have to be round the back of the station for people to think that.'

'Oh really? Down there a lot are you?'

'Yes. I mean no. Oh *come* on.' I was flustered twice over. 'Why is this so stiff?'

'All that talk about stations.'

Lauren was still laughing when the lock finally relented. She was wearing a thick navy blue polo neck, one that covered all but the tips of her fingers. I followed these fingers as they pushed her dishevelled hair back behind her ears. Kind of messy looking, kind of sexy.

'Are you going to let me in then?' Her smile caught the shop light.

'Yeah. Sorry.' I stepped aside, and let her past. 'Look. About the station,' I struggled to shut the archaic door lock. 'The only time I ever go there is when I've got to pick someone up.'

'You said.' Lauren strode down the shop, smirking. 'So where's thingy then, the guitarist?'

I leaned on a guitar, trying to act casual. 'Danny's out the back.' The guitar hit the floor with a thump.

'And Rich?'

'Oh he's late as usual.'

'Saving the best until last, eh?' Lauren slung her camera bag on to the till, stared round at all the guitars. 'I've got to say, Will, as a woman, the atmosphere in here is highly intimidating. I mean, look at all these penis substitutes.'

Penis substitutes? And why did my face go red when Lauren mentioned the word 'penis'?

'I can see now why there's so few female guitarists,' Lauren gave a guitar a playful pluck. 'All that masturbation must give men *such* a head start.'

'That's not true. If it was . . .'

I stopped before I came across as a total wanker.

'Of course,' Lauren smiled, 'the other band members aren't much better. The singer with his microphone, you don't get much more phallic than that. Then there's the drummer, with his endlessly monotonous banging. A very male interpretation of sex.'

'And the bass guitar?'

'The bass guitar is the same as the guitar but bigger. I think the inference from that is fairly clear . . .'

Maybe there *was* something in this Freud stuff after all. All I had to do was find myself a psychology student, then casually mention with a nod and a wink which instrument I played.

'. . . the inference being that the larger musical instrument compensates for a smaller anatomical one.'

Psychology students, they're not really my type. Them and the rest of the fucking world.

'You must be Lauren,' said Danny, reappearing. 'Hi. I've just been out back having a fag.'

'Let me guess.' I could do this Freudian psychobabble too. 'He's been reliving the sucking of his mother's nipples.'

'Hi.' Lauren pulled a puzzled face at Danny. 'He's a bit weird, your friend.'

'I know,' said Danny. 'You should have heard what he was coming out with earlier. Brought the whole shop to a standstill as he described how he . . .'

'Let's play your riff, eh, Danny?' I changed the subject. 'We should get on, if you don't mind, Lauren.'

'Oh don't let me stop you,' said Lauren, unzipping her camera bag. 'You won't even know I'm here. You boys just carry on with whatever it is you boys do.' She winked at me. 'I think I've got some tissues somewhere.'

1

I first realised something might be going on on Christmas Eve. I was balanced on a table in The Queen and Country at the time, as I always was on the night before Christmas. Melanie was next to me, dancing in a drunken sort of way. I was bent double, trying not to bang my head on the ceiling. The pub was within struggling-home distance of my house, and mixed original Edwardian architecture with a fake mock-Tudor extension. The walls groaned with authentic artefacts, lesse olde than they purported to be. Like many of the underage customers.

Every Christmas, the landlord hired a bloke called Donald, who possessed thick glasses, lambchop sideburns and dressed like a member of Showaddywaddy. He'd plug in a PA, hand out song sheets, and proceed to guide the worse-for-wear through a tacky list of festive favourites. Tunes like 'Frosty The Snowman', 'Rocking Around The Christmas Tree', 'When Santa Got Stuck Up The Chimney (We Had To Smoke Him Out)'.

' "Fairytale of New York",' I said, as the Pogues gave way to Sir Cliff, whining on about mistletoe and wine, 'that's got to be the best Christmas record ever. The music. The words.'

'Speaking of which,' said Melanie, groping around by her feet for her bottle of Diamond White, 'aren't you writing them for your band?'

'I am, yeah. Rich seemed to think I'd be brilliant at it.'

'And how did he figure that out?'

'It's all to do with my empathy and understanding.'

That was how Rich had sold it to me. I suspected the delegation of hard work had something to do with it as well . . .

*

'It's to do with knowing your subject,' he'd explained. 'The songs that really *connect* with large chunks of the population, they're all about insecurity, fears and worries, about not being sure what you want from life. Do you know 'Pet Sounds' by the Beach Boys?'

'The Beach Boys? I thought they were all about good vibrations.'

'Bad vibrations too. You don't balloon like Brian Wilson did if everything's hunky-dory.' Rich laughed. 'Chunky-dory more like. Anyway, that album is stuffed with self-doubt – "Caroline No", "I Know There's An Answer", "I Just Wasn't Made For These Times . . ."'

So that's why we're doing all this retro stuff.

'If you're sure of what you want,' I asked, 'why don't you write the words yourself?'

'Exactly that. Because I'm sure. I've got far too much going on to write about being insecure. The words would come out all false. They've got to come from someone like you, Will, someone who knows what it is like to feel unwanted, rejected, insignificant, small . . .'

Rich had come up with a blueprint, a list of lyrical requirements for me to follow.

Will, The image I'm trying to aim for is one of youthfulness and Englishness. I want new listeners to link our music to classic bands like the Beatles, and Beatles fans to link their music to ours. I want a strong sense of identity, a specifically English identity, via a careful use of cultural references (see attached list).

Teenagers (together with twenty- and thirty-somethings yet to grow up) respond strongly to vulnerability, believing they are not the only sad, pathetic, inconsequential suckers around (which is where you come in!). Also, skirt always succumb to men being a bit sensitive, and this should be exploited to the full.

One of each of the following song types should do the trick.

1. Song berating the old for not understanding the youth of today (sung ironically, against a backdrop of Beatles riffs).

2. Song about the joys of getting pissed, taking drugs, or both.

3. Song about the morning after getting pissed, taking drugs, or both.

4. Song about how school, work, whatever is a load of crap and how your teacher, manager, whatever figure of authority just doesn't understand.

5. Song about a foxy female figure of authority (e.g. traffic warden, lollipop lady).

6. Song about how it's great to be single.

7. Song about how you wish you weren't single.

8. Song about London (good for international market).

9. Song about something popular and working class (e.g. football, *Coronation Street*, etc.).

10. Song about wanting to get laid.

Rich had attached a list of cultural references, supposing I got stuck.

GOOD 'UNS:

Double-decker buses, black cabs, beer, nuns, the White Cliffs of Dover, pigeons, sparrows, bank holidays, the shipping forecast, *Bill and Ben*, *Bagpuss*, The Marvellous Mechanical Mouse Organ, DLT, *Dixon Of Dock Green*, *The Sweeney*, *Monty Python*, *Carry On*, Terry Thomas, Twiggy, Spaghetti Junction, Watford Gap, Henry VIII, Ethelred the Unready, Gotcha!, Freddie Starr Ate My Hamster, *Get Carter*, Little & Large, Harold Wilson, Christine Keeler, Cecil Parkinson, Enid Blyton, Quentin Blake, Lewis Carroll, Ringo Starr, the dole, the Arsenal, cricket, darts, snooker (especially on the radio), Peckham Rye, Didcot Parkway, Milton Keynes, Newport Pagnell, Bonfire Night, the Blitz, Dunkirk Spirit, Spotted Dick, Lancashire Hotpot, a nice cup of tea . . .

Some of the songs came together like clockwork. Our anthem, 'My Generation' type number, 'Our Tune', started with Danny playing the opening bars of the music used for Simon Bates's legendary radio feature, before his distorted guitar gave way to a fake letter to Simes, from a teenager who had fallen out of love with modern Britain.

Dear Simon Bates, we're not feeling too great
That's the reason that we're writing this letter
Cos when you play our tune, then we are over the moon
And we know that things can only get better . . .

I was equally pleased with 'Lisa The Lollipop Lady', my tale about a saucy seductress in Milton Keynes, who people were always happy to pull over for.

Cross over the road my friend
Cos Lisa's passion hath no end
And later when the cars have stopped
She'll make your lolly pop!

The problem song was the meaningful one. It should have been the easiest, really, I had enough experience of being alone to make your average hermit look like some sort of networking natural. Danny, I thought, had written a lovely tune. All I had to do was write some words about being lonely. I had plenty of notes, about thirty pages of jottings and ideas but I was becoming increasingly frustrated by my lack of focus.

That and nothing to rhyme with inadequate.

*

'So what Rich was looking for,' Melanie continued, 'was somebody who's an insecure bag of nerves with low self-esteem and no girlfriend.'

'A unique insight into the darker reaches of the human soul. That's how I like to see it.'

'Yeah, yeah. So do you think you can write about insecurity and uncertainty?'

'I'm not sure.'

'Oh, Band Aid! Ace!' Mel wobbled about excitedly, causing the table to do the same as 'Do They Know It's Christmas?' kicked in.

For a song about famine, 'Do They Know It's Christmas?' had turned into something of a crowd pleaser over the years. Any guilt about having a good time had long since gone. A world outside there may well be, but down at The Queen and Country we had the curtains closed and were cheerfully raising our glasses and singing, merrily passing round mince pies without a second thought. But that's the way that charity records go. If they're remembered at all, it's as the festive filler between 'A Spaceman Came Travelling' and 'Stop The Cavalry'.

Would our band ever be up there, raising funds for the one-legged pygmies of Outer Mongolia? I could see Rich now, posing with a pair of headphones pressed to one ear, Danny trading licks with John Squire and Johnny Marr, my presence only required for the terrace chant chorus, sharing a turned-down microphone with Chesney Hawkes.

They may be small, but they must be saved,
They've got their one and only foot in the grave . . .

Melanie looked at her watch. 'Nearly Christmas. What do you hope Santa has brought you?'

'Mel, I don't know how to tell you this, but Father Christmas doesn't actually exist.'

'*No?*' Melanie mocked surprise. 'Seriously, though, supposing he did exist, what would you like him to bring you, more than anything else in the world?'

I'd always known what I'd wanted when I was little. Stephen Mitchell would tell me. *I think Santa should bring you a BMX this year, Saucepan.* As a teenager, what I wanted simply wasn't an issue. Despite dressing in red, Santa was something of a true blue, each year leaving me a volume of Winston Churchill's *Collected Works*. I was currently up to volume six, and having checked at my local bookshop, knew exactly what my Christmas present was going to be for the next seventeen years.

'I bet I know what it is,' Mel said. 'It's a record contract, isn't it?'

'No. What I really, really want is . . .'

And then I realised. What I wanted, as ever, was a girlfriend. But what I wanted was something more specific than that. I wanted a girlfriend who was sharp and funny, someone who was, well, a bit like Lauren. Someone who was tall and sexy, someone who was, yes, someone who was a bit like Lauren. And as I thought about this bit-like-Lauren person waiting for me when I got home, lying on the sofa, feet in the air, helping herself to my father's secret supply of spirits, I felt ever so slightly wobbly. It could have been because I was standing precariously on a dodgy table. But somehow I didn't think so. It felt more like butterflies. Yet different.

'Well?' Melanie asked. 'What do you want for Christmas?'

'. . . another pint,' I lied, as the bell rang for last orders. 'That and a packet of dry roasted peanuts.'

*

Lauren was waiting for me when I got home, lying on the sofa in a white, army-style shirt, feet in the air, helping herself to my father's secret supply of spirits.

'Hi, Will,' she said. 'Happy Christmas.'

'Hang on,' I said. 'How did you get in?'

'Easy. I followed Father Christmas down the chimney.'

'But, but our chimney's blocked up.'

Lauren laughed.

'I'm joking, stupid. You invited me to stay. Or are you too pissed to remember?'

'Oh. Right.'

'I decorated the house while you were out,' Lauren waved a hand in the air to indicate. 'Do you like it?'

I *thought* there was something different about the place. I'd hardly bothered with the festive decorations, there only being me staying in the house. Lauren, though, had harboured different ideas. What had once been drab was now a mass of multicoloured fairy lights and Christmas trees and tinsel and mistletoe. Even the portrait of Winston Churchill above the fireplace had gained a Father Christmas hat and beard.

'I hope that comes off,' I said.

'You're a saucy one.'

'No, oops, no, I didn't mean your bra.' Bra? Why did

I say bra? 'I meant the . . .' I found myself staring at Lauren's chest. She wasn't wearing a bra.

'It feels more natural,' Lauren said. 'And it'll save time later.'

'Later?'

'It's OK, Will, I know you're a virgin. I didn't want to spoil the moment by waiting while you figure out which way round the fastener goes.'

'Hey, er, right, er, what?'

What was going on?

'I'm your Christmas present, Will,' Lauren took another sip of spirit. 'You can unwrap me whenever you're ready.'

'But what about Rich? I thought you were going out with him.'

'Oh, forget Rich.' Lauren hurled her glass into the fireplace. Her eyes were blazing, either with passion or alcohol or both. 'It's you I want Will. And I think you want me too.' She stood up, a little unsteady from the booze. 'Come next door, Will, I've done some more decorating.'

She kissed me on the cheek, took my hand, and guided me through into what used to be my kitchen, but now seemed to be the studio for the teatime TV word quiz, *Countdown*.

'Hey,' I said. 'Where's my kitchen gone?'

'I knew you'd like it,' Lauren said. 'Hey, I want you to come and meet Richard.'

Richard Whiteley, the host, stood in front of the set, waiting to greet us. He was wearing his customary bright green blazer, with a black, lacey bra over the top.

'Is that your bra, Lauren?' I asked.

Richard chuckled wanly, held his hands up in a 'guilty!' pose.

'I'll give it back,' he said feeling his chest. 'It just feels so, so . . . comfortable.'

'Come on,' Lauren whispered in my ear, dragging me round to my seat. 'I bet you're the repressed sort who likes being beaten . . .'

We sat in the contestants' seats, either side of the famous *Countdown* clock. Lauren had a name tag on her desk that read 'Lauren'. I had one that said 'sad, pathetic, inconsequential sucker'.

'And cue Richard!' shouted a voice from the back of the set.

'. . . And welcome back to *Countdown*,' Richard winked at the camera. 'Let's get straight on and meet tonight's contestants. We've got a fantastic pair for you this evening . . . but I'll get on to Lauren's breasts in a moment!'

'In your dreams,' said Lauren.

'I thought this was Will's dream,' said Richard.

'So *that's* where I am,' I said.

'Of course you are,' said Lauren. 'Do you think I'd fancy you in real life?'

'Let's start with a letters game,' Richard said. 'Will, do you want to go first?'

I heard a crack of a whip, and turned round to see Carol Vordemann dressed in a PVC catsuit and brandishing a whip.

'Hello, Will,' she said, cracking her whip again. 'What do you want me to give you?'

'Er,' I thought hard, 'er . . . a consonant, please.'

'D,' said Carol, placing a letter on the board.

'And a vowel.'

'U'

'And a consonant.'

'T'

'And another consonant.'

'C'

'And another.'

'H'

'And a vowel.'

'I'

'And another.'

'E'

'And a couple of consonants.'

The *Countdown* clock ticked down its thirty seconds, hitting its unmistakeable tune.

Ba da da. Ba da da. Ba da! Ba da! Ba da da da. Boo!

'OK, Will, let's start with you.' Richard said. 'How many have you got?'

'I've got seven,' I said.

'Really?' said Lauren. 'I heard you've only got four.'

'What's your seven?' Richard asked.

'Dutchie.'

'Dutchie?' Richard looked puzzled.

'It's a West Indian sort of saucepan,' I explained. 'I saw them tell Simon Groom on *Blue Peter*.'

'It's not in my Oxford English,' said the man in dictionary corner. 'All I have here is, "slang for joint".'

Lauren, I suddenly noticed, was perching on the edge of my desk.

'Is it just me,' she asked, unbuttoning her shirt, 'or is it really hot in here?'

'It's the television lights,' I said.

'Are you sure that's all?' Lauren asked, leaning forward. In the background a phone started to ring.

'Shouldn't we answer that?' I said, as Lauren started to explore my left ear with her tongue.

'I'll get it,' said Richard, lifting a receiver up. 'Hello?' The ringing continued.

'It must be your phone,' said Richard.

'That's OK,' I said, as Lauren continued to fondle me. 'I've got an answerphone.'

Sure enough the ringing stopped and my voice boomed out. *'Hi, you're through to Will Harding. I'm sorry I can't come to the phone right now but please leave a message after the tone . . .'*

Bip. Bip. Bip. Beeep.

'WILLIAM! WILLIAM!'

I froze. A bolt of reality ripped through my dream. Lauren looked up.

'Oh God. That's my mother,' I said.

Typical. Just as I'm about to get laid, the old battleaxe has to butt in.

'William! William! I know you're there!'

'Maybe some other time,' Lauren said, fading away as I came round, discovering I'd never made it to bed, having crashed out in the hallway after returning from the pub.

'William Enoch Churchill Harding! Come to the telephone this instant!'

My mother, most unfortunately, was not part of any dream.

'Hello,' I said, fumbling for the telephone, picking up the receiver and dropping it. 'Er, er, Happy Christmas, Mother.'

'*William! William! Is that you?*' Even from the other side of the world, my mother's voice still split my head in two. '*What on earth are you doing in bed? You'll miss church if you don't get a move on.*'

I tried to focus on the hall clocks. Clocks? I'm sure we only used to have one.

'Mother, it's five-thirty. You've got the time difference wrong.'

'*Five-thirty in the afternoon? Why are you still in bed? Are you ill?*'

'It's five-thirty in the *morning*.'

'*Nevermind*,' my mother said by way of an apology. '*I expect you'll be getting up soon anyway. Now listen . . .*'

By now the hall had gained a fourth clock. My mother said that Aunt Sylvia had promised to cook Christmas lunch for me and blathered on about what time I was meant to turn up and what I was to wear and what I mustn't forget to mention and . . . ugh. In desperation I started to bang the receiver against the table.

'*William, William what's that noise?*'

'There must be interference on the line.' I hummed, whistled tunelessly, then held the phone at arm's length and gargled my best Donald Duck impression. 'Can you hear me?'

'*William! William! You've gone all faint. Typical state-run*

49

*foreign telephone systems, if only they'd had the guiding hand
of the privatised sector then they'd . . .'*

'Mother, are you still there? Hello? Hello?'

I put the phone down, and then disconnected it. I'm
going to bed, I thought. I staggered to the bottom of the
stairs, then paused and went to check the sitting room,
on the off chance.

Lauren, alas, wasn't there.

5

Sometimes when people get drunk, they reveal their real selves. And sometimes they become gibbering gibbons, either telling everyone they're their besht mate, or getting all unhappy and bursting into tears. Or maybe the gibbering *is* the revealing of the true self, the human race showing off its true colours by dividing neatly between the needy and the depressed. I didn't know where that left me, I was probably a bit of both, and I didn't know where it left my thoughts about Lauren on Christmas Eve. Was that the cider doing the talking, or was it me?

I didn't see Lauren again until New Year's Eve. It was about twenty-five to twelve, and I was wandering down the seafront, heading for the pier and midnight with Mel and friends, when I spotted her. Lauren was alone, leaning on the railings looking out to sea, wrapped up warm in a long purple coat with fake fur trimmings. She was clasping the front of her coat in her left fist, and leaning forwards ever so slightly, just enough that I couldn't but notice the sleek arc of her back.

'Lauren? Is that you?'

'Will? Oh hi. *Hi.*' Lauren looked surprised to see me, then slowly her smile broadened.

'Are, er, you all right?' I suddenly had the strangest feeling I was intruding. It was New Year, after all, and if someone as cool as Lauren was on her own, then she was probably on her own for a reason. 'Look, I didn't mean to interrupt or anything, if you're, like, wanting to be alone or something . . .'

'God, do I look that miserable?' Lauren turned round to look at me, and her face caught the light. Her skin looked pale, her cheeks looked cold. 'No, no, I'm fine. Really. How are you?'

'Will,' I heard Mel's voice above the noise of New Year and the sea. 'Are you coming or what?' She was standing on her own, pointing at the rest of my friends who were moving on.

'I'll catch you up in a sec,' I shouted back, and watched her go.

'Don't let me stop you,' Lauren said.

'It's fine,' I said. 'I know exactly where they're going. We've been going there every year since I was thirteen.' I looked at her and felt myself smiling. 'And anyway I haven't seen you for ages.'

'A week and a half,' Lauren replied.

'Really?' Is that all? I thought. It felt a lot longer. 'So what are you doing on your own on New Year's Eve? Why don't you come and join us?'

Lauren smiled. 'That's very sweet of you, Will. No, I like to be alone at this time of year. I prefer to think about the past year on my own. Work out what my plans for the next one are.'

'Right.' My plans on New Year's Eve were somewhat less philosophical. More alcoholical. 'And how's the, er, planning?'

'Oh, you know. *Planned.*' Lauren smiled mysteriously. Whatever she was thinking, she wasn't going to let on to me. 'And how about you? Have you made any resolutions?'

'Yes, I . . .' I stopped myself. My usual resolution was to give up being single. To get myself a girlfriend. I'd been making it for as long as I could remember, but I didn't want to tell Lauren that. It sounded a bit, well, it sounded a bit soft.

'. . . I, er, I'm going to stop biting my nails.'

Lauren looked at me, and put her hand to her mouth to suppress fits of giggles.

'What?'

'*Stop biting your nails?* You're a man who knows how to think big, eh, Will? Come on,' she squeezed my arm, 'live a little. Aim a bit higher.'

'Like what?' I thought hard. 'Stop biting my nails *and* stop picking my nose?'

Lauren looked at me. 'You know, I can never quite tell when you're being funny, and when you're being serious.'

Easy mistake to make, I thought. I'm funny when I'm trying to be serious, and serious when I'm trying to be funny. Lauren looked at her watch.

'Ten to midnight already. I'm going down to the beach. Do you want to come, or are you going to catch your friends up?'

'I really should be getting back,' I said.

'Phew,' Lauren sighed. 'For a moment I thought I was going to be stuck with you.'

'Oh,' I said, deflated.

'Joke,' said Lauren.

'Oh right,' I said. 'I don't think I can tell when you're being funny or serious either.'

'That's because I'm both,' Lauren smiled.

*

It's difficult to explain what happened next. The more I've thought about it, the more I've decided that my behaviour that night isn't something you can put a reason to, not something you can rationalise. Because sometimes life is about instinct, and while you can describe how such emotions feel – giddy, exciting, shit scary, stomach churning – you can't actually put into words the reasons behind them. Sometimes things are the right thing to do (or the wrong thing to do) because they just *are*.

Here's what happened. I'd walked for about fifty metres towards the pier when I stopped and turned round. Fuck it, I thought, I don't want to be with my friends. I want to be with Lauren. And even though I'd been looking forward to New Year for ages, to getting pissed, having a laugh, seeing friends I hadn't seen for ages, right then, I couldn't have cared less. It was ten to midnight, and there was only one place I wanted to be, and that was down on the beach.

I'm not normally a spontaneous person at all, rather the opposite. And maybe if I'd stopped to think about the situation I wouldn't have gone. But that is my point.

I didn't stop to think because there was nothing to think about. There was just that strange feeling in my stomach again, butterflies but different, and I knew instinctively what I wanted to do.

It wasn't a romantic gesture, not consciously at least. I fancied Lauren, sure, I'd worked that much out by now, but I hadn't twigged I was in love with her. I just wanted to *be* with her. The thought of anything else didn't cross my mind, because the chances of anything else, like Lauren, were slim.

And this wasn't a fate thing. I don't think it was *meant to be* or anything tacky like that. You're either a cock-up or a conspiracy person in life, and I'm on the cock-up side – a coincidence and chance person through and through. The fact that Lauren had been staring out to sea that night, the fact that she'd been staring at that particular point, the fact that I'd seen her, the odds against that happening must have been of Loch Ness monster proportions. Fate has to be the opposite of that, surely. If something is so obviously going to happen, the odds would be terrible. Otherwise, what's to stop God cleaning up down the celestial branch of William Hill?

What was I thinking as I ran along the promenade? I was thinking, You're bloody mad. You'll never find her. I was thinking, Why the fuck am I doing this? I was thinking, Running on five pints of cider and an empty stomach is a very bad idea. I was thinking, You know what'll happen? You'll end up missing Lauren, then run back to the pier, and end up missing midnight as well.

But then I saw her, a flash of hair, as she disappeared

on to the beach below me. It was enough. I knew it was Lauren. And I felt myself smiling, pathetically grateful at my good fortune, thankful I hadn't been looking the other way at that instant. I paused to catch my breath, then lunged on to catch up with her.

*

It's kind of strange, down on the beach at night. I guess it's the contrast: so dark out to sea, and so bright the other way, looking back into town. Likewise the noise, the hum of the town, the shushing of the waves. As we crunched along the stones, away from the crowds, I felt ever so slightly excited, touched that Lauren was happy to break her no-person New Year by spending time with me. She seemed different to the other times I'd met her. She was gentler tonight, somehow, though I couldn't tell you why.

Without warning, Lauren suddenly took off, and ran full belt towards the sea. 'Come *on*, Will!' she yelled, as I stood there for a second and watched her, watched her hair in full flight. As unpredictable as I was predictable. I ran after her, playing catch up once again.

'Feels great, yeah?' Lauren asked as I puffed up to her. 'That shot of cold air in your lungs?'

' . . .' I wheezed.

'Are you any good at skimming stones?' Lauren asked. I shook my head.

'Oh, you must be. You've lived by the sea your entire life.'

Lauren crouched down, started inspecting the beach

for suitable stones. She stood up, holding two flat pebbles.

'Ladies first,' she said, skimming a majestic eight.

'Bugger,' I replied, managing a pathetic couple of bounces.

'Typical man. Can't manage it more than twice.' Lauren pushed a strand of hair behind her ear. 'Will, can I suggest a New Year's resolution for you?'

'It was the *stone*,' I said. 'The shape wasn't right at all.'

'No, not that.'

'What then?'

'I think you should forget about not biting your nails and resolve to do something adventurous. You know, like travel somewhere exciting.'

'Like where?'

'Anywhere. Somewhere exotic. Where would you like to go?'

I thought about this. I wasn't what you'd call a good traveller. I wouldn't want to go anyplace that required lots of injections. Or somewhere with insects. Or rats. I explained all this to Lauren. Then I asked, 'Where does that leave?'

'Bognor Regis.' Lauren punched my arm. 'No, there's still lots of place you could visit. America. Japan. Australia . . .'

'New Zealand,' I said.

'Or New Zealand.'

'What's it like?' I asked. 'You never really talk about it.'

'Beautiful,' Lauren bent down, scoured the beach for more stones. I crouched down beside her.

'Do you miss it?' I asked.

Lauren nodded. 'Yeah, yeah I do.' She paused. 'You know, it's funny, but leaving New Zealand is one of my earliest memories. I think it was because we were going on a plane that I remember it so well. I was really excited about travelling by plane. But all I can remember of New Zealand is what I saw from the window. The mountains, the lakes, it all looked so far away.' She turned away from me, stared out to sea. 'We left on New Year's Eve, you know. I guess that's why I always spend the day alone. I'm never really in the mood for parties.'

There was a silence, save for the gentle splash of the waves.

'I don't know what to say,' I said.

'There's nothing to say,' said Lauren. 'I'm a bit sad, that's all. I'll be fine in a while.'

I wanted to touch her. I really felt the urge to put an arm round her and comfort her. But I felt myself stiff and English and desperate not to intrude or impose. So we just crouched there.

'Have you ever moved house?' Lauren asked.

'No,' I replied, 'though I did change bedrooms when I was seven. My father wanted to use my old one for a study.'

Another silence. In the background, a drunken shriek rang out.

Lauren looked across at me.

'Are you OK?' she looked concerned.

'Er, can we stand up soon? My legs are killing me.'

Lauren stared at me for a second, then reached out and pushed me over. As I fell backwards, she started to laugh.

'You prat,' she said, standing over me. 'Why didn't you say anything?'

'Oh, you know. You looked thoughtful. I didn't want to interrupt.'

Lauren smiled, and shook her head slowly as I got up.

'I've got it,' she said. 'Your resolution. I think you should fall in love.'

She skimmed another stone. Seven. I replied. One.

'How can falling in love be a resolution?' I asked. 'Resolutions are all about stopping bad habits.'

'Maybe not being in love is a bad habit.'

Maybe it is, I thought. But I can't say I knew what the alternative was like.

'Even if it is a bad habit, I still say that falling in love isn't really a resolution,' I said eventually. 'It's not something you can do anything about.'

'What if it is, and you're just not doing anything about it? What if you have to make it happen, rather than waiting for it to come to you?'

'And how would I do that?'

'Ah,' Lauren smiled. 'Now that would be telling.'

In the background I could hear lots of cheering. I glanced at my watch. Midnight.

'Well,' I said. 'Happy New Year.'

'Happy New Year, Will.'

I paused, just long enough to be awkward. Should I

hug her? Should I kiss her? As I was working out just what was the correct etiquette, factoring in how long I had known her and how English I was, Lauren answered the equation by hugging me.

As hugs go, it was a friendly one. She went left arm high, right arm low, rather than a lover's embrace of both arms around the neck or waist. It was friendly, and also generous. Lauren hugged tight and long, so much so that I felt she was hugging as much for herself as for me. So I held her back, trying not to notice that her fake fur collar was itching my nose something rotten. Her back felt warm against the palms of my hands, and as I gave it a little rub, I could feel the shape, and the strength of her shoulder blades.

I pulled back slowly, when I thought my nose could take it no longer. Lauren was smiling at me.

'Well?' She asked. 'Do I get a New Year's kiss, or what?'

'Er, yeah. Right.'

A kiss? I'd just about got through the hug without making an arse of myself, but now Lauren wanted more. I'd never been in with the 'in-group' at school, the ones who greeted each other in that ever-so-exclusive 'mwah, mwah' way of theirs. I was more of an anti-social than a social kisser. A drunken slobber on the cheek was normally about as good as I got – the sort of kiss your gran gives you, except without the lipstick. I felt my palms go ever so slightly sticky at the prospect, and prayed I wasn't leaving a pair of sweaty handprints on her coat.

I didn't mean to go for the lips. I was heading for the left cheek, trying to remember if it was left before right, or right before left, when at the last moment Lauren tilted her head. Oh my God, I thought. Just fucking peck her and get out. But as our mouths met, I froze. Our lips were hardly touching, just grazing really, but what I couldn't get over was her breath. It smelt sweet, it reminded me of oranges, and I could feel its warmth gently push its way into my mouth.

And then I kissed her. I think it was partly the nerves, but I found myself pressing hard against her mouth, and really felt the softness of her lips. I half expected her to recoil from the kiss, but she didn't. She kind of kissed back.

All of this couldn't have taken more than a couple of seconds, though somehow it felt like ages and at yet the same time, no time at all. What it felt like was a kiss beyond the bounds of social necessity. Couldn't have been much in it – maybe as little as a tenth or a hundredth of a second, but it was enough. I'd kissed that fraction longer than I should have done.

I stood back. Lauren was staring at me. I could feel my face fizzing red, and was glad it was dark rather than daylight. Shit, I thought. I've overstepped the mark.

'God, I'm sorry,' I said, feeling my various nervous tics coming out to play. 'Look, I've been drinking. My breath probably smelled disgusting.'

Lauren shook her head. 'No, no that was, um . . .'

Then she smiled, put two fingers to her lips and pointed at my face.

'What?' I asked.

'You,' Lauren pulled my hand away from my mouth. 'You biting your nails so soon into the new year. I reckon you should ring Norris McWhirter up, get yourself into the *Guinness Book of Records*. And then, seeing as you've blown your own resolution so spectacularly, I guess you're going to have to take up my suggestion after all . . .'

6

I'd kissed her. Oh my God. I'd got drunk and kissed Lauren, Rich's *girlfriend*. I'd got carried away by alcohol and the occasion and had taken advantage of the situation. How absolutely, utterly, completely and crassly embarrassing. What on earth could I have possibly been thinking of? I'd behaved like some sort of drunken slob. As I hid under the duvet and prayed for 1992 to start again, I cringed at my behaviour.

Lauren, I decided, must hate me. Heck, I know I'd hate me. If I was a good-looking girl and some spotty lamp-post stinking of booze used a New Year's kiss as an opportunity for something more, I'd hate him, too. As I replayed the kiss again and again in my mind, I couldn't think how else Lauren could have interpreted it.

Shit. That was twice in a week that I'd got drunk and my mind had been consumed by Lauren. I was going to have to get a grip. Even if I did fancy Lauren, that was clearly as far as anything was going to go. Firstly, she was going out with Rich. Secondly, there was no way on earth she'd find me attractive. And thirdly, not only did she not fancy me, she probably now thought I was a prick, both a big and a little one at the same time. I could almost hear the conversation that must have occurred between Lauren and Rich . . .

'And then he tried to kiss me, Rich. God, it was awful.'

'I'm sorry Lauren. What can I say? The guy's not used to handling gorgeous chicks. He can't control himself.'

'And his breath too. It was like snogging a cemetery . . .'

I groaned. I was so embarrassed at what I'd done that if I never saw Lauren again, I reckoned it wouldn't be a moment too soon.

*

The next day Rich rang me up to tell me I was going shopping with Lauren.

'No disrespect, mate,' he said in a tone that translated as lots-of-disrespect, mate, 'but when it comes to clothes, some of us have it, and some of us don't. And you don't.'

I looked down at what I was wearing. An unbuttoned red lumberjack shirt. The same 'Cool as Funk' T-shirt I had worn in bed the night before. Cream chinos. A pair of green Converse All Stars, with a hole in the front where my big toe had gone through. He was right. I looked a mess.

'So I want Lauren to go through your wardrobe,' Rich continued. 'And then, when she finds you've got absolutely sod all suitable to wear, she can take you round the shops to find you something half decent.'

For the briefest of seconds I felt my male pride rear up. How dare he say I've got no dress sense? Then I thought, He can say it because it's the truth. I *do* have no dress sense. If I ever had money to spend, it went on records. Clothes buying was closer to some sort of ritual humiliation exercise, a nightmare afternoon that occurred every three months or so when I'd be dragged round with my mother because 'there's no way you're seeing your grandparents dressed like that'. Normally I was so embarrassed by the whole thing that I'd agree to anything just to get out of there as soon as possible.

You might think that with my mother away, things would have been slightly better. But you couldn't have been more wrong.

'Now I did think about leaving you some money, William,' she'd explained the week before she left, 'but I was terribly worried you might go and buy something horrible. So I've planned ahead, and bought you everything you need for the next six months.'

How thoughtful. It was a fashion statement that would have caused a sensation on the catwalk.

'. . . and here comes Will now, modelling the winter and spring collections from the Cynthia Harding collection. Will is wearing a lovely green wax jacket, ideal attire for either the office or the fox hunt. The corduroy collar is a particularly nice touch, going well with his brown corduroy trousers. As Will unzips his jacket, we can see THE fashion accessory for the season, a black waistcoat, which sets off his crisp red and white pinstriped shirt. And look at that daring lack of tie, the buzzword for this look is casual. Underneath, steady girls, Will is sporting a traditional matching set of Marks and Spencer pale blue vest and Y-fronts . . .'

However bad my dress sense was, my mother's was even worse. Man At Eton was not the look that I was keen to follow. But then I remembered she'd kept the receipts, should anything not fit and I had to take it back and swap it for the right size. And as Rich continued talking, I saw a cunning way out of the inevitably humiliating shopping trip with Lauren. I'd return the clothes to Marks and Spencer, then use the money to buy myself something funky. No need for a trip with Lauren. No need to embarrass myself.

At least, that was the plan.

*

The refunds section in Marks and Spencer was well hidden, so well tucked away in fact that I couldn't find it. I searched through menswear, womenswear, kidswear, footwear, dragging my three large carrier bags around, with no luck. And then, finally, I saw it.

Just behind the lingerie section.

Wow, I thought as I wandered through. There were so many bras, more than that dream I'd had about Winona Ryder and Wendy James from Transvision Vamp. Push-up bras to sports bras to sexy bras to training bras. Bras to make your breasts look bigger. Smaller. Firmer. Rounder. Bras that gave you more cleavage, bras that gave you less cleavage, bras that tucked your tits in behind your armpits. Every sort of bra you could possibly think of, and believe me, as a nineteen-year-old male, I'd thought of a few.

There wasn't this choice when you went to buy a pair of boxer shorts. Why were there no push-up pants, or padded Y-fronts for men? Hell, I'd buy a couple of pairs. Men were second-class citizens when it came to underwear, and the women in the shop treated me accordingly. *There's no way he's buying for a girlfriend*, they were thinking. *Look at him. Which right-minded female would go near him? Yup, he's got to be a pervert.* I tried to act all laid back, difficult at the best of times, doubly so when I couldn't shift lingerie from my line of vision.

And then I saw Lauren.

I ducked down behind some sexy stockings, and prayed she hadn't seen me. What the fuck was she doing here? *What do you think she's doing here?* said a voice in my head. *She's buying underwear.* Yes, yes, yes, but why now? What if she saw me? With all my bags of embarrassing clothes? If she told Rich, and Rich told everyone else . . . Oh God. And what would Lauren think? That I was spying on her? I looked across to see what she was buying. Mmmm. *Very* nice. Rich was an extremely lucky man, though he'd deny it of course, dismissing such claims with a wink. *Luck, Will, doesn't come into it* . . .

I saw a fire escape to my right. I could make a run for it, I thought, if she was looking the other way. A little to your left Lauren, I thought. Go on, GO ON, have a look at that display. Yes! Lauren was facing away from the exit, and I had my chance to escape. Go! Go! I tiptoed carefully, no sudden movements now, keeping an eye on Lauren all the time. A couple more seconds, and I'd be there. I double-checked that Lauren wasn't looking and, hello? What's that she's picked up?

Bugger.

'Aiiek!'

I felt my feet go, and grabbed at a mannequin to cushion my fall. A stand of lingerie fell on top of me.

'Will? Is that you?'

Think about the most embarrassing position you could be in with a store mannequin, a mannequin wearing nothing but a matching bra, knickers and stockings set, the perfect present for the one you love, complete with presentation box and chocolate mints. That's kind of where I was, propping myself up on a plastic breast. I stared up at Lauren, gave her my best well-wouldn't-you-know smile.

With a pair of knickers on my head.

'Lauren! Fancy bumping into you!'

'I bet you would,' she smirked. 'Looks like I've been beaten to it.'

I pulled the pants off my head, made to get up.

'Oh don't mind me,' Lauren held a hand up. 'You go ahead. Finish whatever it is you're doing.'

'Wait.' I struggled to my feet, caught up with her looking at some bodies. 'Look, let me explain.'

'Finished already? You don't hang about, do you?'

'It's not what you think . . .'

'Every man's dream. Going out with a model.'

'I'm not! It was an accident.'

'Of *course* it was.' Lauren patted my shoulder. 'You got drunk, one thing led to another and . . .'

'It's not like that.'

'No?' Lauren noticed my carrier bags. 'Been shopping, have we, Will? Let's have a look.'

'NO.' It wasn't the most convincing argument I'd ever come up with in my life, but for want of any better strategy, it'd have to do. 'You can't. Just can't.'

'Oh, come now.' Lauren leaned over. 'Just a peek.'

'Really. I'd rather you *wouldn't.*' I slammed my hand down on top of the bags in a defensive moment as Lauren moved forwards. A receipt popped out. Before I could grab it, Lauren had snatched it away. To my horror, she read it, and smiled.

'Oh, Will,' she said.

'Look,' I said. 'These clothes. I'd never wear them. I'm taking them back.'

'It's all right,' she said. 'Really. You're a typically repressed middle-class, Middle England male. What else are you going to be wearing in private?' She folded the receipt in half and handed it back to me. 'I like the name, by the way.'

Name? I unfolded the receipt. Thank God, I thought. It was the store card slip, rather than the till receipt – my wardrobe of embarrassing clothes wasn't listed. All that was printed was the price, plus my mother's name and signature . . .

'Cynthia Harding.' Lauren looked at me, and nodded. 'Yes, yes. I can see why you chose that name. It rather suits you.'

'Lauren.' I wasn't sure if this was better or worse. 'Look . . .'

'It's OK, I'm not going to tell Rich.' Lauren smiled. 'You can even borrow my lipstick if you're extra nice . . .'

*

Lauren's philosophy for clothes buying was simple. Cut first, colour second. If you get that right, she explained, everything else falls into place.

'Cut?' I asked.

We were stood in a North Laine boutique, where speakers jostled with racks of second-hand clothes: leather and denim and cords and multicoloured shirts. The place was empty, save for a bored-looking shop assistant in goth make-up and purple dye skirt, who'd looked up when we walked in, smiled when Lauren said, 'Hi Sam,' and reached across to turn her Rolling Stones record down from ear-splitting to dead loud. I was three bags of clothes lighter, a couple of hundred pounds richer and ready for my overhaul.

'The cut of the clothes,' Lauren said. 'You know, how they fit, how they hang.'

'Oh right,' I said. 'You mean small, medium or large?'

'Men are simple,' said Lauren. 'But not that simple. You get fat men with thin arms, thin men with fat legs, people big in some places, small in others, never in the right ones. Basically, people come in all shapes and sizes, and rather than fit the nearest approximation, you should search for the garments that fit you best.'

This all sounded a bit like hard work to me. I usually just bought medium and moaned when the sleeves weren't long enough.

'So what would fit me best?' I asked.

'I thought you'd never ask,' Lauren said. 'Let's get you stripped off.'

'Pardon?'

'Come on, Will, I'm not here to mess around. Take your clothes off.'

'Excuse me?'

'Oh don't be so English. I need to have a look at you.' Lauren shook her head at my face, on which must have been a look close to sheer terror. 'Take your coat and jumper off at least.'

I did so, and Lauren stepped back to look at me. Then she came up close.

'May I?'

But before I could say yes, she started stroking my arms, then lifted them up into a crucifix position, started feeling my chest, my sides. I looked round to see if anyone was watching, and thanked God no one was. Lauren's fingers, their nimbleness, their pressure, their sensuousness, it was transfixing. No one had ever touched my body like that before. Please may I not get a hard-on, I prayed. When she reached down and felt my bottom, I yelped and the shop assistant looked up.

'Just relax, Will,' Lauren smiled. 'I'm not trying to feel you up. I'm just working out your physique from underneath your baggy clothes.' She stood up. 'Which is my point exactly. You're a thin guy, but your T-shirt and trousers are so loose, you just end up looking scrawny. What you need are better fitting, tighter clothes, ones that show off your physique.'

'Lack of physique,' I corrected.

'Well, I've never gone for muscle men myself. You've got a nice bum as well, but you'd never know.'

'I have?' I felt myself go red.

'Do you wear boxers or pants?'

'Er, boxers.'

'Buy some pants or briefs or something,' Lauren said,

not remotely fazed by the fact we were talking about my underwear. 'Something to give your buttocks some shape.'

'Um, right. Thanks.'

Buttocks? Shape? I remembered this time at school when I had to do a term of yoga for PE. One lesson the teacher had been showing us some new position, dog with leg up or something, and was explaining how it stretched such and such a muscle, made the buttocks solid. Stephen Mitchell leaned across and sang-whispered 'Solid', a truly terrible hit by Ashford and Simpson, which gave me the giggles. The teacher hauled me up in front of the rest of the class and before I could explain the joke, gave me a lecture about how we shouldn't be embarrassed by our bodily parts.

'You shouldn't be ashamed of your *buttocks*, Will,' she droned. 'Or your *anus*. Or your *penis*.'

'Yes he should,' someone shouted, to giggles from everyone else. 'It's absolutely . . .'

Lauren, meanwhile, was flicking through a clothes rack to my right.

'No, no, no, yes!' She pulled out a pair of purple cords, ever so slightly flared at the bottom. 'What do you think?'

'They're purple.'

'My God, so they are. Do you have an ethical problem with that?'

I shook my head. 'I'd never have chosen something purple myself.'

'It's a strong colour,' Lauren said, 'and with your black hair you can carry it off. Now let's find you a shirt.'

Lauren, you could tell, was completely in her element. She moved between each rack with purpose and with passion, her head bobbing along ever so slightly to the music. By the time she'd finished selecting, I was weighed down by an almighty stack of clothes.

'I'm not sure I can afford all these,' I said.

'Of course you can't. We're going to try them on.' Lauren smiled. 'Are you having fun?'

'Um, yeah. I guess so.'

Was I having fun? I supposed I was. Shopping with my mother had never been like this. She'd have taken one look at the shop, and said something like 'Second-hand? You don't know *where* they've been. We're going to Marks, then we can get something that won't shrink when you wash it.'

I crammed into the cramped changing cubicle behind a psychedelic curtain at the back of the shop.

'Come on,' Lauren said. 'What are you doing in there?'

What I was doing was looking at myself in the mirror. I'd put on the purple cords, together with a tight pink shirt with winged collar. I couldn't get over how I looked. It was surreal, compared to what I normally wore, so different that I couldn't tell whether it was better or worse.

Lauren pulled the curtain back.

'Oh my God,' she held her hand up to her mouth.

'What?' I asked. 'Is it that bad?'

'It's, it's your bum,' Lauren pointed.

'Wh-what about it?' I asked, not sure that I wanted to know the answer.

'You've got one. You've actually got an arse.' Lauren smiled. 'Cute one, too.'

I was speechless. I didn't know what to say.

Lauren prodded the small of my back, pulled my shoulders back.

'Posture. Bloody hell, Will. When you stand up straight you look so much taller. She straightened my collar. 'Do you like the shirt?'

'Well I, er . . .' I wasn't sure. 'Do you?'

'Very much.'

Now I did like the shirt. I felt myself grinning. The female seal of approval, the Lauren seal of approval was all the credibility I craved.

But what was more, my fears about New Year's Eve seemed unfounded. However much I couldn't stop thinking about it, Lauren had forgotten about it. Either she had forgotten forgotten, or she had dismissed it as being unimportant. Either way, I felt pleased, relieved, and more than just a teensy bit thankful. Lauren, I decided, even if it was only a little bit, must like me.

And then two days later she handcuffed me to her bed.

1

The day had started out so well. The band were holding drummer auditions. It had taken a while, but finally the band was going to be complete. We'd taken advantage of Riff Raff being shut on a Sunday, and had arranged auditions all afternoon. Rich had chosen the shortlist of candidates on the basis of their ads stuck up on the 'musicians available' board at the back of the shop, though some drummers were about as accurate in their descriptions as they were with their timekeeping. *A seasoned semi-professional*, contestant number one had claimed. *I have toured extensively throughout Europe and the Far East.* Who with? Johnny Spliff and the Backpackers? I think what gave him away was the fact that he had no idea how to put the drum kit together. From his stressed expression, I reckon he must have had a bad experience with Lego as a child.

'Musical differences,' Rich showed him the way to the door. 'We're musical. And you're different.'

The second drummer was better. Just. We had three instrumentals for him to play, loose jams that Danny and I had been working on. The first was 'Our Tune' or what

Danny had christened 'The *Abbey Road* Rip-off', on account of the fact that my bass line bore more than a passing resemblance to that from the Beatles song 'I Want You (She's So Heavy)'. The drummer played it well, hitting on a groovy kind of beat and shuffling like a card dealer. Less impressive was his offering for our punk rock song, where he hit on a groovy kind of beat and shuffled like a card dealer. As Danny strummed the opening of our ballad, I remember thinking, Surely he can't hit on a groovy kind of beat and shuffle like a card dealer on this one? Of course he couldn't. But it didn't stop him having a damn good go though. Rich smiled, and said we'd be in touch.

'Fuck me! If it isn't Saucepan!'

'Hi, er . . .' Our next auditionee looked familiar but it took my brain a couple of seconds to remember who he was. I worked it out when he came across and gave me a friendly punch.

Ouch.

*

Gary Townsend. Gary 'Townie' Townsend. Squat, squalid, aggressive, he had a neck nearly as thick as his brain. I met him when my parents had sent me to the local comprehensive school rather than the nice, exclusive private one you'd expect from their politics. It's more rewarding, they explained, in a that-five-grand-can-go-towards-our-skiing-trip sort of way; 'Education's more than just about examination grades, William. It's about developing yourself as a person.' For a middle-upper,

upper-middle-class child like myself, this personal development involved the nickname 'Posh Twat', and having my head kicked in by the kids from the estate.

Every lunchtime, Townie ran an expensive little eaterie on the far side of the school playing fields – for the purist, there was Grass Au Naturelle, one hundred per cent pure grass with no added flavours or preservatives; then there was Grass Au Gratin, choice cuts of grass topped off with a crisp, succulent layer of gravel; the house speciality, though, was Grass Au Fumée. This consisted of top-class grass, delicately seasoned with a choice selection of the finest of cigarette ends.

'You're spoiling me again, Townie,' I munched, on this particular lunchtime. 'You should save the penalty area for special occasions.'

'I hate creeps.' Townie delved through my bag, found my calculator. 'What does this do?'

'Everything.' I picked the remains of a Marlboro Light from between my teeth. 'Extended memory, ten decimal places, fractions button, the lot.'

Townie and his pair of sidekicks looked nonplussed.

'And you can get it to say rude words,' I said desperately.

'Show me!' demanded Tweedledum.

'55378008? That's not rude,' said Tweedledumber, as I passed the calculator back over.

'You've got to turn it upside down.'

'Ah,' said Tweedledum, twisting his head round rather than the calculator. 'BOOBLESS!' He started laughing. 'That's rude!'

'T-o-w-n-i-e!' Tweedledumber moaned. 'I want to hit him.' He jumped up and down on the spot in frustration.

'Cost you,' said Townie. 'Ten pee.'

Tweedledumber turned to me.

'Got ten pee on you, Saucepan?'

Hey, have a pound. Treat yourself. I stood up and handed Tweedledumber the money, who gave it to Townie, who nodded back to Tweedledumber, who turned back to me.

'Right then, Saucepan . . .'

He clattered my legs away like a lower division defender, then he showed me the various wrestling moves he'd learned from watching *World Of Sport* on a Saturday lunchtime. It's a fix on the telly, everyone just screams and shouts and pretends that they're injured. Tweedledumber, though, was more Little Shit than Big Daddy, and some way from such professional standards. Years on, I can still feel a twinge from his half-cocked half nelson.

Townie, meanwhile, was playing around with my walkman.

'Frigging aces,' he said, putting the headphones on.

'I'll pay you double tomorrow.' Townie's sidekick twisted my arm into a position I didn't know it could go. 'Aieeee!' My voice reached similar unexplored territory. Tweedledumber took a step back and covered his ears. Townie, bobbing away to the music, was oblivious.

'Aw, come on, Townie. It was a birthday present . . . WAH!' Tweedledumber grabbed me by my legs, started shaking me upside down. 'You don't really want it,' I continued. 'The treble's gone and the headphones are loose and every time you press rewind the tape unravels. And, um, I'll tell my dad! He's really big, like a cross between a gorilla and a brick poo house . . .'

That didn't sound as scary as I'd hoped. I changed tack, and had a go at flattery.

'Think about it, Townie. Someone like you deserves something far better than such a cheap and nasty model . . .'

'Oh, your Walkman's crap.' Townie nodded to Tweedledumber to put me down. Thud. 'It's the music that's wicked. Who is it?'

'Oh, just some songs I like.' I picked myself up off the floor. 'Really old stuff. The Beatles, the Who, no one you'd know . . .'

'I know ALL about the Who!' Townie started jabbing at his chest excitedly. 'I'M their biggest fan!' He leaned towards me, and I pulled back. 'The name of their drummer,' he whispered to me like it was some big secret, 'is Keith Moon. There. Bet you didn't know that.'

'Did too,' I said. 'And I know how he joined the band.'

'Oh yeah?' Townie looked worried. 'Er, I don't believe you. Prove it!'

'He went to watch the Who play and then once they'd finished he got up on stage and kicked the drum kit to bits. Then he told them that he should be the drummer because their drummer was really rubbish, and he was loads better.'

'Really? Er, I mean, that's right!' Townie was grinning at me now, not a pretty sight with saliva dribbling through the holes where various teeth had been knocked out. 'Can I borrow this?' He ejected the tape, and threw the Walkman back at me. I doubled up as it winded me.

'Please,' I said. 'For as long as you like.'

'Ta.' Townie slapped me on the back playfully. Playfully like a lion cub pawing someone's arm off. 'Soz about the grass. You're all right, Saucepan, for a posh twat.'

'That's OK,' I smiled, feeling all personally developed

*

'Townie! What are you doing here?' I asked. 'I, I thought you were in prison.'

'Got out for good behaviour, didn't I?' Townie was wearing a T-shirt that read 'Love hurts' in bright red letters, except with the word 'love' crossed out, and replaced with the word 'pain'.

'Smart,' said Rich. 'So you know each other.'

'Not really . . .'

'Oh, we go *way* back, Saucepan and me.'

Townie gave my shoulder a squeeze.

Ouch.

'Saucepan?' Danny started to giggle.

'Yeah,' said Townie. 'Do you remember that song . . .'

Why had I ever bothered watching Blue Peter? If only I'd done what *Why Don't You* had said, and switched off the television and gone and done something less boring instead, I might have had a reputation that didn't rely on pieces of drug-related kitchenware.

Knock, knock! Twenty minutes early. Why can't drummers come in when they're meant to? Contestant number four was bony, a four-foot thug in condensed form. Dark hair, Ned's Atomic Dustbin sweatshirt, he had a goatee that was an insult to goats everywhere.

'Best make a start,' Goatee said. 'He's obviously missed his go.'

'Listen, mate,' Townie patted him on the back. 'You might as well head on now. Once I've played, they're not going to need to hear anyone else.'

'Says you,' Goatee squared up to Townie.

'Says me,' Townie squared down to Goatee. And headbutted him. It was a low thud, like a bass drum, and one that caused Goatee to wobble backwards. Townie pointed a thumb to the door. 'Now,' he said, in a matter-of-fact way, 'fuck off out of it.' And Goatee duly did.

There was a pause, and then Rich walked across and slapped a still bristling Townie on the back.

'Mate,' he said to my horror. 'I've seen enough. You're in.'

*

I wouldn't say it was a nightmare, because I'm not sure my subconscious is capable of coming up with something so twisted. But there he was, this horrible blast from my past, twirling his drumsticks and laughing that laugh, the one that normally meant I'd have to buy a new calculator. Townie had always been someone with rhythm. The first time he collared me, I remembered that he had a really strong beat. The head slapping was a fraction late, but I wasn't going to suggest he work on it. He might have used me for practice.

Townie had obviously been honing his head slapping

in prison, because his drumming was good. And hard. I couldn't help thinking of the drummer in the Police, who used to hate Sting so much, he had the words 'Fuck', 'Off', 'You' and 'Cunt' written across his tom-toms. I don't know if Townie hated Sting as well, but the way he was bashing the drums about, he sure as hell hated someone.

It sounded good, it had to be said, the band being complete. Instead of playing along to Danny and working out in your head what the drums would sound like, you could now hear the whole thing in glorious 3D Technicolor sound. And it sounded better than what I'd been imagining. Bigger. Better. Beefier. That makes it sound like some sort of bacon double-cheeseburger, but in fact it couldn't have sounded more different. It sounded *real*. And looking round, at everyone playing, everyone together, it felt good, like the beginning had ended, and the real fun was about to begin. One door closing, and another one about to open.

With all the noise, nobody had noticed there was someone knocking on the door. I left Rich and Danny explaining to Townie what beat they wanted, and went to see who it was.

'Lauren!' I smiled, once I'd mastered Riff Raff's stiffer than stiff door lock. 'I didn't know you were coming.'

'Hey there, Cynth. Thought I'd get a few of those work in progress shots.' Lauren unzipped her bag, pulled her camera out. 'So who's your drummer then?'

'He's called Townie.'

We looked across to where Rich and Danny were

describing what they wanted, and Townie was struggling to understand.

'Isn't he sweet?' Lauren slipped the lens cap into her back pocket.

Sweet? The only thing sweet I'd ever known about Townie were his pockets, bulging with someone else's penny chews and cola bottles.

'If I'd known Rich was going to wear that shirt, I'd have bought another film,' Lauren glanced up from behind her lens. 'He's fucking sex on legs today.'

Snap, I thought.

The jamming resumed. I had one eye on the music, one eye on Lauren as she zipped around, photographing the band from different angles. I couldn't help noticing the way she twisted a loop of hair round one finger, then absent-mindedly untwisted it, then twisted it again. I couldn't help her noticing that I couldn't help noticing either.

My mind kept on replaying that kiss on the beach at New Year. I remembered the softness of her lips, and then a split second later, the warmth as she pressed them strongly against mine. And I remembered my confused conclusion: was it a good friends' kiss, or was it just good?

It didn't seem fair, somehow. Rich could get all the stunning girls he could handle, yet he'd moved in on people who were intellectually stimulating as well. No wonder there was no one left for people like me. Why, I wondered, was he going out with Lauren? Practice? To be worshipped? Lauren was not that sort of person.

Maybe she was blessed with some fabulous technique, was ridiculously supple or something. I thought about this and caught Lauren's eye as I was doing so. I turned as red as the word 'hurts' on Townie's T-shirt.

*

Why what happened next, happened next, was as much because of where I lived as anything else. The rehearsal finished, and everyone made to go home. Rich, Danny and Townie were heading townwards, whereas Lauren and I went the other way. Just me, her, my bass guitar and her camera. And as we walked and talked, the conversation came round to Rich.

'Tell me to sod off if you like,' I said, 'but it seems strange you and Rich being . . .' What was the word she used to describe their relationship? '. . . *partners*. You're so different.'

'In what way?'

'Well, Rich's very sussed, very happening and you're . . .'

'I'm what?' Lauren looked up. 'A bit square?'

'Hardly. Hey, *I'm* square. You're more kind of . . .'

'Triangular? Octagonal?'

'. . . more well-rounded is what I'm trying to say. You've got your principles, your politics, your photography. There's something more *permanent* about what you do.'

'Permanent? What am I? Some sort of ink stain you can't get out of your clothes?'

For a second I had an image of Lauren getting out of her clothes. 'No, er, what I'm *trying* to say is . . . oh I don't know. What I'm trying to say is that you're,' I was back to where I'd started, 'different.'

'That's not necessarily a bad thing,' Lauren said. 'Different people can clash, or they can complement each other. Rich is big on show and appearance, on making the most of his good looks and shagability. Whereas what I do, my photography, my art, is aiming for an authenticity.'

'And how do you do that?'

'Well, I strip them of their everyday baggage, expose their true self, and then try to capture their bare essentials in some way.'

'And have you done that with Rich?'

'I certainly have. Let me tell you, his bare essentials are very impressive . . .'

So that's why he walked like that.

'You know, Will, you're not the sort of person I'd expect to find in a rock band at all.'

'No? What sort am I? The accountancy sort? The librarian sort?'

'Oh you're not *that* bad,' Lauren laughed. 'I don't know, what did your careers adviser suggest at school?'

'An accountant at a library. A librarian at a firm of accountants.'

'You shouldn't take too much notice of those people. I reckon you can be whatever you want, if you put your mind to it.'

'What did your careers adviser suggest?'

'Didn't have one.'

'Oh, that's right,' I remembered. 'You grew up at Greenham Common. What did you do for education?'

'There was this professor from some local university,' Lauren explained, 'and she used to come down, do all the teaching. A really interesting woman, made learning fun. She taught us in the morning, then we shouted abuse at the American bastards all afternoon.' Lauren laughed. 'Contemporary History, I think we used to call it. We did that most days for the best part of five years, and eventually the missiles got sent home.'

'Not because of your protest, though.'

'*Don't* you belittle it. Our protest, however small, had something to do with the decision. Better that than sitting at home doing nothing about it. I bet you've never campaigned about anything in your life.'

'I've campaigned about lots of things,' I said, struggling to think of one. 'I, er, followed the example of Band Aid and Live Aid, and set up a group to raise money for famine relief.'

'Called what?'

'Lemon Aid. I sucked a citrus fruit for every pound of sponsorship I got.'

'And how much did you make?'

'Three pounds fifty. I would have made more but I had to go to hospital and have my cheekbones straightened.'

Lauren laughed. 'I guess your heart's in the right place, even if your brain isn't.'

We walked on in silence.

'Tell me. Why are you doing the band?' Lauren asked. 'Is it the fame that motivates you? The money?'

'Kind of, but not really.'

'What then?'

'Well, it's more to do with . . . no, it'll sound stupid.'

'I bet it doesn't,' Lauren flashed a look across. 'Come on, try me.'

'I don't know,' I paused. I never really told anyone what I thought. I'd done it once at primary school, and had the piss ripped out of me so mercilessly I'd decided from then on to keep my feelings to myself. There was something about Lauren, though, that made me want to open up. I stared straight ahead and said in a rush. 'I, I'm hoping the glamour might rub off on me, help me get a girlfriend.'

'There,' said Lauren. 'That wasn't so hard, was it?'

And then it all came out. How my sex life was permanently in a coma. How phone-sex girls hung up on me. How rubber dolls deflated on me. How my treasured copy of *Swedish Nuns IV* had unwound itself inside the video. How all I had left were my fantasies, and even they were erratic at best. The last time I'd tried it on with Carol Vordemann, she'd got bored and started practising her long division instead.

I paused for breath, and realised we'd stopped walking. I waited for her to suggest the name of a therapist she knew, but instead she smiled and said, 'I think you worry too much. Something will turn up. You're a nice bloke.'

I think it had been a long day, what with seeing Townie again and everything, because I just flipped. 'That's right. I'm a nice bloke. And do you know where nice blokes finish, Lauren? I'll tell you. Last. L-A-S-T, last. It's started to get to that stage where people are spreading rumours. *That Will, he's never had a girlfriend* . . . People start to think that you're gay and then it's even *more* difficult to find yourself a girlfriend, and then everyone is *sure* you're gay and then it's *impossible* to get a girlfriend. And then! Then people start noticing you've never had a boyfriend either, so all these new rumours will start surfacing, about how Will gets his kicks by wandering up into the fields and shagging the . . .'

'Sssh,' Lauren put a finger to my lips. 'It's all right. You'll find someone. All you've got to do is be yourself.'

'Be myself?' I pulled a face. 'Why would I want to do that? Who on earth finds *me* attractive?'

'I can think of one person.'

'Sure,' I said. 'And who's that?'

Lauren pushed a curl of hair back behind her ear. 'OK. You want to know what I was thinking earlier on, when I was photographing you playing your bass guitar?'

'What a jerk? Where's that smell coming from?'

Lauren shook her head, beckoned me closer. I leaned forward. Lauren whispered into my ear, speaking so close I could feel the warmth of her breath.

'I want you.'

8

'I want you,' Lauren said.

'What?' I asked.

'I want you.'

I looked at her, surprised. Girls weren't meant to be like this. I didn't mean to be sexist about things, but I'd always marked such statements down as a strictly male preserve. Part of me felt threatened, the rest excited, that here was a secret fantasy of mine for real: a female so anal that they knew that I'd lifted the bass line for 'Our Tune' from the Beatles' *Abbey Road* classic.

'I want you,' Lauren continued.

'All right,' I said, 'there's no need to go on about it.'

I wondered if anyone else had recognised my steal?

'Are you not interested?' Lauren asked.

'Oh very much so.'

I certainly was. If Lauren had twigged, then there must be other people as well.

'Do you think Rich's had the same thought?' I asked.

'I doubt that *very* much,' Lauren smiled.

'Why? I thought he was a massive Beatles fan.'

'Beatles? Will, what the fuck are you on about?'

'Music? What are you on about?'

And then she leaned across and kissed me. From the moment I smelled her breath, everything blurred. I can only really remember snatches: Lauren taking my bass guitar out of my hand and leaning it against a wall; my fingertips tentatively touching the top of her jeans, Lauren's hand guiding my hand down on to her arse, which felt soft, felt warm; Lauren murmuring that I was 'cute', which I think is girl's talk for 'You know, you're not a *complete* bastard are you?'; me kissing Lauren back, in a way that would make her say 'You know what I said earlier about you being sweet? I was wrong. You're an *animal . . .*'

Somehow, we made it back to Lauren's flat. Once inside, Lauren made quick work of my clothes. Such a physique, she'd groaned, which I really should have been more suspicious of. As it was, my mind was on other things. Like Lauren pulling off her shirt, and revealing a navy blue vest top, her gawky bone structure and her *breasts*. She pushed me down on to the bed, put a hand on my groin.

'It's so *big*,' she said.

I really should have been on to her at this point. No one would ever, *ever*, say 'take me big boy' in my presence. Take-me-slightly-above-average-if-it-will-make-you-feel-better boy was exaggeration enough. Lauren, I should have realised, either had a problem with the concept of size. Or she was lying. As it was, I was more concerned with trying desperately not to come. Bryan Adams, I thought. Bryan Adams, Bryan Adams, Bryan Adams, Bryan Adams . . .

'Aha,' Lauren said, pawing my pants down. 'Another offering for my collection.'

Lauren certainly knew how to deep throat someone. Her throating was so deep that it was almost philosophical.

Lauren reached under the bed, produced four pairs of handcuffs.

'Let me tie you up,' she nibbled in my ear.

Ah. I'd thought this was a no-strings-attached sort of evening. Lauren looked at me, all mock-disappointed.

'You *are* sexually liberated, aren't you?'

It seemed a funny way of proving your liberation, by allowing yourself to be tied down.

'Er. Um. I guess so,' I said.

And in a way I was. Kinky threesomes. Mile High Club applications. Steamy sauna sessions with the entire Spanish volleyball team. These were all sexual experiences that I could imagine myself enjoying. I'd enjoyed myself imagining them, anyway.

'So what's the problem, then?'

'It's just that, um . . .'

Like most blokes, I was incapable of putting into words exactly what it was I was feeling. Like most blokes, if there was one thing I was even worse at than putting my feelings into words, it was admitting I was scared.

'No problem,' I lied. 'Go ahead.'

*

Fifteen minutes later. There was something about the way Lauren had said, 'Aha! Another offering for my collection' that worried me. That and the fact that she'd gone off looking for a knife. It was then that I remembered not only that she studied photography, but also the title of her thesis. Portraying the Fallacy of the Phallocentric Morality. Oh my God I could almost picture the chief-examiner's face, as he turned to chapter one. Excellent, Miss Miles, a thesis *and* a pop-up book. Would my contribution be big enough, I wondered, to entitle me to an honorary degree? Looking down at my member, I decided not. Educational standards may have slipped, but there was still some way before my manhood was worth an upper second.

I'm being stupid, I thought. Lauren doesn't want to cut my knob off. I glanced round her bedroom to reassure myself. See? She's normal. She likes plants: I noticed the bizarre-shaped cactii on the window sill. She appreciates art: I spotted the framed print of *The Scream*. She's into music: I peered to see what the record was on the record player. A singer-songwriter who committed six harrowing records to vinyl before, gulp, before being committed herself.

I could feel my heart racing. I tried really hard to convince myself that I'd misheard what Lauren had said. Instead of saying 'Aha! Another offering for my collection,' she'd in fact said something similar, but with slightly less pain involved. 'I've got some chilled champagne in the fridge.' 'Hang on a second, Will, I'll get my massage oil.' 'Do you mind if I call a friend over? She's a Swedish porn star . . .'

Try as I might, I couldn't convince myself that any of these possibilities were possible. I was about to eunuched, cut down to size, have my man-mantle dismantled whether I liked it or not. And surprisingly enough, I found myself leaning ever so slightly towards the latter. My penis wasn't a world-beater, apart from in the Best-funny-dangling-thing category, but I still felt rather attached to it.

What had I done? Maybe it was the masturbation after all. God had given up with the eye for an eyeful, and gone for a more brutal punishment instead.

'Lauren? Mr Big here. I've got a small problem I need dealing with. A persistent self-abuser.'

'I keep telling you, boss, blindness isn't enough for his sort. Let me handle this my way. I'll give him a punishment that fits the crime, a message he can't interpret in any other way.'

'You're going to break his wrist?'

'I'm going to cut his dick off.'

'OK, but keep it clean. I don't want any *complications . . .*'

The door to the bedroom was shut, but I could still make out a series of weird noises coming from the kitchen. Clank. Whirr. Badump. Then there were the snatches of sentences. '*Fuck, I knew I should have written the recipe down. Why is it so lumpy?*' Now I may not have been an expert on having my knob cut off, I was quite happy being a beginner, but I hadn't thought it would be like this. Call me naive, but I'd always thought it'd be, ouch, one, *wince*, slash of a knife. And that'd be it. It seemed to be more complicated than that. A bit of preparation beforehand. A softening up of the, shudder, victim.

I decided I would reason with Lauren when she

returned. She studied philosophy, she would bow down to a good, well-structured argument. I would explain, very clearly, that enough was enough, and although I'd had a very nice evening, I never went too far on a first date. And, anyway, I really must be going. My dinner was in the oven. I had a plane to catch in the morning. My library books were extremely ill. I had a grandmother to take back. Outside, I could hear footsteps. Keep calm, I thought. There's no reason to get carried away. Lauren pushed the door open, stood there. A silhouette in the doorway. Calm, I thought. Calm.

Deep breath.

'I'm sorry!' I screamed. 'I don't know what I've done, really I don't, but however I've offended you, I apologise. Men, we're all bastards, yes, every single one of us. And yes, I'm sure I let my dick do the talking but I don't think that every woman I meet wants to shag me, really I don't . . .'

I didn't as it happened. I wasn't *that* stupid.

'. . . and yes I'm sure I deserve everything that's coming to me, I am a man after all, and yes, I'll admit to having treated women as sex objects, which is wrong, very wrong, but springs from the inadequacies of my own sex rather than any attempt to undermine yours, after all, women are wiser and better than men, at every academic subject and in every walk of life, and if only we hadn't oppressed you for quite so long then the world wouldn't be in the awful mess it is now . . .'

I paused for breath, and looked at Lauren.

'Will, are you all right? I only want to preserve your penis for posterity.'

Preserve? In my mind I imagined a chip shop, on a rainy Friday night. *The usual, Mrs Morrison, and one of your pickled penises, if you please. No, not the big one. I'll take the small, funny-looking one at the end . . .*

'How long does this take?'

'Normally about three to four hours.'

Three to four hours? I could have bled to death by then.

'Why?' I said. 'Why do you have to cut it off?'

Lauren smiled, as though the thought had only just occurred to her.

'The thing is,' she winked, 'it does make it a lot easier to mould.'

Now I was dazed *and* confused.

'*Mould?* Lauren, what are you on about?'

Today, viewers, I'm going to show you how to make a plastercast penis. For this you will need some plaster, something to make a cast with, and, how did you guess? A penis. The size of the penis isn't that important, nevertheless, in order to make it easier for you to see at home, I'm going to be helped by Simon the soundman, who is, so I'm informed, hung like the proverbial donkey. As for the cast, there are various things you can use to make it: aluminium foil, moulding clay, melted wax and so on but if you can get hold of some, I'd recommend a can of dental mould. You should spend some time perfecting the mix for this, otherwise you'll end up washing your model with a vat of lumpy water.

OK, so first, it is necessary to lubricate the penis. Oh, come on girls, I think we all know how to lubricate a penis. Simon, if you'd just like to come and lie down here. As you can see, this is one that I prepared earlier. Next, you need to slap the mould on, carefully, men do have SOME feelings, and then wait for it to set. This should take about forty-five seconds, and it's important that your assistant remains hard at all times. So a bit of seductive dancing, a few sweet nothings, I'm sure you can think of something to stimulate your model.

Once the forty-five seconds are up, thank you Simon, you were wonderful, then let him go floppy and slide out. There we are, I'll see you in the dressing room in a minute, OK? Right, now you need to fill your mould with plaster, like so, and then leave it for about four to five hours. Now it may be that when you break the mould, the plaster hasn't quite set. In this case stick it back together, no, NOT with double-sided sticky tape, and have another go. Let's have a look at a finished one. This is John, Camera 2. Look at the zoom lens on that, eh, girls? There are various things you can do with your plastercast at this stage. You can paint it, this green one here is Crispin the researcher, something of a disappointment that one. You can put it your mantelpiece, though if it's like Crispin's, I wouldn't bother, frankly. Alternatively you can, well, I'm sure we can all think of another use for a life-size model of a penis. That's all from me for the moment. Let's go back to Chris and Catherine, who are hard at it in the garden . . .

'Oh,' said Lauren.

'Oh? What do mean, "oh"? Why isn't it coming off?'

We were both staring at my penis, which had disappeared under a large pink lump of dough.

'I'm not sure,' said Lauren. 'This has never happened before.'

Oh great. My first ever sexual experience, and not

only had I pulled myself Little Miss Weirdo, I'd now won myself a lifelong supply of Plasticine as well.

'Maybe I didn't lubricate you enough.' Lauren giggled. 'Will, I think your pubic hairs have got stuck in the mould.'

Double great.

'OK, this might hurt a little . . .'

'Ow. *Ow*. OW. *OW!* Can you be careful? *OWWW!* No, you can't be careful. OWWWWW! I've changed my mind. I know it looks silly, but I'd rather carry round a lump of Play-Doh than go through, *OWWWWW!*'

'Finished!' Lauren said.

I looked down to assess my damage. *Ouch*. My pubic hair now boasted a circle, like the ones that aliens make in corn fields. I was going to have to keep this very quiet. Otherwise I'd have a queue of ufologists, demanding access to my private parts.

'Can I go now?' I said.

'*God* no. We've got to wait for the plaster to dry. If it goes wrong, we'll have to do it again.'

Ah.

'Does it go wrong often?' I tried to remember what daylight looked like.

'Sometimes, but I think yours should be OK,' Lauren slipped off the bed. 'I guess you're wondering what the finished product will look like.'

No, actually. Call me Mr Stick-in-the-mud, but I was more bothered about when my groin would stop aching. Lauren, meanwhile, was rummaging around in a cupboard.

'Here's one,' she planted a fluorescent green penis on

the bedside table. Without a man attached, it looked lost, vulnerable, alone somehow.

'A glow in the dark dick? Nice touch.'

'This one was the first, Steven I think his name was. I got him drunk down the pub and dragged him back. A bit like you, in fact. And this one,' she produced a smaller model, painted in red and yellow stripes, 'this is a tutor from college. He used to teach me philosophy.'

'A hard subject, I've always found.'

'Ha ha. Actually, I was a bit disappointed with him, I thought he was going to be a lot deeper. Still, at least my exam grades held up.'

'So what do you do with them?'

Lauren stared at me.

'What do you think I do with them?'

Penis three, penis four, penis five appeared. Then penis six. Penis seven. With a flourish, Lauren unveiled penis eight, the sort of penis that would make Errol Flynn feel self-conscious. Lauren stroked it fondly.

'This one's my favourite, though.'

'So who does that belong to?'

She smiled. 'You know him already.'

And then it hit me. What had not crossed my mind as the evening had lurched from surprise to snogging to sexual excitement to blind fear to painful pubic plucking.

Of course, of course, of course.

Rich.

Oh shit.

9

You can always tell when I've been sick, because the blood vessels burst around my eyelids. It's the velocity of the vomit that does it, the pressure leaving a cascade of bright-red pin pricks, long after the nausea has died down. It's bad, but it could be worse. The first time Melanie got really drunk, she chucked so much an artery burst *behind* her eyes, and the whites of her eyes went red. For weeks. I might look ill occasionally, but I've never come across as an extra from the video for *Thriller*.

I've been sick many, many times over the years, but there are some incidents that still stick out. One of my personal favourites was in hospital, when I was recovering after having my wisdom teeth out under general anaesthetic. It was meant to be all four, but the surgeon took so long chipping out the bottom pair, he took an executive decision to leave the other two where they were. Anyway, there I was, all woozy and 'where am I?' and 'why can't I move my mouth?' and said surgeon comes round, impressing the arse off an impressionable group of students. Did his best *Blue Peter* 'and here's one

I did earlier' impression. Halfway through his account, he brings me into the conversation.

'And how are we feeling now young man?'

He quickly found me a bucket.

I don't like being sick – who does? – but because I do it so often, it's not a big deal. And I know I've got it easy really. I once did a biology project on nausea, and let me tell you, however much I hurl, it's nothing compared to some poor creatures. Like cows, chewing the cud, having to barf up their last meal so they can swallow it again. Or baby birds, who for breakfast have to eat what their mother has already eaten. And no one has it as bad as flies, having to retch on their food before they can digest it.

Travel sickness is one of my particular specialities. I've been sick at sea many times over the years, but one experience in particular always stands out. It was on a holiday to some obscure island in the Inner Hebrides, don't ask, on a day when only the driest wit would describe the sea as 'mildly choppy'. And as we cleared Mull and Morvern, left Tobermory for the full force of the open sea, the contents of my stomach, despite being allegedly pacified by a variety of sea-sickness tablets, wanted out.

I think my plan had been to 'get some fresh air'. But on the way, I knew I wasn't going to make it, and veered left for the toilets. I bagged the last cubicle, for I was not the only person whose stomach was being whipped away. A large Scottish bloke in the next cubicle – I knew he was Scottish from the way he kept on saying 'Oh

Jesus' – was my chucking companion. Every time he went, my stomach was sure to go.

But here's the best bit. After what seemed like forever, the captain announced that the sea was too rough to attempt to dock. He had no option but to turn the boat round and head back for the open sea.

How me and my Scottish friend laughed.

Elizabeth I once said, 'I may have the body of a weak and feeble woman, but I have the heart and stomach of a king.' I'm kind of the opposite. I may have the bodily bits of a king (if not the blood), but I have a stomach as weak and feeble as they come. Whilst some people respond to stress with sweats or headaches, migraines or palpitations, my stomach simply shuts up shop. I'm left with a sort of nausea tinnitus, a consistent low-level sickness that never quite goes away, humming away softly in the background.

You can always tell when something big is going down in my life, because I start throwing up. And you can always tell when I've been throwing up, because the blood vessels burst around my eyelids. And as I walked back from Lauren's, rubbing my eyes from my lack of sleep, rubbing my wrists where the handcuffs had marked, both my stomach and my eyelids knew exactly what was coming next.

*

'Will?' Rich asked. 'Are you with us? Anybody there?'

'Yeah. Uh.' I came to, finding myself sitting in Barneys with the rest of the band. 'Sorry Rich. I was miles away.'

'Yes, well you will be if you don't pay attention.' Rich shook his head. 'I'm trying to tell you my fantastic strategy for success. Danny, do you want to summarise for Mr Head-in-the-clouds here what I've said so far?'

I wasn't miles away at all. I was right there, but my mind was only capable of switching between two basic thoughts: Oh my God, I'm going to be sick and, It's all right. Deep breath. Relax. My pint of cider sat untouched on the table in front of me, as earlier on had my breakfast and lunch. My stomach was doing its level best to put the retch into wretched. I looked, and felt, like Keith Richards on a bad hair day.

Ow.

And that was the other thing. There was no way I was going to be allowed to forget about Lauren, because on the few occasions I didn't feel like I was living my life on the high seas, my chopper was chipping in. I'm sorry, I thought, as my sorry-looking member twinged for the thousandth time. *Ow.* My ring of missing pubic hair was feeling especially sore. Somehow it was now even whiter than the rest of me, almost glow-in-the-dark white. If – and as ifs went, this was a ruddy enormous one – if I actually managed to pull anyone in the foreseeable future, I was in danger of going down in history as Mr Polo Pants.

'First thing we've got to do is record a demo tape,' Danny recapped. 'After that, Rich reckons we should start flogging it around. That, and building up our ability to play live . . .'

As Danny outlined Rich's vision for global domination, I couldn't but think about the tenuousness of my position. I may have been new to all this band business but even I knew that copping off with your lead singer's girlfriend was not the best way of promoting intra-band harmony. It didn't take a rocket scientist to work out what would happen if he found out.

'Will, mate, fucking great news! I've only gone and got us a multi-million-pound deal with Parlophone Records.'

'Brilliant. Er, Rich, I think there's something you ought to know. Last night I got off with your girlfriend.'

'Sorry, is there any reason why you're still here?'

We hadn't actually had sex. I tried to work out if there was any mileage in this, if it somehow lessened my wrongdoing. Not really. My actions had sod all to do with some principled stand. If Lauren had suggested we had sex, we'd have had sex. As it was, her motives had been artistic. Mine, however, were nothing like as profound.

'. . . we should push the tape to promoters,' Danny continued, 'people in the know. We want to create a bit of a buzz, get our name known before we launch ourselves properly . . .'

My stomach lurched. Oh my God, I thought. I'm going to be sick.

'That's right, Dan,' Rich took over. 'The new music scene in Brighton has got to go off with a bang. It's got to look like something brilliant is happening out of nothing. And that level of performance involves practice playing live . . .'

It's all right. Deep breath. Relax.

'. . . what we're going to do is cut our teeth by playing some small low-key shows until we're really ready to rock. Then bang! We have the Brighton Rocks gig, launching both us and Loz's band in one triumphant fanfare. It'll be the gig that defines the scene; the sort of gig that people will pretend they were at even when they weren't . . .'

It's not all right. I'm going to be sick.

'. . . it's like the Beatles said. You take your hometown first. Then the rest of the country, then the rest of the world.'

Deep breath. Re*lax*.

'You know what I think would be really good?' Danny said. 'We should try and get a single out quickly, you know, some sort of limited edition thing.'

'I like it,' said Rich. 'We can do a tour to promote it, by which time the big record companies will be coughing up the . . .'

Coughing up. That did it.

''Scuse me,' I screeched my chair back and headed for the toilets.

*

A few minutes later, I was stood on the toilet seat, poking my head out of the cubicle's small, square window. The fresh air was cold and slightly seasidey, but its chilly blast went down a treat. I was feeling much, much better, but for how long was anyone's guess.

I breathed out deeply. It was in these brief moments, the moments when my stomach was still, that my thoughts about that night with Lauren weren't dominated by guilt, or by wondering if I could reach the toilet bowl in time. Instead my mind was consumed by other things. Different things. Nice things.

Like the way Lauren kissed me. The way it felt when her lips were pressed against mine. The thrill of pushing into their lushness, into their warmth. Of touching her teeth with the tip of my tongue. Of brushing her hair off her face. The way that the harder I kissed her, the tighter Lauren grabbed my hair – pulling it, twisting it, squeezing my scalp with her fingers.

I'd never forget the way her waist felt in my hands, its lightness, its litheness. Likewise the illicit thrill of pulling Lauren's top out of her jeans, and feeling my hand touch her warm flesh. This is real, I remember thinking, this is fucking real. And for the first time, I felt a flicker of manhood. It was kind of like when you strike a match, but without it catching. There's that tension as it scratches along the matchbox, and the anticipation that next time round, the match is going to splutter into life.

I heard the door to the bar open, then the sound of someone walking across to the urinals, a sharp *zip* followed by an audible groan of satisfaction. What was I going to do? I stepped down from the window, and sat on the toilet seat. There were so many conflicting thoughts spinning in my head. What did that night mean? What did Lauren think? Was it going to happen again? What was I going to do if it did? How I could have done this to Rich? Would Rich find out? What would he do if he did?

What *was* I going to do? I heard the bloke zip up, wash his hands, dry them and leave. I didn't know. I just didn't know.

*

'. . . it's all to do with timing,' Rich's big speech was still going strong as I sat down. He had become increasingly animated in my absence, was wagging his cigarette at Danny, dropping ash into my pint. At least it gave me an excuse not to drink it. 'It's all to do with being in the right place at the right time. You can fanny around for as long as you like, but if you don't know how to sell yourself to the people that matter, you can kiss your contract goodbye. That's why me and Lauren and Loz are working so hard on images, making the whole project a coherent package. Lauren is going to have an exhibition of her photos and artwork, showing the Brighton scene as it really is . . .'

Lauren's artwork on display? Oh my God, I thought. My plastercast.

'Are, are you sure that's a wise idea?' I interrupted. 'I mean, exposing the bands as they really are, doesn't that, er . . .' I was thinking fast now, '. . . doesn't that shatter the mystique of being a rock star, removing the myth that separates the celebrity from his fans?'

I'd lost Townie with that last sentence, I could tell. Either that or he'd just swallowed a large wasp.

'That's not a bad point for you,' Rich drawled, 'but I'm not stupid. This is going to be a celebration of a movement, not some sort of piss take. I'm hardly going to let in anything that reflects badly on me.'

'And the rest of us?'

'Relax, Will. All Lauren wants to do is to capture the band as we really are.'

That's what I was worried about. My penis in the corner, a sad reminder of the small-town boy, dumped just as the band made it big.

'It's important that the scene is seen as being more than just music,' Rich continued. 'We need images that will tie the whole thing together. That's what Lauren's job is.'

'So what do we do whilst you're sorting out these images?' I asked.

'You write lots of great songs,' Rich said. 'The stuff you've written so far is fine, but I know we can do better. Then you practise them like mad.'

I was slowly beginning to grasp the gist of Rich's great idea. Townie, Danny and myself worked our arses off for hours on end in some godforsaken rehearsal studio. Rich swanned around having his photo taken by Lauren.

Lauren. Lauren, Lauren, Lauren. Everything came back to her. I tried to take my mind off the situation, and picked up Townie's copy of the *Sun*. No such luck. IT'S PADDY PANTSDOWN! The front page screamed. I read the story. With the general election just months away, the leader of the Liberal Democrats had gazumped a forthcoming tabloid exclusive, and confessed to cheating on his wife.

'They're all at it, aren't they?' Townie nudged me. 'That's why there's so many people like me on the dole. Instead of working to make work for people, they just sit there and shag their secretaries.'

'I bet he's gone up in your opinion, hasn't he, Rich?' I asked, optimistically. 'Someone who was once a bit of a boring prat turns out to be a right Jack the lad.'

'Not really,' Rich shrugged. 'I think he's made a massive error of judgement.'

'You reckon?'

'Oh yeah. If Paddy's going to play the field he might as well pick up some skirt who's half decent. Porking his secretary, to me it says "Hi, I'm a philanderer *and* I'm half blind."'

'Phil?' asked Townie. 'I thought his name was Paddy.'

'It's a typical Liberal Democrat compromise,' Rich continued. 'The Conservative policy of banging your secretary coupled with the Labour desire to do something for the disadvantaged.'

'Oh I get you,' I said. 'It's his choice of woman you disapprove of. Being a rock-and-roll sort of a guy, you don't have problem with Paddy sleeping around. Free love for all, eh?'

Just maybe, I thought to myself. Maybe Rich had the same attitude as the apocryphal story of the Rolling Stones, Marianne Faithfull and the Mars Bar. If the band were going to replicate sixties music, maybe we could go the whole hog and borrow the girlfriend-sharing bits as well.

'Let me put it this way,' said Rich. 'If I was going out with someone and I found out they were seeing someone else, I'd be off to see that someone else as well, and it wouldn't be for a crafty fuck on the side. There'd be none of this "I'm standing by my man in this time of crisis" bollocks. If I was Ashdown's wife, I'd be round to give his secretary a good hard slap.'

Ah.

'I think there's a lot of dignity in the way Mrs Ashdown has behaved,' I tried to temper the panic creeping into my voice. 'Drawing a line under the affair, carrying on like sensible adults, that's a very mature approach to take.'

'Bollocks to that,' said Rich. 'I'd make sure the only note the secretary was capable of taking was a doctor's one to the local chemist, you know what I'm saying?'

I didn't like the way this conversation was progressing. Rich's ethics, as far as I could work out, were that everyone should conform to the highest of all possible standards. Apart from him, who could do whatever he wanted.

'Isn't that a bit hypocritical?' I felt myself getting desperate now. 'I mean, I'm sure you've had the odd bored housewife in your time.'

'Will, you're missing the point. Do you know what the basic principle of morality is?' Rich asked.

'I've never thought about it.' I thought about it. 'Being nice to everyone? Doing unto others as you'd like them to do unto you?'

'The principle,' Rich said with a wink, 'is not to get caught. Once that happens, you deserve everything that's coming to you. The skill is to not to be so stupid that you get yourself in such a situation in the first place. Learn how to get away with it, and everybody's happy.'

'Even Mrs Ashdown?'

Rich sighed. 'Yes, Will. Even Mrs Ashdown. She can't be angry about her husband having an affair if she doesn't know he's having one.'

I'd never studied philosophy myself, but felt that Rich wasn't about to replace Rousseau in the pantheon of great minds. Not getting caught? That might be fine for a smooth operator like Rich, but for someone as cluelessly clodhopping as me it simply wasn't workable. If I actually got away with getting off with Lauren, I reasoned – and my stomach insisted – the only sensible course of action was to thank my lucky stars and quit while I was ahead. Otherwise, my place in the band, and in rock history, would go the same way as my ring of pubic hair.

As it was, I got off with Lauren again.

10

It happened the following Saturday, the day we were down to record our demo. Rich had booked an out-of-town recording studio, and at ten o'clock picked me up in a clapped-out Ford Transit he'd borrowed for the occasion. I sat in the front, whilst Townie and Danny rattled about in the back with all our gear, occasionally banging on the partition in fits of giggles. And just before we left Brighton, we picked up one more passenger.

'Lauren? What, what are you doing here?' My reaction to her turning up was not as friendly as it might have been, especially considering the fact that I hadn't seen her since, well, you know. As we'd turned into her road, so had my stomach in recognition. But when I saw her, and she smiled that big warm smile of hers, it had wobbled in the other sort of a way.

'Thought I'd get a few of those in-the-studio shots. Now,' she looked at me in a way that couldn't help but make me flush red, 'are you going to budge up? Or do you want me to sit on your lap?'

Rich laughed his seventies laugh, thank God. I joined

in, and hoped I didn't sound too high-pitched and hysterical.

The studio can't have been more than a forty-five minute drive out of Brighton, but the journey there seemed to go on forever. Partly it was Rich, who drove like he led his life; fast, swaggering, with little consideration for others. It was also partly Lauren, who chatted away to Rich about fashion and shops and ideas and music, while at the same time taking every opportunity to brush her leg against mine. I could feel its warmth beneath her brown cord skirt, the coolness of her long leather boots against my shin. I kept shuffling along until Rich shouted at me for sitting on the gear stick.

'It's all right mate,' he laughed. 'She doesn't bite.'

On the contrary. I had the teeth marks to prove it.

'Loz said you've found the joke band,' Lauren asked Rich.

'Certainly have,' said Rich. 'Monkey Boy. They're going to be perfect.'

The joke band, he explained, was as crucial in establishing a music scene as the proper bands themselves. They hammed up the worst points of the sound of the other bands, thus reinforcing the overall style. Their shelf life was short, once the scene was over they were taken off the shelf and dumped in the bargain bucket. They were the band by which the other bands in the scene were measured and thus looked good. They were easy for the music papers to make jokes about. They were the joke themselves.

'I saw them last night,' Rich said. 'They were really, really shit. They started off the gig as some bad baggy band, and then for the last three songs turned into cod Nirvana. No idea whatsoever about style or image. I reckon we could turn them our way, give them our cast-off songs. Smooth talk them into jumping on the bandwagon.'

'I've been busy too,' Lauren said. 'I've been having a think about the image.' She pulled an A4 pad out of her bag, the pages full of sketches of figures, kitted out in cool-looking sixties stuff.

'Lauren, these are really good,' I said.

'The idea is that it should be retro to go with the sound,' Lauren explained. 'We're talking mid-sixties here, mixing in a bit of mod stuff, Fred Perry shirts, that sort of thing. Tight jeans or corduroy trousers, no trainers, Doc Martens to give the thing a bit of a kick. We want to look sharply dressed, no flares or flower power or hippy stuff. Well, except for the joke band, obviously. They've got to take the whole thing a little too far.'

'You know what I thought?' Rich said. 'I reckon we should try and do something with the Union Jack, reclaim it, make it look cool. This is an English sound we're going for, and I think it would symbolise being proud of our culture. A Union Jack guitar for Danny. A Jackson Pollock style Union Jack record sleeve . . .'

'A Union Jack minidress for you,' Lauren nudged me.

'Look! I don't wear women's clothes, all right!'

'Jesus, calm down, Will.' Rich and Lauren swapped raised eyebrows.

'Isn't all this flag waving,' I asked, 'isn't it a bit right wing?'

'That's why we've got to change perceptions,' said

Rich. 'There's no reason why patriotism should be a right wing preserve. I tell you this, Will, when Neil Kinnock and Labour get into power in a few months time, the country is going to feel refreshed, it's going to feel young and dynamic again – and we're going to be ready to capture the moment. Who was in power when the Beatles were at number one? Labour. Who were in power when the Sex Pistols were around? Labour. And who's going to be in power when we top the charts? Neil Kinnock and Labour, that's who. Good music and leftie governments go hand in hand, mate. And I'm going to be ready to exploit it.'

Lauren, I noticed, was rubbing her leg against mine *again*. I shuffled away. 'You seem a little nervous,' she smiled innocently. 'Is it the recording, Will?'

'That'll be it,' I lied.

'I wouldn't worry about it,' Lauren squeezed my leg with a little too much familiarity. 'I *know* you can deliver the goods when it's required.'

What was Lauren up to? I couldn't but feel she was playing with me. In different circumstances, what she was doing could have been described as teasing, friendly, affectionate. But with her boyfriend sitting the other side of me? I just didn't get it. Was she was taking advantage of the fact I fancied her to show off to Rich? Or did she find the risk thrilling, sexy, funny perhaps? I don't know. What I did know was that I was finding it anything but.

*

The recording studio Rich had chosen was called the Funny Farm, which funnily enough, was on a farm. Its owner and engineer was ex-rocker Rob Hutch, who had the sort of sideburns that won prizes at village fêtes, and a Pink Floyd T-shirt that had been washed so often, it should have read Gray Side of the Moon. He had a philosophy to recording that he described with the faintest trace of a West Country accent.

'I've recorded a lot of bands in my time,' Rob drawled, 'and believe you me, it's worth taking our time over the drums.'

The fact that we were paying Rob by the hour, I'm sure, had absolutely nothing to do with this attention to detail. I soon understood why it took the Beach Boys the best part of six months to record their classic single 'Good Vibrations'. It was nothing to do with the complex instrumentation and arrangements. It was because they were stuck with the mid-sixties Californian equivalent of Rob Hutch, refusing to let Brian Wilson anywhere near his harmonies until the snare sound was *just* so.

Rob was sat to my left wearing a pair of posh headphones, behind a mixing desk that had so many knobs and buttons and levers, it wouldn't have been out of place in Cape Canaveral. Townie was on the other side of a glass screen, sat behind his miked-up drum kit in a small boxroom with padded foam walls. The padding was all about acoustics, apparently, although looking at Townie's pained expression I reckoned it might serve a second purpose should things get nasty.

Rob leaned into his thin, slinky, bendy microphone, which was connected through a series of leads to Townie's headphones.

'Townie, mate, can you kick the bass drum again?'

Boom, Boom, Boom, Boom, Boom, Boom . . .

'There,' said Rob, taking his headphones off, passing them over to me. 'What d'you think?'

Boom, Boom, Boom, Boom, Boom, Boom . . .

It sounded exactly the same to me. As it had done for the previous two and a half hours. It was a bass pedal. It went thud. I tried to sound knowledgeable in front of Rob.

'Very, er, rhythmic,' I passed the headphones back. 'Just remind me what you've done to it.'

'Well, I wasn't quite happy with how I'd set the parameters,' Rob put his headphones back on, launched into his studio gobbledegook. 'So I've modulated the resonator, resonated the modulator, then multi-tapped the configuration of the matrix. Otherwise,' he laughed, 'it would have bled all over you.'

'Phew,' I laughed back. 'And it can be a devil to shift. Shall I get the others?'

Danny and Rich were out the back having a cigarette.

Rob rolled his eyes.

'Don't bother. We've still got the snare, the hi-hat, the cymbals and the rest of the drums to do.'

'Is that going to take long?' I had a feeling I knew what the answer was going to be.

'Well, I wouldn't want to rush it.'

Heaven forbid.

The door opened, and I looked round to see Lauren, camera in hand.

'Hello, Cynthia,' Lauren pulled a light meter out of her bag, wafted it around the room. 'How is the master-piece progressing?'

'Sssh,' I held a finger to my lips, nodding at Rob.

Lauren looked at Townie.

'Oh, look at that expression,' she whispered. 'The tortured artist.'

Not really. The nearest Townie got to a tortured artist was when he threatened the painters by the seafront for money.

'What are Rich and Danny up to?' I whispered back. 'Have they finished their fag yet?'

'They've finished all their fags. They've wandered off to the village to find some more.'

Leaving me behind as per usual.

'Don't look so down,' Lauren sat down next to me. 'I'll keep you company.'

That was what worried me.

'So how are you?' Lauren unzipped her camera bag. 'How are things?'

'Fine,' I lied. My stomach flipped. My groin twinged. 'Yes, fine. Terrific. Wonderful. Thank you.'

'And *downstairs*? Is everything OK?'

No. It hurts. It stings. It looks freakish.

'Never better.'

'Thank God for that. I've been a bit concerned, about the fact that it got stuck. You know the tutor from college I told you about? He had to go to the doctor, to get some ointment.' Lauren smiled, leaned close and whispered in my ear. 'I've painted it pink, by the way.'

Pink?

'I've only had it a few days, but I'm *very* fond of it. It's got a lot of character.'

I looked up to see if Rob was listening, but he had his own knobs to deal with. Character? Was that a back-handed compliment? Unattractive people are often sold as having a great personality. Did penises suffer the same scale of description? I wasn't sure I wanted to know.

'Right,' I whispered. I pulled back from Lauren. 'Er, look,' I cleared my throat as if to say, 'I'm being serious now'. This was my moment. Lauren looked at me intently and I tried to sound coherent. I failed. 'That night, you know, with er, and we, the *pink* thing, and Rich and your *artwork* and . . .'

'Oh *I* know what this is about,' Lauren whispered.

She did?

'Rich told me about your conversation in the pub, the one about my exhibition. That you were, what was it? Worried that by exposing the bands as they really are, you shattered the mystique of being a rock star, removing the myth that separates the celebrity from his fans.'

She didn't.

'I've nothing against your exhibition,' I whispered. 'It's more certain exhibits I have a problem with. Well, one to be precise.'

'Ah.' Lauren leaned forward. '*Now* I understand. You're worried about having your plastercast on display.'

I glanced up again to see if Rob Hutch was listening. He wasn't.

'Yeah,' I whispered.

'Relax,' Lauren smiled. 'I can assure you, that's staying in my own *private* collection.'

You know how Sting can have tantric sex for six hours at a time? Well hearing Townie's drum kit come together must have been close to matching Sting's climax. All those painstaking hours of tweaking, fine-tuning, trying different positions and taping down those funny sticky out bits. All of it had paid off.

For Rob.

It was somewhat depressing to discover that after six and a half hours of waiting for the drums to be done, my bass part needed the best part of twenty-five seconds of attention.

'Bass players are always a bit simple,' Rob smirked as he plonked a mike in front of my speaker.

*

'You were very slick back there,' Lauren commented, as we headed back to Brighton, numerous hours later. We were squashed between the drum kit and amplifiers in the back, perched on a wooden ledge above one of the wheels. Danny and Townie were sat in the front with Rich, along with the rough mix of our demo tape, whose muffled sounds you could just about make out through the partition. 'Back there in the recording studio. I thought you were very manly.'

'Really?'

'Very quick. Over before you'd begun.'

I had Townie to thank for that. The first time the red light had gone on, my brain had frozen, my hands playing every possible note but the right one. Townie, though, used all his diplomatic skills to coax out a decent performance.

'Jesus! I'm going to go nuts in a minute, Saucepan,' he growled. 'If I have to play this again, I'll fucking brain you. Understand?'

Two takes. It was impressively professional, were it not for the fact that Danny and Rich did theirs in one take each.

'Instinctive,' Rich winked at me. 'Now let's mix this baby down and bugger off home.'

'In a minute,' said Danny, in what proved to be one of the understatements of the year. 'I've just got to do the guitar.'

'What was that you just played?' I asked.

'Oh that was just a guide part, so Rich would have something to sing against.'

'Absolutely,' Rob slapped me on the back. Danny was the kind of customer he liked. 'It's crucial to get that guitar sound right.'

Rob's smile didn't last long. I remembered thinking it odd when we unpacked the van that Danny had brought so many guitars with him. Must be paranoid about breaking a string I thought. It hadn't crossed my mind that he was planning to play them all.

'So how many tracks has this studio got?' Danny asked innocently.

'Forty-eight,' said Rob, proudly.

'And how many have we used so far?'

'Six.'

'Forty-two to go,' I joked.

'Don't be daft,' Danny said. 'I'm only going to need about twenty.'

What followed, simply, was a masterclass in recording. Townie, Rich and I, it turned out, were just the foundations for Danny to build his wall of sound. Acoustics, electrics, six strings, twelve strings, overdubs, underdubs, Danny recorded and re-recorded them all: forwards, backwards, even sideways. At first Rob tried to blow him out with the same studio gobbledegook he'd given me, but Danny knew what he was talking about and we settled down contentedly to watch Rob meekly following his instructions. Several hours later, Danny woke us all up to tell us he'd finished.

'He was amazing, wasn't he?' Lauren said as the van sped on. 'An absolute natural.'

'It runs in the family,' I explained about his mum.

Lauren's eyes lit up. 'Penny Martin? You're kidding me? Danny's her son?'

'You know her?'

'I *love* her. I must have, what, three or four of her albums or something.'

'You should tell him,' I said. 'I reckon he'd be dead chuffed to know that.'

There was a crunch as the van went over a pothole, followed by a muffled, 'Sorry' from the front.

'So am I a natural as well?' I asked. 'I recorded my part in two takes.'

'I thought you could have relaxed a bit more,' Lauren

decided after a pause. 'There was something about your body language that suggested that you were concentrating really hard to hold something in. It was a shame you couldn't have shown what you were feeling.'

Yes, well. I'd considered that, but reckoned that vomiting all over Rob's expensive recording gear was not the best contribution I could make to proceedings. It was Sod's fucking Law. I'd been feeling a bit wobbly on the drive there, but then my nerves about recording had kicked in, and my stomach had settled down. Then Rich walked into the control booth as I was about to play and that was it.

'It, it was the pressure,' I said. 'You know, with the red light and everything.'

'Such a shame you find the red light so intimidating,' Lauren smirked. 'You could have made a lot of money in Amsterdam. Especially with your alter-ego.'

'Alter-ego?'

'You know,' Lauren winked. 'Cynthia.'

'How many times do I have to explain this? I haven't got an alter-ego. There is no Cynthia.'

Lauren hadn't moved, but suddenly she seemed to be sitting a *lot* closer. She was winding me up and she knew it. 'Methinks the lady doth protest too much.'

'For the last time, I AM NOT A . . .'

'Ssssh,' Lauren leaned forwards, put a finger to my lips. 'We don't want them to hear us in the front.'

Her mouth, her lips were inching inevitably towards mine. Instinctively, I realised I was responding.

'I'm . . . not . . . a . . . transvestite.' Her lips felt soft and warm as they grazed against mine, dry and cracked.

'I have . . . no problem whatsoever . . . with people who are . . . what they . . . do . . .'

And then we were all over each other. Lauren hooked a leg over mine, her hand scrunch pulling my hair. My left hand was doing likewise, my right was yanking her top out of her jeans, pulling her waist towards me, feeling a frisson of excitement as my fingers found her bra strap. We were kissing like crazy, both pushing against the other's lips with real passion, tonguing and biting with abandon.

'God,' I pulled back, catching my breath. 'God, Lauren.'

Lauren stared at me. I tell you, her eyes were *alive*. She was still playing with my hair, twisting it, pulling it. I could feel my dick starting to strain. And before I knew it, we were on top of each other once again. It was all happening so fast, I can only remember flashes of what happened. Lauren grabbing my arse. Biting my ear lobe, licking my ear. Me squeezing her breasts, feeling their warm softness through her bra. Lauren's breath catching and quickening.

Then I heard Rich laugh.

'Wait,' I said, pulling back suddenly. The van swerved round a bend, and my stomach lurched. 'I can't do this.'

'Do what?' Lauren's face was close, her pupils enormous.

'This. You know, *this*.' I could taste the sick in the base of my throat. 'I can't do it, Lauren, not with Rich three metres away.'

'Will,' Lauren said. 'There's a solid partition between us. He can't see anything.'

'That's, that's not the point.'

'What is the point?'

'The point, Lauren, the *point* . . .' My stomach twinged. The point, Lauren, is that you're going out with the singer in my band. 'It's Rich.' How could I put this? 'The band means a lot to me. I don't want to do anything that would jeopardise it. If you and Rich weren't partners, things might be different.'

Lauren pulled a face. 'You expect me to give all that up? All the publicity and plans for my photographs? What are you? Nuts?'

I shook my head.

'I don't see why there's a conflict,' Lauren said. 'All we have to do is make plans for when Rich isn't around.'

This was so hard. Lauren was up for it. She did look gorgeous, really gorgeous. There was such a strong sexuality about her, the sort you get off someone's elder sister, the kind of person who was that crucial couple of years more experienced than you. I'm sure the illicitness made it exciting too, the danger of getting caught adding an extra edge to affairs. Without thinking, I found myself being drawn towards her once more, when there was a knock from the front. I jumped back, banging my head.

'It's no good,' I said, my morality kicking back in. 'Rich knows something is going on.'

'It's all right, Will,' Lauren pointed at the orange indicator lighting up the road behind us. 'We're just turning into my street.'

'It's not all right,' I said. My *stomach*. 'Look, you're really attractive and this is great and everything, and I mean *everything*, but . . .'

'Woah. Hang on.' Lauren pulled me round, literally held me in her gaze. 'Are you brushing me off? Have I read this all wrong?'

My stomach twinged sharply. I really, really wanted to stop feeling sick. I couldn't deal with this. I looked away, tried desperately to compose myself.

'I see,' said Lauren. She breathed out deeply.

'Lauren . . .'

'Forget it,' Lauren said as the van came to a halt. 'It's my fault. I clearly made a misjudgement.'

'No. No, you didn't . . .'

'Will, I don't want to hear it.' She leaned forwards and kissed me on the cheek. 'Really. It's just fine.'

'But can't I . . .'

'No.' Lauren opened the back door. 'I think here's where I get out.'

11

Well, I stopped throwing up. Almost overnight, my stomach righted itself, deciding that I lived on dry land rather than the high seas after all. The guilt vanished, as did my nausea tinnitus. I woke up, and I didn't feel sick. I could eat food. *I could eat breakfast again.* I can't tell you how good that felt: I'd been feeling so dreadful for so long that I was almost pathetically grateful for feeling normal again. God it was nice. Lurching, hurling and retching became vocabulary from a previous existence.

But that was as good as it got. My stomach may no longer have been upset, but my mind – and my heart – most certainly were. Jesus, I'd turned Lauren down. I had to keep telling myself that she didn't want to go out with me. She was staying with Rich, Will, she'd made it perfectly clear. What she was offering me was to be her bit on the side, her sneaky snog when Rich's back was turned, or when he was in the front of the van. She would be taking advantage of me. And I didn't want that. Absolutely not! Wham bam? No thank *you*, ma'am. Not for me. *No* way. Not at all. Um.

I wasn't sure why Lauren wanted to do this. That

was the one bit of the whole thing that didn't make sense. I didn't know her that well, but from what I did, I didn't think her the type of person to mess around. Rich, sure, I could imagine doing so, but not Lauren. Was it political, Lauren trying to get back at something Rich had done by showing him that anything he could do, she could do better (or worse in my case)? It made a sort of twisted sense. It also made sense for me to keep well out of the way. For if Rich found out, as he inevitably would, then it would be me who got it in the neck.

But this makes it sound as though I was thinking like Rich, with his Youngian morality of don't get caught. Not true. For better or for worse, I seemed to be the only one round here with a strong sense of what was 'the right thing to do'. Cheating, infidelity, going behind a friend's back – and a friend who was offering me a springboard to a better life at that – it wasn't in my make-up. Not that I wear make-up, of course. I may have disagreed with much of what my parents had taught me but not messing about in other people's affairs was one rule I was going to stick by. Call me wet behind the ears – perhaps this was the way that the adult world really worked – but I was going to stick to my old-fashioned beliefs that relationships were about staying loyal to one person and one person only.

After all, if Lauren was only prepared to offer me a bit part in her love-life, what did that say about what she thought of me? Had she sat there, and thought, he's so desperate that he'll take anything he can get? I tried again, really hard, to make myself believe this was possible, because if I could find that chink in the armour, the *amour*, then I could convince myself that Lauren wasn't the sexiest, sunniest, funniest, funkiest girl I'd ever met in my life. And if I could do that, and focus really, *really* hard on that flaw, then the fact that I'd turned her down might not hurt quite as much as it did.

But I couldn't. The more I thought about her, the more I searched for something to damn her with, the more I remembered things about her that I liked. Her hair. Her lips. Her humour. Her charm. The curve of her back. The sharpness of her words and her shoulders. And all I ended up doing was going round and round, thinking how amazing she was and how her offer to cheat on Rich just didn't make sense.

*

Can you remember the moment when you first realised you were in love? I'm not talking about the moment when you fall in love – I still hold that it happens pretty instantaneously, that if you sift through your memories, you'll be able to pinpoint your starting point, a starting point I'd hazard that is earlier than you think. No, I'm talking about that moment weeks later, when your brain finally catches up with your heart, and the sheer enormity of your emotions dawns on you. It's a false epiphany in a way – nothing new has happened, all you've done is place the pieces in the right order – but I don't think that detracts from the moment. Self-realisation is always a wonderful thing, and when it involves the richest feelings of them all, it's a memory you're unlikely to forget. In fact, I'd go as far as to say that if you can't remember the moment – or if your recollection is vague or hazy – then maybe you weren't in love after all.

I was doing the washing-up when I realised I was in love with Lauren. I was doing the washing-up and Phil Collins came on the radio.

Doing the washing-up itself was an occasion. It was the first time in weeks that I'd thrown caution to the wind and cracked open a bottle of Fairy. What with my parents being away, and with the state of my stomach and my soul to contend with, housework had not exactly been a top priority. I'd let it get on top of me, and then I'd buried myself underneath it, hoping the world would go away.

With my stomach returning to normality, however, I felt it was time to begin again. It was a revelatory experience. In the sitting room, for example, under a mound of clothes and magazines, I discovered a sofa my parents used to own. And in the kitchen – well. The crockery was so homesick, having not seen the inside of a cupboard for weeks, that most of it had gone green. I had only one washing-up trick – leaving things to soak, and I'd done it so well that there were enough pans of water for the kitchen to start its own weather system. It was time to act.

It's not that I hate washing-up. As I put on a pair of pink rubber gloves and tuned into Radio One (Simon Bates. Batesy. Simes), I remembered that I quite enjoyed it, pottering around the kitchen, dancing to myself. And cleaning, I felt, was therapeutic. And therapy was exactly what I needed.

There must have been a lot of washing-up, because I began as Simes was finishing the Golden Hour (1984 – I knew that as soon as I heard '99 Red Balloons') and was still going strong as he segued into Our Tune an hour later. Our Tune. That one moment every day, when the nation came together as one. So much so that beneath the gentle strains of the love theme from Franco Zeffirelli's *Romeo and Juliet*, if you listened carefully, you could hear the sound of truck drivers pulling into lay-bys across the country, Kleenex at the ready.

Bates didn't disappoint. The letter he read out was from 'Sally' from Staffordshire, Sally who was trying to overcome the triple heartache whammy of being dumped by her boyfriend, Steve, being disowned by her mother Pam, and then discovering that Steve had been bonking her mum the entire time she'd known him. If that wasn't enough, her only loyal friend in the world – her pet poodle, Fifi – had developed the canine equivalent of measles and didn't look like he was going to pull through. But Sally was determined not to lose the one true friend she had left in the world, and remembering that Fifi was a big fan of Phil Collins, she began a basketside vigil that was to last many weeks, playing him his favourite songs in the hope that it would inspire a recovery.

It was hard not to be moved, and as Simes spun Sally and Fifi's Our Tune – the power-ballad 'Against All Odds' – I found myself feeling ever so slightly wobbly. As the piano intro began, I felt my face flush. When the vocals came in, I could feel a small but definite lump forming in my throat. And as the wash of synthesiser strings came in, and the verse built into the chorus, what I had to face was the fact that I was blinking furiously.

My heart was thumping. Jesus, I thought. Get a grip, Will. This is *Phil Collins* you're listening to. For God's sake. Get through this.

But then the heavy thump of an echo-laden mid-eighties drum kit kicked in. And so did my tears. A trickle, then a stream, and finally a fucking flood of the things. I cried, I sniffled, I howled in a way I hadn't since I was a small child. And it was then that I realised. 'I love you, Lauren,' I yelled at no one in particular, as huge teardrops of despair splashed into the washing-up bowl. 'I love you *so* much.' And with that acknowledgement came a release of emotion. This may sound strange, but what I remember feeling is a tremendous sense of relief. It was like, I'm not going mad after all. I'm in love. And that knowledge gave me some sort of comfort to cling on to. That and the fact that Phil Collins had a hotline to my heart. Phil understood. He wasn't singing to anyone else. He was singing to *me*.

I let it all out. I cried and cried until my heart hurt and my eyes stang. I was madly in love with Lauren, and there was nothing I could do about it. It was awful. I felt like a pining, lovestruck, pre-Raphaelite princess trapped inside the body of a skinny, spotty teenage boy. And there was no way I was going to be allowed out.

Fifi, Bates regretted to inform, did not pull through.

*

Crying wasn't enough. However much I howled, I still had the need to get *more* out. I needed to purge myself.

I needed to express myself. And if you want proof as to just how caught up in Lauren I was, then here it is: I started writing her poetry.

I know. I *know*. It was terrible stuff, too, the worst kind of turgid, self-indulgent, self-pitying verse. As a poet, I was pretty much in the category of fell off the back of a laureate. My ability to find rhymes verged on the laughable. Why wouldn't Lauren go with anything apart from 'warren'? I can't tell you the number of sonnets I wrote that ended up having rabbits in them.

Let me give you an example of my crimes against literature. Here's one that started about the time I bumped into Lauren in Marks and Spencer . . .

I want to tell you, tell you how I feel,
I don't want a model, I'd rather someone real.

Then I went on to talk about New Year

I want somebody year in, year out to be there,
to be with me at midnight with moonlight in her hair.

. . . before moving on to *that* night . . .

You drive my heartbeat faster,
make me feel good about my flaws.
Cast things in a way that I've never seen before.

. . . the fact that I realised it was love

If I had a fortune, kooky,
I would make you rich.
Cos when it comes to love and lust
I know which is which

. . . and how I'd tell her how I felt, if only the situation allowed.

> You're special cos you're different
> Different cos you're special
> I want so much to tell you, and if I can I Will.

I Will. That's me, I thought. So I wrote it again at the end, like I was, well, signing it.

*

But did Lauren deserve to suffer my bloody awful poetry?

The thing was, it was early February, and being a romantic, I guess I felt the same way about Valentine's Day that Christians did about Christmas. For me, the essential message of the day had become increasingly lost, deluged under an avalanche of commercial possibilities: everywhere you went, every magazine you opened, you couldn't move for love; restaurants recommending early booking for Valentine's Day; huge red heart-shaped displays in card shop windows; newspapers offering to print your romantic messages. But even so – like Christians still turning up to church – as a romantic, I felt honour-bound to celebrate the occasion. If I didn't mark my love for Lauren in some way, I'd be doing myself down.

I agonised. I typed the 'I Will' poem out on my father's computer, in a suitably anonymous font. I bought Lauren a card: a small, purple, fluffy home-made one, with a pink velvet heart in the middle. It was a bit girlie, perhaps, but Lauren was big on texture and I thought she'd like it. I would have posted the card, but after a frustrating evening with the computer, I concluded I was not going to be able to print the envelope. There was no way I was going to write it myself: she'd know who it was from straightaway and anyway, I liked the mystique and mystery of it being anonymous. And, apart from anything else, that's all I could really offer her. I wasn't going to go out with her behind Rich's back, so all I could do was let her know that someone, somewhere cared for her. A love quite unrequited.

One final thing. Ever since my application for the Tears For Fears fan club went missing, I'd never trusted the post office with anything important. I was going to have to deliver the card by hand. This wasn't *so* bad, I decided. It spared me my normal Valentine's morning ritual of waiting despairingly for the postman to appear, only to be desperately disappointed after he'd gone. Each teenage year, I'd willed things to be different, but it had never happened. I thought briefly about how brilliant it would be if Lauren had sent me a card, I grinned hugely at the merest possibility, but quickly tempered myself. However optimistic being romantic can make you, I wasn't *that* stupid.

With my poem, and the padded fluffiness, the card felt heavy in my coat pocket as I set out on the twenty-minute walk to Lauren's house. Maybe heavy isn't the right word. Substantial, perhaps. Significant. I felt a little light-headed as I recognised the route leading to Lauren's house. The last two times I had been here had not exactly been without incident. I saw a white van drive past, and couldn't but remember that night I'd turned

Lauren down. As I turned the corner into Lauren's street, I felt my stomach lurch ever so slightly.

The white van that had passed me a moment before had stopped halfway down the street, and as I continued walking, I realised that it had stopped outside Lauren's house. I heard a side door slam shut, and then – to my horror – saw a man in blue cap and overalls, *carrying an enormous bouquet of flowers*. I blanched. I felt sick for the first time in days. Rich, Rich, Rich. I crouched down behind a car and steadied myself, not bearing to look. I heard the deliveryman laugh, then a front door slam. I stayed crouched as he returned to his van, then drove away.

'Are you all right there, son?'

I glanced up, and saw a beefy, burly postman smiling down at me.

'Er yeah, thanks. Um, cramp,' I smiled back.

'Here, let me help you up.'

Go away, I thought, as the postman held out a helping hand. I creaked upright.

'I know how you feel, mate,' the postman banged his bulging bag. 'Bloody busy morning for me. I'll be glad to get shot of this lot.'

He reached into the bag and pulled out a multi-coloured stack of cards, held together with a rubber band. I must have only looked at the top envelope for a split second, but it was more than enough.

The cards were for Lauren.

'I don't know how some of these birds do it, I really don't,' the postman winked, then slapped me on the back and crossed the road.

My legs felt weak again. I felt nauseous. The card in my pocket, which had once felt worthy and essential, now seemed thin, trifling and pathetic. As I watched the postman post card after card after card through Lauren's letterbox, I felt extremely small. And very, very lonely. For either Rich was so in love with her that he was sending her a heap of cards, or I was just another of Lauren's long, long list of suitors. Either way, it was mind-numbingly depressing and I didn't want to know.

I turned, and slowly began to walk away, quickening slightly when I heard the postman shout after me. As if on cue, Phil Collins started singing in my head. Not now, Phil. *Please.* My walk became a jog until I was running, just running down the pavement, as fast away from Lauren and from Phil as I possibly could, running until my lungs hurt as much as my heart did.

I didn't know where I was going. I saw a red postbox ahead of me and with one last burst of energy I ran to it and kicked it. It fucking hurt. Then I leaned on the postbox, put my head on my arms and let out a string of wheezy sobs. It was so, so fucking unfair. How could I feel so strongly for someone and for it not to mean anything? I grabbed my card out of my coat, and tore open the envelope. I took out the poem, shoved it back in my pocket. Then I looked at the card, ran my fingers across its soft, fluffy padded exterior, watched as the velvet heart reflected in the light. Then I put it back in the envelope, which I closed as best I could.

I held it to my chest. What the fuck had I been thinking of? Lauren had Rich. Rich clearly adored Lauren. What had I been hoping to achieve with my card? I sniffed. She was just the same as everyone else, just as uninterested in me. What was it about me that made me so unattractive? Why could I not find anyone to love me? Would I ever find anyone to love me? I pulled out a pen, and wrote an address on the envelope.

> Someone, Anyone.
> Somewhere, Anywhere.

Then I shoved it in the letterbox and hobbled away.

12

In sharp contrast to my private life, everything about
the band was clicking into place. Rich had made Danny,
Townie and I rehearse like bastards – four hours a night
after work – and the results were beginning to show.
The music sounded tight, together and ready to rock.
We knew when to come in, when to turn up, tune in
and drop out, when to turn the volume up to eleven
and tweak it down to two. I'm sure Rich would have
joined in the sessions had he not had his vocal chords
to protect. As it was, he was forced to spend his evenings at Barneys, 'keeping the landlord sweet' before our
forthcoming gig.

The band had finally got a name. I was glad, as I'd
got bored with saying, 'We haven't actually decided on
one yet,' and then some smart Alec quipping, 'Ooh, isn't
that a bit of a mouthful?' In a rare and almost unpre-
cedented display of power sharing, and one, I realised in
retrospect, that was entirely for show, Rich had decided
to let everyone suggest a name, the chosen one being
picked out of the metaphorical hat (in reality, torn-up
beer mats out of a coat pocket). I'd tried to come up

with something clever, a name that would go down with the groupies after the gig.

> ME: *It's actually the robot in a late-forties post-modernist science-fiction film. The robot is really smart, but has a malfunction when it tries to understand love.*
> GROUPIE: *Will, that is so beautiful. Would you like to have sex with me now?*

I couldn't think of one, though, and after careful consideration, plumped for one that highlighted my role in the band.

'First Bass?' said Rich, as he picked it out. He looked disappointed that his choice, Double Top, hadn't been picked. Danny (Three Chord Trick) and Townie (Knuckleduster) looked similarly narked off.

'Sorry guys.' I felt myself fighting a smile. 'That's democracy for you.'

'Exactly,' said Rich. 'And that's why there's no place for it in a rock group whatsoever.' He tore my suggestion in two. 'I think we've all learnt an important lesson today, about how a band should be properly run. Double Top is my band, and anyone who doesn't like it can leave now.'

*

With the big Brighton Rocks gig less than three weeks away, Rich had set up a suitably low-key, out of the way warm-up – at a ball in London. 'Most bands don't dare tackle the Big Smoke until they've cracked their hometown,' he explained. 'But we're so fucking good, we're going to use the capital as our practice show.' Whether where we were playing actually counted as London was open to question. Rich claimed the venue was in 'zone seven', though I couldn't find it on my *A–Z*.

'Are you sure this is the right place?' I asked, as we turned down a gravel, tree-lined driveway that appeared to go on forever.

'Absolutely. This is Piers's pad,' Rich pointed at a stately-looking home in the distance.

Piers, it transpired, was an old school friend of Rich's. He'd swopped university for making money, running private balls for the extremely well to do.

'This is his house?' I asked.

'It's his parents'. They're away,' Rich shrugged.

Bloody hell, I thought, looking round. Where did you go to school?

We drove for an age down the driveway, before swinging the van round a well-kept piece of circular lawn, empty save for signs threatening people who dared to walk on it. We pulled up outside an ornate building that wouldn't have been out of place in *Brideshead Revisited*. Tied to the front of which was a banner that read 'Welcome to the Centennial Ball'.

A bespectacled, dinner-jacketed bloke appeared in the doorway. He had a long, blond floppy fringe which he flicked back with haughty arrogance.

'Charlie? Charlie! *Wie geht's?*'

Charlie? *Wie geht's?* What was this? Some old school greeting?

'Piers! Good to see you,' Rich opened the door and rushed across to shake him by the hand. 'How's it going?'

Rich's voice had changed. It had gone plummy. Posh.

'Fine, fine. It's a bit of a tight finish, but I think we should be ready.'

'How much did you charge in the end?' Rich asked.

'Only one hundred and fifty.'

One hundred and fifty quid?

'For a double ticket?' Rich said. 'Very reasonable.'

Piers agreed vehemently. 'You know, I think it's pretty bloody reasonable considering what a damn fine spread we've put on.'

'Absolutely. Piers, I must introduce you to the rest of the band.' Rich waved his hand vaguely in our direction. 'Danny, Townie and Saucepan.'

'Yes of course.' Piers didn't turn round. 'Delighted, delighted, delighted.'

'So is anyone else from the old school here?' Rich asked.

'Oh they're *all* coming. As soon as they heard you were going to bring your beastly racket, the tickets went faster than those for Glyndebourne. Giles, Quentin, Jeremy, they're all here.'

Rich seemed particularly excited about the last name.

'Just back from Columbia,' Piers tapped the side of his nose. 'I think he's brought you a little present.'

'Well I'd better say hello, then, hadn't I?' Rich waved in our direction again. 'You lot can sort the gear out, can't you?'

Danny nudged me. 'Sounds like his mate Jeremy has beaten us to it.'

*

But however well things were going with the band, it wasn't long before Lauren reared her far from ugly head. It was funny: I'd been desperately relieved when I learned she wasn't coming – 'no press', Rich had explained – but at the same time I was almost pathetically disappointed at her absence. I know that had she been there, it would have been weird and awkward and knotted my stomach into something a scout master would have had problems undoing, but I still wanted to see her. Maybe wanted isn't the right word. Maybe needed is better. I needed to see her. A look. A flash of hair. A smile. It didn't matter what. As long as I got my fix, I didn't mind.

I got a fix all right, but not the sort I craved.

Danny, Townie and I unloaded the van, minus Rich, soundchecked, minus Rich, then killed two hours in our dressing room, minus Rich. Townie was so bored, he picked the locks to all the cupboards to see if there was anything worth stealing.

'Something's better than nothing,' he said, examining a gold-plated toaster, 'especially as those cunts at the DHSS won't give me any more benefit.'

Townie described how he'd been down the council, trying to add invalidity benefit to his housing and unemployment benefit. He'd been practising his cough all week, and could produce a furry ball of phlegm on request.

'The guy looked at my form, went, "It says here that you are blind." So I went "Who said that?"' Townie laughed at his own joke. 'Had him there, Saucepan. Then he went, "What about your arm?"'

'Your arm?'

'Said I'd caught it in a combine harvester. So he asks

me how high I could lift it.' Townie raised his right arm slowly and not very far. 'I was grimacing and everything, like this.' Townie screwed his face up like he was David Mellor. 'Then he went, "And how high could you lift it *before* the accident?"' Townie shot his hand up like a swot at school. He looked at me and shrugged. 'Don't know how he guessed.'

'What a shame,' I said. 'And you didn't even get to show off your phelgm,'

'Oh I did,' said Townie. 'When he said I couldn't have any money, I gobbed the bastard.'

The ball, meanwhile was beginning to kick off at last, and I slipped off to investigate. It was the damn fine spread Piers had promised, but with £150 per person to play with, what else would you expect? 'Fire and Ice' were the themes, with rooms decorated in hot reds or cold blues accordingly. Ice sculptures lined the grounds outside. Doors were manned by jugglers breathing fire. Inside, the banquet hall had food roasting on spits, and waiters dressed as penguins and snow queens. The main stage and bar were decked out in crystals like Superman's icy hideaway. We were playing on the smaller second stage, which I couldn't help noticing was decked out as hell.

At the far end of bar, by a large inflatable devil's fork, was Rich's friend, Piers, waiting to be served.

'Oh hello,' Piers shouted at me above the music ('Fire' by that bloke with the burning bush on his head). 'You're Danny? Townie? Saucepan?' Before I could answer he'd caught the barman's attention. 'Hey you! Yes, a bottle of bubbly, and whatever this fellow is having.'

'Cider, please.' I ignored the barman's expression.

'So tell me about Charlie,' Piers asked. 'I bet he's having a ripping time down in Brighton.'

'Of course he is. You know what he's like.'

'I certainly do. I had to share a set with him.'

A set of what? Scrabble? Monopoly?

'A set of *rooms*,' Piers said, seeing my confused face. 'Ah, happy days. Biscuit games, soap bars in the showers . . .'

If only my parents had been able to afford the fees.

'So why do you call him Charlie?' I asked, as the drinks arrived.

'It was a nickname from our Friday night sessions.' Piers tapped the side of his nose. 'Look do you mind taking these round to him. I've just seen someone I need to talk to.'

I found Rich slopped lazily in an armchair round the corner, the top three buttons of his purple-and-pink-striped shirt undone, puffing away on a fat, expensive-looking cigar and looking very pleased with himself.

'Hi,' I said. 'How was your friend? Jeremy wasn't it?'

'Top,' Rich's grin, not to mention his swagger, seemed bigger than normal. 'I tell you. That Jeremy, he's a fucking mate.'

'Right. He brought you your present?'

Rich sniffed. 'It's all going rather nicely. Jeremy's present, those lyrics you've just written . . .'

'Lyrics?'

I looked blankly at Rich. I hadn't written him any lyrics. And here's where it all went horribly wrong. Rich pulled a piece of paper from his trouser pocket and handed it to me. I unfolded it and started reading its neatly typed, disturbingly familiar words. *I want to tell you, tell you how I feel, I don't want a model, I'd rather someone real . . .*

Oh my God. It was my Valentine's poem to Lauren.

'How, er, where . . .'

'I found them when I was looking in your coat pocket for a light,' Rich explained.

'You were looking in my coat pocket for a light? But I don't smoke.'

'Well you should. It's fucking annoying sometimes.' Rich took the words off me for a second time. 'When we get back to Brighton, I'll get Danny to put them to music.' He shoved the words into his shirt pocket, patted himself in congratulation. 'What a fucking great idea of mine that was. Getting you to write the words.'

Shit. How could I get them back? What could I say? You can't have them, I wrote them about your girlfriend? 'I'm really not sure about them, Rich,' I pleaded. 'They're a bit sentimental aren't they? Maybe I should take them away and work on them a bit.'

'Hey, are you questioning my judgement?' Rich suddenly sat forward, pointed his cigar at me.

'Er, um, well . . .'

'They're good, all right? Jesus, learn to take a compliment why don't you?'

I don't get much practice, I thought.

Rich, meanwhile, had sat back, and was puffing fat rings of expensive smoke into the night sky. He turned to me and winked. 'Oh yes. I'll tell you this for nothing, mate. When those words come out of my mouth, there's no skirt in the world who's going to be able to turn me down.'

Brilliant, I thought. That's just bloody brilliant. Not only had Rich got the girl I wanted to go out with, now he had his hands on the words I wrote to tell her how I felt. And every time we played a gig, I was going to suffer the humiliation of hearing him sing just how much I loved her. I wasn't going to be able to forget about Lauren, even if I wanted to. I watched Rich puffing away and I thought, yeah, my life's going up in smoke too.

*

I needed help.

Not in that sense. I needed help in the form of divine intervention, a miracle, a helping hand. A big fat thunderbolt was something of an urgent necessity. And you know what? For once in my life, God came up trumps.

My thunderbolt arrived after the gig. It was a warm-up, so I won't bore you with the details – that's the point of a warm-up, isn't it? – but considering we were in 'hell', I'd thought it was inappropriately lukewarm. We'd been scheduled at the same time as the main act on the main stage – some cheap Abba impressionists – and so had been slightly shorn of audience. In fact, almost completely clean shaven.

Danny and I were talking about this later, sat on stools by the bar. We'd cleared away all the gear (minus Rich), whilst Townie, after his success with his cupboard picking, had gone on a tour of the house's bedrooms.

'You enjoyed it, didn't you?' I asked.

Danny shrugged. 'Well, you know. It was all right.'

Now this was bollocks. Danny had *loved* it. The moment he got on stage, his persona had changed completely. Gone was quiet, retiring modesty. In came cool, confident, rock-god savvy. Five people, fifty-thousand people; Danny, you felt, would be right at home.

'How about you?' Danny asked. 'You seemed a bit preoccupied.'

Absolutely. I was so wrapped up in Lauren and the lyrics – I could even see the piece of paper poking out of Rich's pocket as we played – that I couldn't really tell you how it had gone. I'd played on autopilot, and if it hadn't shown, then certainly it had been heard.

I really liked Danny. He was a nice guy, but in a gentle, unassuming way, rather than my nervous, neurotic variety. He had nothing to prove, he had his guitar, he knew he could play, and that was that. If I'd known what he was thinking, I'd have unburdened myself to him about Lauren. But his fringe was the problem. I couldn't see his eyes, so I couldn't tell what he thought.

'How do you do it?' I asked. 'How come you're so comfortable on stage?'

'I'll tell you,' said Danny, 'but you must promise not tell the others.'

'Sure.'

'Well, you know the acoustic guitar I had on stage?'

'Acoustic?' I thought Danny had played electric all night. Then I remembered. 'Oh right, the one on the stand?'

'That's my mum's,' Danny said, slightly bashfully. 'With the guitar there, it's like she's with me, you know?'

I thought briefly about following suit, bringing one of

my mother's prized possessions to the next gig. Somehow, though, a framed photograph of Margaret Thatcher sitting on top of my amp didn't quite cut it.

I was feeling a bit cold – for a mock-up of hell, it had to be said the bar was somewhat chilly – so I nipped back up to our dressing room to get a jumper. The corridors were littered with public schoolies and sloanes, occasionally slumped on the floor in inebriated semi-consciousness, but mainly snogging each other in such a slobbery, salivary way that you couldn't but agree that drink loosens the tongue. Indeed, virtually the entire place appeared to have coupled off. Even the really ugly people had pulled. Everyone, it seemed, except me.

Which only added to my sense of self-pity. I know it's not an attractive state, but when I'm down that's what I'm like. It's so un*fair*, I thought. I'd spent so long deliberating about whether to show Lauren those words, and only hadn't because I'd seen the postman stuffing valentine after valentine through Lauren's letterbox. Was that not punishment enough? What right had Rich to override my decision, to steal my words and humiliate me with them night after night? They were only ever intended to be seen by Lauren. Now, though, they'd be heard by God knows how many people. A terrible thought flashed through my mind. What if we actually *did* get famous, and my words were the lyrics for a massive hit single? Every time I turned on the radio it would be there, every café and clothes shop I entered would be blasting out the painful truth of my unrequited love for Lauren. I'd have to move abroad. But what if we got really famous and the song got heavy rotation on MTV? It was no good. There would simply be no escape.

I'd worked myself up into such a state that I reached the dressing room with something approaching relief. I opened the door, switched the light on, and there, on the sofa, was Rich.

Naked.

Well, almost. He still had his socks on. But otherwise he was in the buff, butt naked right down to his butt. I gasped. His chest, I noticed, was matted with thick clumps of hair. On the top of his left arm was a tattoo. The word Rock curved above a picture of a rose. And, I couldn't help noticing, you'd have to have been blind to have missed it, the size of his dick. Fucking hell. It was the Penis de Milo.

But that wasn't what made me gasp. What made me gasp was that on Rich's left was a girl, similarly bereft of clothes. She had her head flung back, her long blonde hair hanging down, and Rich's tongue nibbling away at her neck. She had Rich's hand placed firmly on her arse, and her own hand touching her not inconsiderable breasts.

But that wasn't all that made me gasp. For on Rich's other side, in Rich's other hand, was another similarly unclad girl. She was nibbling on Rich's shoulder, and running her red fingernails across his chest.

I blinked. I gasped. I blinked again.

Rich was cheating on Lauren. Twice over. And I'd caught him red-handed.

Rich looked up. 'Don't you knock?' he asked. Then

he turned back to the girl on his left and French kissed her. The other girl was eyeing me up with interest.

'Don't bother with him,' Rich murmured. 'You'll be *very* disappointed.'

He squeezed her arse, and the girl giggled, returning her attentions to him.

'Is this important, Saucepan?' Rich winked at me. 'I've kind of got my hands full here.'

'I, er, I, er . . .' I was dumbfounded.

I rubbed my forehead. I was, simply, stunned. Stunned at just how *blatant* Rich was. 'Sorry,' I mumbled, and left.

I stood outside the door for a moment, trying to take it all in. Did I really just see all that? From inside I heard a thump and a squeal, and someone moan 'Oh *Rich*.'

I'll take that as an 'oh yes'.

I stumbled back along the corridor. I tried to get things straight in my head. I loved Lauren. Lauren loved Rich. And Rich loved, well, any girl he could get his hands on, by the looks of things. I suddenly remembered those two girls from Melanie's party – Tasmin and Camilla. What had he said about them? 'They'd drop everything for me. And I mean, *everything*.' I'd thought at the time he meant they were really good friends. Now, though, I realised exactly what he was on about. God, I could be so fucking naive sometimes.

Lauren had cheated on Rich. Rich had cheated on Lauren. What kind of a relationship was this? Did Lauren know about Rich's infidelities? Was this why she'd been so keen to get off with me, to level the score? They just – it was strange – neither of them seemed to care.

I wished I could be so laid back about the situation. Instead, whether I liked it or not, I was massively involved. For both knew I knew about their indiscretions, just not each other's. Rich didn't know I'd got off with Lauren. Lauren didn't know Rich had got off with someone else. And what didn't I know? Simple. I didn't know what the *fuck* was going on.

I wandered back down to the bar in a daze, and sat down next to Danny. I must have carried on chewing things over in my mind, for after, well, after I'm not sure *how* long, I looked up to see Danny staring at me in a vaguely amused manner.

'Where's your jumper?' he asked.

'Jumper?'

'Yeah. I thought you went to get your jumper.'

'Right,' I said.

'Well, where is it? You've been gone for . . .'

'I just walked in on Rich with two girls,' I blurted out. 'What are we going to do?'

There was a pause. I drained what was left of my cider.

'Do?' Danny asked.

'Yes, do. About Lauren.'

'What about her?'

'About the fact that she's tucked up in bed back in Brighton,' I snapped, 'while Rich is cavorting around with half of Sloane Square.'

'I thought Lauren was up in Manchester, having some late birthday bash,' Danny shrugged.

'Is she?' Was she? 'Well anyway, that's not the point. The point is, that Rich is cheating on her and . . .'

'OK,' Danny said. 'Now you've *really* lost me. He's *cheating* on her?'

'I think cavorting around with a couple of naked girls just about constitutes cheating, yes.'

Danny lit up a cigarette. 'Well this is all news to me. How long have Lauren and Rich been going out?'

'Ages,' I said. 'As long as we've known them.'

'Are you sure?'

I sighed.

'Of *course* I'm sure. Lauren told me. She and Rich are partners.'

'*Business* partners,' Danny said.

'And the thing is,' I continued, 'it was like Rich didn't care. There was no "keep this to yourself, Will," or "we need to talk about this later, Will," he didn't even stop while I was in the room, Danny, he just carried on letting his you-know-what do the talking and . . .' I stopped. 'Hang on. What did you just say?'

'Rich and Lauren are business partners,' Danny said. 'And Loz for that matter. The whole Brighton Rocks thing is a joint venture between the three of them. They've devised, planned and financed the whole thing between them.' He smiled. 'A *manage à trois* if you like.'

I was dumbfounded. Dumbstruck. Dumb. I opened my mouth and shut it again, like some sort of indie goldfish.

'Has Rich or Lauren ever told you they were going out?' Danny asked.

'Well, well I thought so, but . . .' I racked my brain for an example. There must be hundreds. But I couldn't think of a single one.

'Have you ever seen Rich and Lauren kiss, or hug, or do anything couple-like?'

I thought again. At the pub. In the park. At the guitar shop. The studio. No, no, no, no. The best I could come up with was Rich kissing Lauren on the cheek. But that, I saw now, could have been a friend's kiss.

The full enormity of the situation was just beginning to dawn on me. Everything was clicking into focus. Rich and Lauren weren't going out. It all fitted into place. With a headrush, I realised I'd misinterpreted, misconstrued and misunderstood. I'd got it into my head from day one that Rich and Lauren were going out. I'd never considered I could've got it wrong.

Suddenly it all made sense. Rich wasn't cheating on Lauren. Lauren wasn't cheating on Rich. No one was cheating on anyone. I felt an almighty rush of relief as the guilt at going behind Rich's back evaporated. I felt like a weight had been lifted. I felt light-headed.

And then another realisation hit me. And it hit me hard, like a cold slap in the face. I'd turned Lauren down because of my mistake. The only reason I'd rejected her advances was because I thought she was going out with Rich. My God. I could be going out with her. Fucking hell. I *should* be going out with her. Jesus fuck. If only I hadn't been so stupid, I *would* be going out with her.

But what about Valentine's Day? The flowers? Then I remembered something Danny had said earlier.

'Did, did you say Lauren was belatedly celebrating her birthday?' I asked.

Danny nodded.

'So when *was* her birthday exactly?'

'It's the fourteenth,' Danny said. 'She was telling me how she's never worried about Valentine's Day, because she knows she's going to get lots of cards.'

Was this for real?

I sat back in my chair and breathed out deeply. I didn't feel so cold anymore. I glanced around the room and saw people smiling, laughing, having fun. Seated at the table to my right were a particularly amorous couple; a rugby-playing type with his bow tie undone – a dark-bobbed girl with an electric-blue ball dress. They were leaned back on their sofa, nose to nose, not kissing, just whispering and laughing. Barely minutes earlier, I would have dismissed them as nauseous – another couple whose sole point was to ram home how single I was. Now though, I found myself smiling. I'm one of you, I thought. I know where you're coming from.

And just as soon as I can, I'm going to get myself there too.

13

Do you believe in love? Do you really? I'm not talking about liking the idea of love – everyone does that, in the same way that everyone thinks world peace is a great idea. I'm talking about *believing* in love, about being passionately willing to go that extra mile for romance, about allowing your life to be run by your heart and your feelings and your instincts, whatever the consequences.

Because it's not all fluffy bunnies and a dozen red roses. There's likely to be as much heartbreak and heartache as there is heartskipping and heartgiving. More so, in all probability. But if you're a real romantic, then you're prepared to take the bad with the good, the rough with the smooth, because being with your bit of rough, or bit of smooth (delete as appropriate) makes it all worthwhile.

I can only speak from experience, but for what it's worth, I love being in love. It's when I feel *alive*. It's when everything is bigger, brighter, better; more colourful, more vivid, more exciting. I love that: the elation, the intensity, the joy. And it doesn't stay within the confines of your relationship: Climie Fisher may have been the dodgiest of mid-eighties pop duos, but they hit the spot with their massive hit single 'Love Changes Everything'. The excitement and exhilaration of being in love is so all-consuming that it permeates throughout your entire life; you actually start to enjoy work, you shrug off missing your bus with a rictus grin on your face; what do you care? You're in love. You cook in the evening, and the food is just fantastic; fresher and sharper and tangier and tastier. You go to sleep, and you sleep like you've never slept before.

Yes, as far as states of being go, being in love just can't be beaten.

Of course, you may disagree with what I've just said. You may be sitting there, snorting through your nose, mumbling words like 'pah' and 'poppycock' under your breath. You may dismiss me as the soppiest of sentimentalists. You may think that what I'm talking about is the stuff of Mills and Boon and Lionel Richie love songs. Well, if you're thinking like that, all I can say is this: you've never been in love. You've never allowed yourself to fall, to really *fall*, to let yourself go without knowing what's going to happen next.

I'm not saying it's going to be easy. If you're with me on this, then you'd better fasten your seat belt, because it's likely to be a bumpy ride. If it's contentment you want, if it's a smooth state of affairs you're after, well you'd better keep clear of us romantics. Find yourself a low-maintenance lover with a steady job who likes order and routine and everything just so, the sort of person who thinks going out on a 'school night' is a bad idea, who thinks it is better to save than to spend, who is private even in their private life, who doesn't drink because they like to be 'in control'. I hope you'll be happy. And you may well be, in a low-maintenance sort of way. But you won't be *really* happy, and I think that's a shame.

When did I become a romantic? I think I always have been. I remember getting misty eyed over Sleeping Beauty and the Frog Princess as a small child, and it all kind of went from there. But there's no reason why you can't make the change, however old you are. Everyone has the capacity to be romantic, be they young or old, ugly or beautiful, left wing or right wing, rich or poor. That's one of the beauties of love – anyone can be touched by it. Even the most uncommunicative, unfeeling, unemotional, unresponsive types can fall in love. Yes, even men.

*

I had my chance to tell Lauren two days later. It's going to happen, I thought, the moment I woke up and saw the sun was shining. A big, bright, brand spanking new spring sun, with a spring in its step and a smile on its face. The sort of sun that when I got out of bed and opened the curtains, filled the room with thick rays of warmth and splendour. It was like living in a washing-powder commercial. I wandered over to the stereo, and put on 'I got you (I feel good)' by James Brown. Now I don't know exactly how good the Godfather of Soul was feeling when he wrote that song, but as I danced around the room, I decided he'd have to be pretty fucking happy to be half as chuffed as I was.

Lauren was doing a photo shoot with the band. She was going to go snap happy, and snap! So was I. I turned the radio on in the shower and sang along very badly to 'Deeply Dippy' by Right Said Fred, using the showerhead as a microphone. I washed myself like I'd never washed myself before. If nothing else, Lauren was going to be bowled over by how immaculate I was going to look. Every nook. Every crevice. Every cranny. Behind my ears. In between my toes. Up my . . . well, you get the picture.

I got out, wrapped my father's bath towel around me, then walked across to the sink, and wiped my hand across the steamed-up mirror. I examined my face. Spot count low. Should I shave? Should I look rugged? What did Lauren go for, I wondered. Was stubble trouble, or would it make her heartbeat double? The fact that I was trying to look rock and roll tipped it for me. That, and the fact I was petrified of cutting myself in an embarrassing adolescent way. Turning up with a small square of toilet paper stuck to my face was not going to be good for business.

I flossed. I gargled Listerine. I stuck cotton wool buds in my ears, in my nostrils, up my, well, you get the picture. I blow-dried my hair in as rough and manly a way as I could manage. I talked to myself in the mirror, imagining what I was going to say.

Hi, Lauren. Looking hot.

No, she might think I thought she was sweaty.

Lauren, long time, no see. We're going to have to make up for lost time.

Ugh.

Is that a camera in your pocket, or are you pleased to see me?

Christ, if that was the best I could come up with, maybe I should go for the non-verbal approach. I tried raising an eyebrow. I looked like a bad imitation of Roger Moore. I tried winking, pointing with my index fingers. I came across as an American game-show host. I licked a finger, ran it along an eyebrow seductively. If I did that in public, I might be locked up.

How do you woo someone? It depends, really, on what you've got to offer. With someone like Rich, it's easy to see where his appeal lay. One, he was good-looking. Two, he was endowed in donkeyesque proportions. Three, he was supremely confident, though given points one and two, maybe that's no surprise. What it meant, though, was that Rich had a range of wooing weapons in his armoury. He could pose. He could preen. Hell, if all else went wrong, he could pull his trousers down and slap his tackle on the table.

I couldn't really compete on any of those fronts. And I couldn't woo with expensive gifts, not on the sort of money I was earning. Maybe I should go for a more amusing approach? Women are meant to love blokes with a great sense of humour: to wit, to woo as a wise owl once said. But did I have a great sense of humour? Women, I sensed, liked to laugh *with* their boyfriend, not at them. Maybe I should leave the joke book behind.

What did that leave me with? Well, it left me with

what I felt for Lauren. That strength, that intensity was as strong a card as I had in my hand. I couldn't see the point of putting on an act, pretending to be something that I wasn't. Lauren was so sharp she'd see straight through it. Better to be exactly who I was, to rekindle how things were before my misinterpretations had made a mess of things. If I could get things back to how they were then, my feelings would be able to take things from there.

I got dressed in my finest rock clothes – the cords and the shirt that Lauren had picked out for me – she'd said how much they flattered me, hadn't she? I went down to have breakfast, but being paranoid I might spill egg or tea or something down my front, I ran back upstairs and got changed into something scruffy. I went back downstairs, had my breakfast, then went back upstairs and got changed back into my rock clothes. I looked at myself once more in the mirror.

Showtime, I mouthed, and breathed out deeply.

I felt a twinge of apprehension, sure, as I locked the front door, but that was easily overridden with my very own feelgood factor. As I thought of Lauren, I felt my rare and beautiful breed of butterflies in my stomach. I imagined Lauren and I laughing and kissing in all sorts of exotic places. Paris. New York. Tokyo. Hawaii. We were in restaurants, in cars, on trains, drinking, eating, talking, reading, and whatever we were doing, we were unable to keep our eyes, and our hands, off each other.

After ten minutes of waiting at the bus stop I decided a bus was never going to come. I was going to be late, but I didn't care. It's such a lovely day, I thought, I'll walk. Well, walk*ish* – I couldn't deny there was a skip in my step. I was so *excited* I didn't want to just hang around, I had to keep moving. I couldn't wait to see Lauren, to tell her how I felt. I tell you, it took immense self-control not to swing round each and every lamp post that I passed.

The photo shoot was in the Pavilion gardens. It seemed particularly apt, I couldn't help thinking. Here was where I was going to ask Lauren out. And here was where I first met her. I remembered the way she'd sat on the bench, grasped the front of it with her hands, and leaned forwards. The way, the *way*, her hair had swung down. Was that when it had all begun? My stomach felt fleetingly odd at the memory. Yes, I thought. You know, I do believe it was.

Like before, the gardens were occupied by a cross-section of the daytime TV audience. The grannies, the girls who should have been at school, the students, and judging by their familiar faces, the long-term unemployed. Except this time, there was one important difference. Lauren was there before me. She was kneeling on the path, her face hidden behind her camera, as she snapped away at Rich, Danny and Townie sat on a bench.

I tiptoed up, so as not to disturb the shoot, pausing behind Lauren. She flicked her head ever so slightly, causing her hair to ripple halfway down her back. Townie was the first to see me, and winked. Danny probably saw me next, I could never quite tell behind his fringe, and then finally Rich. He looked up at me, just as Lauren pressed the camera button.

'What did you do that for?' Lauren asked.

Rich nodded at me. 'Because his lordship here has finally got himself out of fucking bed.'

For someone who was so often late for things, Rich, I felt, was hypocritically unforgiving when someone was even later than him.

'Rich. Danny. Townie.' I smiled, but it wasn't them I was pleased to see. I looked down at Lauren.

Here goes.

'Hey, great to see you, Lauren. It feels like ages since I've seen you.' I sighed. 'Isn't this just the most lovely day?'

'Was,' Lauren replied, without looking up.

I was still on my nervous high, so I didn't realise that something wasn't quite right. Not even when Lauren stood up, and didn't turn round to look at me. Instead she picked up a light meter, looked up at the sky. I followed her gaze.

The sun had gone behind a cloud.

'When was the last time I saw you?' I asked. 'Gosh, let me see . . .'

'Will,' Lauren turned round to look at me at last. The paleness of her skin. The fullness of her mouth. The cut of her cheekbones. All exactly as I'd remembered, and then some. I smiled. Lauren smiled back. It was the same big, gummy smile she always gave me, and yet somehow it wasn't. This was when I realised something might be up. It wasn't as welcoming. It wasn't as warm. And as Lauren put a cap on her lens, she fixed me with a look. 'Sorry, Will. I'm afraid you're just that little bit too late.'

*

Late?

Late?

Was Lauren talking about the shoot? Or about us?

'It's the light,' Lauren explained to everyone else. 'You see that big cloud sat in the sky? By the time it's moved off, the shadows are going to have moved too far round.' Then she turned back to me. The way she was looking, she wasn't talking about the weather. 'I think you've missed your chance.'

I looked up again at the cloud. Grey. Imposing. Sloth-like. Cumulus Nimble it was not.

'What do you think, Rich?' Lauren asked.

Rich was helping himself to one of Townie's fags.

'You're the photographer,' he shrugged.

'The key thing is you, Rich,' Lauren said. 'You look great anyway, but in the sun you looked bloody gorgeous. I can't see the point of shooting another reel in the shade. It won't be as good.'

I've pissed her off, I was beginning to understand. I've really pissed her off by turning her down.

'Absolutely,' Rich pointed at me with his fag. 'It's got to be all about the singer, hasn't it? It would be a sorry state of affairs if things revolved around a bass player.'

'Quite,' Lauren said. 'That wouldn't do at all.'

Ouch.

'I thought this was a band thing,' I said. 'Danny and Townie are in the picture.'

'Oh, it's nothing *personal*,' said Lauren, which translated as, oh, it's completely personal. 'They just happened to be in the right place at the right time.'

'And I wasn't?'

'The moment's gone.'

'We've got to give the thing focus,' Rich explained. He began one of his cliché-riddled lectures about the rock-and-roll law of the jungle, about how it was dog eat dog and survival of the fittest and all that. He described how the episode with the band name should have taught me that band democracy didn't work.

How did I feel? Crestfallen is one way to describe it. Deflated is another. The sharpness of Lauren's words had punctured me. She'd been talking about her photography, but I knew what she was really saying. You've had your opportunity, Will, and you've blown it. Hell hath no fury like a woman scorned, and like any cliché, it was a cheap, annoying, overused thing to say, but it still contained an inescapable nugget of truth. I'd scorned her – for Rich, mistakenly, and for the sake of my stomach. And now the scorning was seriously on the other foot.

I put myself in Lauren's shoes. No, I wouldn't want to see me either. She was pissed off, and understandably so. She didn't know what I'd thought about her and Rich. Without that piece of knowledge, it made sense that she was mad at me. She thought she'd come on to me, and I'd turned her down. Actually, it was worse than that, wasn't it? She thought I'd felt the same way about her (which I had. Which I did). By turning her down, not only did she have rejection to deal with, but also the fact that she'd completely misread the situation. Except she hadn't misread the situation – I did fancy her. God did I fancy her.

Confused? I would be.

'. . . if I didn't impose some sort of control on proceedings,' Rich concluded, 'we'd be struggling under some terrible name. What was it?'

'First Bass,' Danny reminded him.

'You see? That says it all. We'd never even get to first base with a name like that.'

I looked at Lauren, who was kneeling down packing her camera gear away. I'm not going to get to first base either, I thought. Not the way she was playing hardball.

14

If I was going to get through to Lauren, I was going to have to follow in the footsteps of someone who knew what he was doing. I was going to study the skills of one of my long-time heroes, imitate his techniques, and hopefully copy his every last success. He was a man who I'd admired for many a year, a man I looked up to, a man I'd always wanted to be.

My hero was one of the most famous men of the 1980s. Not a household name admittedly, but definitely a household face. And a household body as well. I'm talking about the person who adorned *that* Athena poster. No, not the tennis girl scratching her arse, but the bronzed, beautiful, six-packed, sexy-pecced, bare-chested bloke cradling the oh so cute baby in his arms. A picture that, so I'm told, adorned many a teenage girl's bedroom wall. He's my hero – handsome and muscular, yet caring and sensitive. An animal in bed, yet happy to change the baby's nappy in the middle of the night. He was every woman's ideal man. And mine as well.

Now don't go getting me wrong here. *I don't fancy him.* He's not some kind of gay icon for me. And anyway, this particular chap isn't like that. Far from it. And I don't look up to him as some kind of symbol for new men. What is a new man? I've certainly never met one. No, the reason I admire this bloke is for decidedly 'old' mannish reasons: he has had sex with several thousand women. The sexual exploits of this beefcake Casanova have resulted in an average that is, well, anything but average. A different woman approximately every day and a half to be precise. That's four and two thirds every week (the rounding up each fortnight must be fun). I know all this because I read an interview with him once, when he discussed his success with women, the fact that he never washed with soap or shampoo, and the special energy drink he drank most days for breakfast.

A mouth-watering tall glass of cold carrot juice.

Topped off with just a dash of his own spunk.

Was that it? No two hours a day in a gym? Could I look as pathetic as I would in the equivalent poster – pale and skinny holding a pooping baby at arm's length, and still women would want to have sex with me? Just as long as I'd remembered to wash down my morning cornflakes with a glass of come and carrot juice? I didn't know how essential the daily drink was, but anything this bloke did was worth a go, considering how many women he'd scored. Revolting as it sounded (and tasted) it had to be worth a shot.

Gulp.

Have you ever tried to land come in a glass? No, I don't suppose you have. Believe me, it's easier said than done. I'm no novice when it comes to wanking, but even so, precision was not exactly one of my fortes. My efforts all went a bit Shrove Tuesday – when it came to that all important toss, the bloody stuff got stuck on the ceiling. I stood underneath for five minutes, wondering if it was going to fall off, or whether I would have to stand on something and scrape it down with a knife. As I was walking off to fetch a chair, I saw it start to move out of the corner of my eye. I dived full stretch, like some sort of goalkeeper, catching it in my hands.

Talk about a comedown.

It's funny stuff, spunk, I thought, as I carried it down to the kitchen. It looks – and feels – a bit like gloopy shampoo. *New Come & Go! One rinse and your hair will be full of life!* I've got to *down* this, I thought, holding it up to my nose. Urggh. Never again would I criticise the Lord Almighty for creating my body in such a way that I was unable to give myself a blow job.

Carrot juice. I rummaged through my parents' pantry, found a bag of carrots. I put the edible ones in a blender, threw the rest away. One carrot in particular was impressive: flowering at one end, decomposing at the other, it was the entire life process in one root vegetable. I wondered why it had to be carrots, as the blender whirred into action. Was there some equilibrium being established? Wanking is meant to make you go blind. Carrots are meant to make you see in the dark. Maybe the two together restore some sort of balance in your life.

I looked at the sperm sitting in the bottom of a glass. How much carrot juice should I add? A lot, so I can't taste the spunk? A little, so I get it over with as soon as possible? I dribbled a little carrot juice on to the come, turning it a sour, lumpy sort of orange. A single pubic hair rose to the surface. I added some more, stirring it with a teaspoon. Most of the spunk, thankfully, decided to dissolve, but there were a few sticky lumps that were going to float around for the duration. Those must be strong ones, I thought. The ones that could swim for England.

I sniffed the drink, which smelt vaguely acidic. No wonder this guy got through so many women, I thought. Sure, it might have helped him pull, but perhaps it explained why no one ever stuck around. I mean, think about breakfast the morning after.

'Morning, darling. Sleep well?'

'Not really. I was up half the night, thanks to you! Rrrrrr! You're such an animal. I can't understand all those women who leave you after just one night. I know it's early days, but you're so different to all the other men I've ever been out with. I could really imagine us settling down, getting married, having children . . .'

'Yeah? Me too. I'm so bored with all these one-night stands, honey. All I really want is a decent long-term relationship.'

'You do? Oh that's fantastic. I thought you were great last night, but this morning you're even more wonderful! I'm so happy. You're, you're just perfect.' Sighs. 'Now, what's for breakfast?'

'Whatever you want. Coffee, toast . . .'

'I fancy a glass of that fruit juice you're drinking. Is it freshly squeezed?'

'You could say that. Try some.'

'Mmm, it's quite thick isn't it? What is it, some health drink stuffed with proteins?'

'Sort of.'

'That taste is really familiar, too. No, you're going to have to tell me what it is.'

'Carrot juice and come.'

'Carrot juice and WHAT?'

'Come. My come.'

'You drink your own come for breakfast?'

'Are you all right, honey? You've gone all white.'

'Oh I'M fine, but then I'm not the one drinking his own fucking sperm.'

'Wait! Where are you going? Why don't you sit down and . . .'

SLAM!

I put the glass to my lips, was just about to drink, when I heard a loud banging sound coming from outside the front of the house. Huh? I put the fruity juice down, had a look through the hall curtains. Someone was erecting a large posterboard in my front garden. I slipped some slippers on and hurried out. A bloke in a pinstripe suit with a blue rosette and clipboard waved at me.

'Ah, you must be William,' he smiled, shaking my hand. 'Now if you wouldn't mind standing there, by the edge of the board, that's it, splendid, now look at the photographer.'

'What photographer?' I turned round, saw a man with a camera.

'Say cheese.'

Flash!

'Now hang on,' I said, turning back to the clipboard man. 'I don't know what's happening, but I think you must have made a mistake. What are you doing in my garden? What do you think my parents would have to say about this?'

'I'll tell you.' He smiled smugly, pulled a letter out of his jacket pocket, began to read. '*Dear Godfrey, we regret to inform you that Cynthia and myself will not be around to help you in your battle to keep those dreadful socialists out of office, on account of our round-the-world second honeymoon. In our absence, however, we would be delighted to donate our front garden to the Conservative Party's election campaign. It is a prime site, and passed by numerous motorists on their way to and from work, work I might add, created by the prudent economic policies of three successive Conservative administrations. Yours sincerely Peregrine Harding.*'

'You're joking,' I said. I glanced at the poster. KEEP THIS COUNTRY IN THE RIGHT HANDS. SAY NO TO KINNOCK'S COMMUNISTS. Jesus. Even fifteen-thousand miles away, my parents were still more than capable of making my life an absolute misery.

'I'll see you later,' the photographer said to Godfrey.

Hang on. Didn't he just take my picture? Standing next to the board?

'Who's he?' I asked.

'He's from the *Brighton Evening Argus*,' said the clipboard man. 'Fingers crossed it'll go on the front page tomorrow night.'

Me. On the front page. Next to that board. Oh my God.

'Now.' Godfrey flicked a page over on his clipboard. 'Your father said we could stick some posters in your front windows, maybe get a flag flying on your roof, and that you'd deliver some leaflets for us.'

Hi, I'm Will Harding, your local Young Conservative bass player . . .

'William, are you listening to me? Tamara's just gone back to the office to pick those up. She'll be along in a minute . . .'

Who's next at the bar? I'd better serve that lanky Young Conservative at the end, so I can have his money before someone beats him up . . .

'. . . with your help, William, we're going to stop those communists once and for all. Look, I don't suppose I could trouble you for a drink, could I?'

This was bad, very bad. It was a hard enough battle for credibility at the best of times, without having such a photo sprawled across the local rag. What if Lauren saw it? I'd be finished.

'William, a drink?'

A drink? You're ruining my life and now you want a drink as well? You've got to be taking the . . . *hang* on. I had a thought.

'Er, how about something cold?' I suggested. 'Some fruit juice, perhaps?'

'That'd be delicious.'

'No, no, no, don't you move.' I held a hand up. 'Please. I'll bring it out to you.'

*

The next day I rang Lauren up. It took me three attempts to get through, not because the line was busy, but every time I got to the last digit, I hesitated.

Please don't be in, I thought, as the phone finally started ringing.

'Hello?'

Bugger. She was in.

'Hello? Lauren? Hi, it's me.'

There was a pause at the other end of the line.

'Me? Me who?'

'Will,' I said, deflated she didn't recognise my voice.

'Will who? Will Jennings or Will, Saucepan Will?'

I felt even more disappointed. Not only was there another Will in her life, but he came before me in the pecking order of Wills. Not only that, but he didn't have an embarrassing nickname.

'Will Saucepan Will,' I said weakly. I hated my voice on the phone. It sounded tinny and tiny.

'Oh, *that* Will.'

Lauren's inflexion worked in the same way you'd say 'oh *that* moron', or 'oh God, not *that* idiot'.

'Yes, *that* Will.'

There was a pause. Phone silence can be the most romantic moment in the world, two lovers happily sharing an instant of contemplation with each other. I may have loved Lauren, but this was anything but one of those silences.

'And?' Lauren asked. 'Did you want something?'

'Yes,' I said.

There was another pause.

'Will, are you ringing from the other side of the world? Because there seems to be a time delay between each of your answers.'

It was funny. My throat was as dry as my palm was damp. I can't do this over the phone, I was thinking. I should meet her face to face, and talk it through.

'Is this about the *Melody Maker* photo?' Lauren asked.

What *Melody Maker* photo?

'No,' I said.

There was another pause.

'It's so hard to get a word in edgeways once you get going, isn't it?' Another pause. 'Is there anything specific you wanted, Will? I'm not too hot on telepathy.'

Finally I took the plunge.

'I, er, I wondered if perhaps you'd go for a drink with me?'

'I see.' Now it was Lauren's turn to be quiet. 'And when exactly were you planning to have this drink?'

I tried not to sound too desperate.

'Now?'

'Let me just check my diary. Oh damn. I'm washing my hair.'

'Right. Well how about later?'

'I think I'm still going to be washing my hair.'

'Um. Tomorrow?'

'I'm still going to be washing it, I'm afraid.'

I knew women spent a long time in the shower, but this was ridiculous.

'Just how long is your hair?' I asked.

'Believe me. It's very, *very* long.'

'So long you'll still be washing it at the weekend?'

'You know what? I think I might be.'

I paused. 'OK. Well maybe I could bring some shampoo round?'

'Shampoo?'

'Yes, if you're going to be washing your hair for that long, you're going to run out of shampoo at some stage. Maybe I should bring some round?'

Lauren laughed. 'I'm going to go now, Will. Let you get back to your canvassing.'

'Canvassing?'

'At least you've got the balls to stand up for what you believe in. Most people are too embarrassed to admit it.'

'Admit to what?'

'Very good.'

And then the penny dropped. The photographer. The newspaper.

Lauren laughed again. 'I can't pretend I'm not disappointed, though. I really thought you'd know better than that.'

The phone went dead. She's turned me down, I thought, as I stood there, and that annoying woman whined, 'Please hang up and try again.' I hung up. Should I try again? I redialled, but lost my nerve at the last digit. I placed the receiver down. I mean, what was the point? Lauren had made it perfectly clear what her position was. She'd warned me off on the day of the photo shoot, and now she was doing it all over again.

Photo shoot. Oh fuck. I tore off for the newsagents, praying like mad that it wasn't too bad, please God may it not be too bad. But when I got there, all such optimistic thoughts evaporated.

My picture. On the front page on the local paper.

THE 'WILL' TO WIN!

Teenage Tory 'Board' with Politics!

Who says that young people aren't interested in politics anymore? It's certainly not true in the case of nineteen-year-old William Harding, doing his bit to keep the Tories in power. 'I don't understand people who don't vote,' he said yesterday. 'It's a democratic privilege, an honour to keep those dreadful socialists from office.' William has erected a huge poster board in his front garden, to remind motorists which way to vote; 'The right way', he joked.

Fucking Godfrey! I'd never said that. I'd never said anything of the sort. No wonder Lauren was so funny with me: she thought I was some sort of Young Conservative. There was nothing I could do to sort it out. Even if I did ring the newspaper and complain, all they'd do would be to print a tiny apology, weeks later. Who'd see that? All anyone would remember was the original photograph.

Photograph. I picked up a copy of *Melody Maker*, to see what Lauren was on about. I flicked through, until I found a page called Upcoming Gigs. Rich had done his homework, all right, for there was a plug for next week's Brighton Rocks gig, together with a photo of the band.

Well, three quarters of the band, anyway.

It was a great photo, I'll say that much. It was one of the shots from the morning in the park. Rich was leaning forward on the bench, his head in focus, Danny and Townie fashionably blurred behind. And me? Well they say that life imitates art, or is it art imitates life? I can never remember which, but it doesn't matter anyway. Whichever way you looked at it, I was out of the picture.

15

I wasn't finished. Next time, I decided, I'd tell it to her straight. I was going to pluck up my courage and go for it. I was going to have to – for my next chance would be the Brighton Rocks gig itself – and what with Rich and Loz and everyone around, we were unlikely to get more than thirty seconds alone together. And in a strange way, my mishaps didn't downhearten me: I was so convinced of my feelings for Lauren that they only made me more determined. As someone once wrote, the art of romance is to take your chance. And mine, I decided, simply hadn't arrived yet.

At about five-ish on the big day, Danny, Townie and I were setting our stuff up in Barneys' back room. We'd moved the pool table out of the way, despite the protests of the two people playing at the time, and dumped our gear on the stage. It wasn't much of a stage to be honest, more of a piece of hardboard nailed to the pub floor. The 'stage' raised things all of two inches, except for the hole at the back where successive heavy drum kits meant the rhythm section still had its feet firmly on the ground. It was a funny venue, I thought, looking round. The lack of daylight coupled with the bar running all the way down the left-hand side distorted perspectives, made the room look smaller than it was. But what was really noticeable about the room was the fact that it stank of stale Guinness.

Danny and I were unravelling our many ravelled-up leads when Frug arrived. You could tell who played what just by looking at them. There was a short guy in denim, who quickly asked Danny for a tour of his amplifiers. A squat guy with a facial tic, cracking his knuckles in 4/4. A skinny, spotty guy, who looked both awkward and reliable, who wandered nervously around, refusing to make eye contact with anybody. And last, and by anything but least, was Loz, with his golden hair, his chocolate-brown cord suit and cheekbones which almost looked as though they'd been touched up.

The way Loz spoke, it was clear that all the camaraderie and chummy friendship of the Brighton Rocks partnership had been put to one side. We'd reached the moment where private dreams had become public property, and as far as Loz was concerned, it was every band for himself.

'It can't be easy for you,' Loz ran his hands through his hair, 'being our support band. I hope we don't show you up too much.'

'We're not your support band,' Danny responded. 'Rich said this was a joint headline.'

'Yeah, yeah, yeah.' Loz rolled his eyes and the rest of his band laughed. 'That Rich Young, he's so full of . . . Rich! Hi!' Rich swaggered out from behind the bar, grabbing a beer on the way. 'How's it going?'

'You know how it is,' Rich flicked the top off, raised his drink as if in celebration. 'Just had a word with the landlord, Loz. Seems your lot are going on first.'

'Yeah right,' Loz brushed his jacket. 'We're head-lining.'

'Not any more,' Rich nodded at Danny, who threw him a cigarette. 'Go on. Ask him.'

Loz did. He wasn't happy. 'You bastard,' he said. 'How the fuck did you manage that?'

'Oh. You know. Contacts.' Rich drew an imaginary 'one' with his cigarette smoke.

'We'll still blow you off stage,' said Loz.

'Of *course* you will,' Rich slapped him on the back. You could tell he was just loving this. 'Listen, you can stick around for our soundcheck if you like. You'll learn a lot.'

So will you, Rich, I thought.

'Oh, I don't take lessons from your sort,' Loz snubbed. 'And anyway. I've got to go shopping.'

'What kind of shopping?'

Loz tapped his nose.

'A trip to the old Superdrug.'

'How's Biz?' Rich asked, without missing a beat. 'Haven't seen him for weeks.'

'Oh, *Rich*.' Now it was Loz's turn to be sarcastic. 'You're not doing this gig *clean* are you?' He pretended to yawn. 'And I thought you lot were rock and roll . . .'

Rich bristled. 'You're going to see Biz? Biz is coming to see me.'

'Of *course* he is,' said Loz. 'Tell you what, why not come with me now? If we score the same gear, you can't go round making excuses. You'll have to admit we're the better band . . .'

*

'. . . cake, coke, E and whizz.' Rich returned an hour later, waving his brown paper-bag of tricks. 'Biz was doing a pick-and-mix special. Buy any three different drugs, get a fourth free. So. Who wants the cake?'

'What's in it?' Danny asked.

'It's a hash brownie.' said Rich. 'What do you think is in it?'

'Oh, right,' said Danny, suitably chastened.

'Whizz?' asked Rich, passing the brownie over.

'Smart,' said Townie, hands out.

'Wanna get loved up Will?' Rich asked.

Loved up, loved down, loved sideways, loved anything . . .

''Course you would,' said Rich, passing me the E. 'Cos this baby's all mine. They didn't call me Charlie at school for nothing, you know.'

I had my first drugs experience aged ten, taking the adult dosage of paracetamol by mistake. I was convinced I was going to die, that I'd have to have my stomach pumped and my parents would find out I'd been lying to them about not eating sweets. And then this amazing sensation took over. I don't know, it's so difficult to put into words, exactly what it was I was feeling. It was my head. It just felt so, so . . . *clear*.

Once I'd popped, there was no way I could stop. Migraleve, Panadol, you name it, I took it. I moved on to powders, Lemsips, stuff like that, and was just getting bored when the second summer of love came along, opening up a whole new range of pharmaceuticals. I know some people thought the flower power stuff a post-modern sham, but for me there really was something in the air that year. Until mid July anyway, when the pollen count began to die down.

I smoked my one and only joint in the sixth form. And yes, I did inhale. The whole fucking joint as it happened, badly burning the roof of my mouth. Proper drugs, though, I've always left well alone. Partly because I'm one almighty chicken, but mainly because of *Grange Hill* and their double whammy of drug horror; the terrifying plotline of Zammo's smack addiction. And even more harrowing, the Grange Hill Cast's top five anti-drug single, 'Just Say No'.

If you're someone like myself, there's always an added danger when it comes to taking drugs. If you're hip and happening, you're never likely to come down with anything nasty from doing drugs. Like, I don't know, *death* or something. However, if you're a dorkish dullard, the first time you try *anything*, you're all but guaranteed to drop down on the spot. And then there you'd be, the figurehead of the next anti-drugs campaign, your face plastered across the front page of the *Daily Mail*.

I was thinking about this as I slipped inside the toilet cubicle. The *Daily Mail*! It's my friends that I'd feel sorry for. First, they'd have to do all that lying stuff about how I was an incredibly gifted individual, a tragic loss to society, a glittering career cut short etc. No one in these situations ever has the honesty to say, 'To tell you the truth, Will was so anonymous I'd be surprised if many people realised he's dead. He had future accountant or librarian written all over him.' And secondly, my poor friends would feel obliged to take part in the obligatory anti-drugs campaign. *HAVE THE WILL TO SAY NO!* My picture would be everywhere, oh *God*, probably that horrible one from school when the photographer turned up unannounced, and I hadn't washed my hair for a week and had that awful spot on my chin. As legacies went, I really couldn't think of one that was less rock and roll.

Anyway. Like I said, I slipped inside the toilet cubicle, and before I knew it, the matter was out of my hands. Out of my hands and into the toilet to be precise. Shit. I thought briefly, *very* briefly, about plunging in after it. Then I pulled the chain, and tried to ignore any symbolism with regards to the gig.

*

'Rich, you're not going to believe this. You know that E?'

'Yeah. Did you drop it?'

'Right there, in the toilet.'

Rich slapped me on the back.

'That's what I like about you, Will. You're *reliable*. The others said you'd bottle it, but I knew better.'

I tried again.

'You don't understand. I DROPPED AN E IN THE TOILET.'

Rich put a hand to my mouth.

'All right, Will, you don't have to tell the whole pub. This place is due for a raid.'

I had a funny feeling as to how the evening was going to pan out.

'Do you feel any different?' Rich asked.

'Pretty much as I did before.'

'It'll kick in in a minute.' Rich felt in his pocket for some change. 'Now. Do you want a drink?'

'Cheers.'

'Ice?'

I was obviously behind on the latest way of drinking cider.

'Since when did you put ice in my drink?'

Rich pulled a face, like I was the thickest man on earth.

'Mate, you're off the alcohol with what you've taken. Now. Do you want ice in your water or what?'

All of a sudden, drug taking did not have quite the appeal of earlier. Although I'd avoided becoming a figure of pity for Middle England teenagers, I now had a gig to play, stone-cold sober. What about my nerves? Then there was Rich. What if he twigged I hadn't taken that E? I had no choice but to pretend. Pretend I'd taken a drug I'd never touched before, a drug that by my reckoning should kick in about . . .

'Hi, Will. Feeling nervous?'

Lauren. *Shit.*

'H-h-hi.'

Oh my God. I looked around. We were together alone. Was this it? Was this my big chance?

'H-h-how's everything going?' Lauren mimicked.

'Yeah. Um, fine.'

Lauren looked great. Her hair was up in that sexy messy way of hers, a thick red ribbon threading through the strands, matching her T-shirt, the 'Kinky' one she'd been wearing the first time I'd seen her. A second red ribbon made do for a belt, keeping up her jeans, figure-tight at the top, flared as they hit the floor.

The same T-shirt. It was a sign. It had to be a sign.

Go on, Will. Tell her about what you'd thought about her and Rich, about how you thought they were going out, about how a misunderstanding is making you miss out on love.

I cleared my throat. 'Lauren, there's something I've got to tell you.'

Bloody hell. I think I surprised myself more than I surprised Lauren. I was speaking to her. The words were actually coming out.

'Yeah?' Lauren asked.

'Well, it's like this.' Now I had her attention, now she was looking at me, I could feel myself getting hot. I could also feel myself speaking really quickly, to get through this before I bottled it. 'There's something I should have said to you weeks ago, and I don't know why I haven't. I've tried, really I have, but every time it's all come out wrong. But anyway I'm prevaricating again and I don't know why, I should just come out say it, yes why don't I do that, you see, Lauren, the thing is, the thing is . . .' I shut my eyes and took a deep breath. 'I love you.'

'What?' said Lauren.

'What?' said Rich.

What?

Rich. Back from the bar. How long had he been there? I'd been so focused on Lauren, I'd no idea. Rich was staring at me in bemusement. Lauren was likewise.

If this was my chance, it was the Monopoly card equivalent of going directly to jail, without passing Go, without collecting £200.

I was bust. I urgently needed a double to get myself out of the shit.

'I love you,' I said to Lauren again, then without pausing, I turned to Rich. 'And I love you too.' I gave him a bear of a hug and took my water off him. 'You're a really good mate, you know that?'

'Christ!' Rich pushed me off, straightened his sheepskin. 'Maybe I should have given you half.'

'Half?' Lauren asked. 'Hang on. Will, have you taken something?'

I beamed at her, jiggling along to the PA.

'This music's so good, doesn't it just make you want to dance?'

'Will, it's just Frug tuning up,' Rich said.

'Everyone's SO nice.' I ploughed on. This is terrible, I thought, but I might just get away with it. 'I mean, I know that they're strangers yet they're not strangers at the same time.' I put my hands in the air and waved. 'It's like we're long lost brothers and sisters but brothers and sisters you can get loved up with without getting arrested for incest . . .'

God. Somebody shut me up. Please.

Rich gave me a long hard stare. The smile on my face was beginning to hurt.

'I don't believe this, Will.'

I grinned an extra ten per cent praying he hadn't twigged as well.

'I could have sworn Biz palmed me off with paracetamol. You lucky *bastard*.'

Lucky? *Lucky?* I was stone-cold sober, had a gig to play, two hours of bad acting to go, I'd just blown yet another chance with Lauren, who now thought I was a fraud as well as a fascist and a pervert, my jaw was aching, my head was throbbing, and what I needed more than anything in the world I'd had the foresight to flush down the toilet.

Oh yeah. You lucky bastard, Will.

*

The gig was an equivalent disaster. The warm-up act, Monkey Boy, weren't bad, but Frug, to my horror, were fantastic. Loz came across as real rockstar material, preening, swooning, causing one girl to faint (a fix, I'm sure, but it looked great). The crowd loved it, whooping, like the moronic audience on *Stars in Their Eyes*, as Frug started each song. I was impressed, and by their drug taking too. They took their stimulants in their stride, almost as if they hadn't taken anything at all.

I don't know if it was an attack of nerves or the amount of water I'd been drinking or both, but my bladder suddenly felt like the Thames Barrier at a spring high tide. The pub's bogs were not going to win any awards for size, and with Rich disappearing into the last available cubicle, I made for the urinals. I unzipped, my hand carefully hiding my missing ring of pubic hair, when to my left appeared a damp, but definitely full-of-it, Loz Green.

'Hey there, Saucepan,' he slapped me hard on the back causing me to splash all over my shoes. 'Was that brilliant or was that brilliant?'

'Yeah,' I said. 'Er, great.'

'So where's Rich?' Loz asked.

'In the toilet,' I pointed.

'Bricking himself, I'll bet.' Loz laughed. 'You guys are on to a hiding.'

'Like fuck.' Rich joined us, rubbing his nostrils. 'Loz Green, you're about to be blown away.' He sniffed loudly. 'Woah. This is fucking good stuff.'

'Yeah? I'll look forward to snorting mine.'

'Forward?' Rich scrunched his face up. 'Have you forgotten our bet?'

'Of course not.' There was a smugness to Loz's smile I didn't like. 'But that's not until later.'

'*Later?*'

'Sorry, did I not make that clear?' Loz knew perfectly well he hadn't. 'Rich! You *haven't*, have you . . .?'

There are some times in life when you know that however badly things are going wrong, they're about to get worse. You've reached that point when you are so far up shit creek, have thrown the paddle out with the baby and the bath water, that you might as well sit back, enjoy the ride and wait for the waterfalls. As I followed Rich on to the stage and plugged my bass in, that's exactly how I was feeling. And if there was any doubt, it disappeared the moment Rich opened his mouth.

'You're a lucky bunch of fuckers,' Rich told the audience. 'In twenty years time you can tell your children that you were there! When a rock-and-roll legend was born.'

'Fucking stillborn,' said a voice from the bar. Loz if I wasn't mistaken.

If only Rich hadn't claimed we could handle twice whatever Frug took. And if only we'd taken the same drug. Townie's whizz had left him feeling the pace was too pedestrian. So he speeded up, accelerating until he was firmly into techno timekeeping.

'Shift it, Saucepan!' he shouted. 'You're dropping behind the beat!'

Danny's dabbling, meanwhile, had rendered him giggly, with a fascination for particular notes and chords. Some long after the next chord had come along. Some not in the original song at all.

'Relax, mate,' he said. 'What's all the hurry?'

Rich, meanwhile, was lording it up at the front.

'We're Double Top and we're fucking great!' he announced, as the silence gave way to caterwauls of laughter. 'The next big thing in motherfucking rock and roll.' Then he launched into his own reworked a cappella version of 'Special', the song my Valentine's poem to Lauren had become.

'I'm special cos I'm different
I'm different cos I'm special

You'd like so much to tell me
And you can, and you will'

Lauren. I scanned the audience to see what she was making of all this. I caught sight of her at the side of the stage, her camera lowered, her jaw likewise.

Rich turned round and looked at me.

'Loosen up, Will. Jesus.'

Loosen up? I smiled, and tried to look relaxed. As far as you could when you were nervous, bursting once again from all the water you'd drunk, aching from pretending to be high and acutely aware as to how bad things were going. I wasn't exactly strutting with confidence, but given the circumstances it was the best I could do. Rich, meanwhile, was continuing to lecture the audience as to how great he was.

'I know what you're thinking,' he said. 'You're looking at me and thinking sex god.'

The audience howled with laughter. I risked a smile too. Maybe the evening wasn't all bad, after all. I looked around at Lauren, to see what she was making of it. Tactfully, she'd disappeared.

'Will!' Townie hissed. 'Are we going to play an encore?'

We were only ten minutes in, but I realised that he'd already reached the end of the set. In real time we were about halfway through the second song, though Danny, I noticed, was still having fun with the introduction to the first.

'Not tonight, Townie,' I shook my head. 'Let's leave them hungry for more.'

'This is fucking rubbish,' said a perceptive voice from the back, followed by an equally perceptive beer bottle. It missed my ear, and smashed as it hit the wall behind me.

'Get off!' Another bottle hit the stage. Then another.

'Fuck off, you talentless cunts.'

I nodded at Townie, then unplugged Danny and bundled them both off stage.

'You may mock,' Rich said, 'but let me remind you they criticised Jesus Christ too . . .'

'Come on, Rich. Show's over for tonight,' I said, taking the microphone off him and dragging him off stage.

'Hoo fucking ray.'

The crowd cheered sarcastically, which Rich took as a compliment. He made to accept his applause, and I wouldn't have been able to hold him back had not another hand appeared.

Lauren.

'Come on,' she said, nodding to the fire escape. 'Let's get him outside.'

Rich was still telling us how brilliant he was as we hit the smack of cold air and the pub car park.

'Was I great or was I great?' he asked Lauren. 'It's all right, you can tell me.'

'You were *shit*,' Lauren shook her head. 'You stupid coked-up prick.'

'What is this?' said Rich, snapping from satisfaction to aggression. 'Why are you always so prissy about drugs, Lauren?'

'Because I've seen what they can do to people,' Lauren snapped.

There was a pause. I held my breath as Lauren and Rich glowered at each other.

'I don't need this,' Rich relented. 'People love me.'

'Oh, well, fuck off back in there for all I care,' Lauren barked. 'I can't believe that after all these months of preparation, you're prepared to blow it all for a quick sniff.'

Rich pulled a face and stormed inside. Lauren just stood there for a minute, staring at the stars. A world of her own. I don't even think she even realised I was there.

Was this my chance? This time, there would be no Rich to interrupt. Fuck it, I thought. What have I got to lose?

'Lauren,' I said, eventually. 'Lauren, I love you.'

There was a pause, then Lauren turned round slowly. 'And you,' she said, 'you are no better. What the fuck are you doing, trying ecstasy on tonight of all nights?' She shook her head. 'Oh, go tell your loved-up bullshit to someone else. I've had enough of all this.'

Before I could say anything, she'd stormed back inside.

'I love you,' I said again. But this time Lauren wasn't around to hear it.

16

The ninth of April was always going to be a red-letter day. And red in more ways than one, I hoped, for 9 April was election day, the day when John Major and his sorry Tories sodded off, and Neil Kinnock and his shadow cabinet stepped into the spotlight. It was a day steeped in potential and possibilities, and not just on a political level. The fact that the launch of Lauren's Brighton Rocks exhibition was scheduled for the same night was not a coincidence. I couldn't help but be caught up in the buzz myself. If 9 April was the day for new eras and new beginnings, what better date could there be for Lauren to learn that I loved her? A new Britain. A new relationship. A new Labour government. A new romance.

Oh yes. I felt buoyed up, for the ninth was decidedly the day when eleven miserable years of Tory rule were upended into the historical dumpbin, when Neil Kinnock stood on the doorstep of Downing Street, punching the air, shouting 'We're all right!', and John Major disappeared, his eighteen months going down as one of the shortest and most pointless pieces of Prime Ministership ever to have disgraced this country. People were sick and tired of being sick and tired. People who'd voted Tory, who'd voted for Thatcher, these people had seen the error of their ways and were voting for Labour. Oh yes, as John Major would say. The true blues were turning. Middle England was bringing in the new.

People like my parents.

It sounded strange, I know, but even my parents had decided to vote Labour. For the first time, for the only time in their lives. Neil Kinnock was their man. And how had this bizarre turn of events come about? Was it because they approved of Labour's policies? Not quite. Each time they'd discussed Labour's plans, 'the Communist Manifesto' as my father called it, they used a unique series of adjectives containing the names of former Soviet dictators. Was it because they admired Neil Kinnock as a man, a man of vision with strong leadership whose depth of character transcended party politics? That neither; 'They should've put him down the pit and left him there,' my father once said. Maybe it was part of some clever right-wing plot to make Major lose, so a true believer, a Michael Portillo or a Peter Lilley, could be shoehorned into the succession? Possible, though my parents didn't trust Portillo (Por-tee-yo as they pronounced it, to accentuate his origins). My father described his prospective leadership as 'the Spanish Armada by the back door'.

No. The reason my parents were going to vote Labour was simple. They were in the middle of the Pacific, and had elected to vote by proxy. This involves handing your part of the democratic process to someone you could trust, someone you knew was reliable.

Hello!

Was I going to fulfill my parent's wishes and carry out my duty as a firm, upright, upstanding citizen of the community, voting Conservative on their behalf?

Was I buggery.

The polling station was at my old primary school, the sign tied to the railings like I'd been many years before, in a lunchtime game of *Star Wars*. The usual scenario was that Stephen Mitchell was Luke Skywalker, his six-year-old girlfriend Katie Mandelson was Princess Leia and I was Darth Vader and the evil empire rolled into one.

'You lose again, Darth Vader!' Luke Skywalker shouted. 'My force is too strong for you! And by the time you escape, it'll be too late! Princess Leia and I will have had lots of children, and their force will be too strong for you, too!'

Return of the Jedi hadn't come out yet, so Luke didn't know who Leia really was. It was just as well she threatened her Jedi knight with Mrs Baxter the dinner-lady, otherwise the next generation of Jedi knights would have been lacking more than the force. Thumbs, for example.

'William! How good to see you!' Standing by the door was the God-awful Godfrey, the Tory man with the clipboard. He slapped me on the back with a firmness reserved for those who believe in capital punishment and cold showers. Ow.

'Good morning!' I beamed back. 'Isn't it a wonderful day?'

'Well, the weather's not that nice,' Tory man peered out of the door.

'I'm not talking about the weather,' I smiled, 'I'm talking about the election.'

'Ah. Yes.' Tory man winced. 'Glad to see you're so confident.'

'I certainly am. By this time tomorrow, this country will have the government it deserves.'

'Good for you, William,' Tory man slapped me with his clipboard again. 'Dunkirk spirit and all that. Your father would be proud of you.'

I doubted it very much, I thought, taking his voting slip into the booth and putting a thick pencil cross next to the Labour candidate.

'Should I bother asking you which way you voted?' Tory man stood expectantly, pen poised in hand, as I returned.

'I wouldn't,' I smiled.

*

I should have suspected something was up the moment I stepped into Lauren's exhibition. The first thing I saw, on a round table, was a display of plastercast penises.

My buoyant mood, the optimism of having voted Labour three times, the crackle of anticipation from watching the night's political events unfold, all of it vanished in an instant. I stared at the table. Where was it? Lauren said mine was pink, didn't she? I couldn't see it. I scoured again. No, no sign. I checked round the back, under the table, and then over the display twice more before I concluded, with a sigh of relief, that my own contribution was not on show. However much I may have pissed her off, Lauren had been as good as her word, and had kept my model in her private collection. I was so relieved that I barely noticed that the centrepiece of the entire display was Rich's far from modest manhood.

I wandered into the exhibition. It wasn't a bad space, white walls, authentic wooden floorboards, a half-decent view of the seafront, but space wasn't the word I would use to describe it. It was *rammed* with people. Some I recognised – indie folk I'd seen at gigs. Most I didn't – arty types with strange hairdos and weird multicoloured clothing. I spotted Rich, standing in the centre of the room, chatting to Loz from Frug and one of his friends from Mel's party, the snotty one who looked like she could have been in Abba. Behind them were blown-up poster-sized photographs of Rich and Loz, both singing into microphones, which had been put together as though they were staring at each other. Down the middle was a red neon strip, flashing the words Brighton Rocks.

And the noise. Danny had rigged up a powerful sound system, with speakers virtually everywhere you turned. He was crouched behind a set of decks in the corner and I wandered over to say hi.

'Good stuff, isn't it?' Danny shouted above 'So Tired of Waiting For You' by the Kinks. He pulled a copy of *Abbey Road* out of its sleeve, held it up to the light to find the track markings. 'Any requests?'

I flicked through his box of records. It was all sixties stuff: the Stones, the Who, Hendrix, Cream, Dave Dee, Dozy, Beaky, Mick and Tich.

OK, so I lied about the last one.

'What's this?' I asked, picking out one I didn't recognise. Its cover was a black-and-white photo of a striking and vaguely familiar dark-haired woman.

'That's my mum,' Danny said proudly. He took it out of my hands and flipped it over to show me the track listing. 'She does a great version of "In My Life". I thought I might put it on later, as a chill-out tune.'

I made my way over to the bar, which was being run by some of the staff from Barney O'Blarneys, all dressed up to represent different eras of rock music, one as a punk, one as a glam rocker, one as a mini-skirted sixties groover. The drinks themselves were a similar cocktail of styles. Wine for the artists, beer for the bands (they'd remembered my cider, I was pleased to notice), and for a real touch of class, the Barney's version of an ice cream 99. This consisted of a pint of Guinness with a stick of Brighton Rock stuck out the top.

On the side of the bar, I noticed a pile of copies of *Rock Face*, a local Brighton music magazine. I say magazine, it was more a couple of sheets of badly photocopied A4 stapled together. Nevertheless, it was the must-read for any local muso. Its normal cover style was some sort of bastardised Sex Pistols style photo of a famous person, with the lettering cut out of newspapers like it was a ransom note. This issue, though, was different. It was a review, under the banner heading BRIGHTON ROCKS!

Through my mind flashed the seminal articles of rock journalism: Jon Landau's 'I saw rock and roll future and its name is Bruce Springsteen'; Nick Kent's *NME* review of *Marquee Moon*, a '24-carat inspired work of genius'.

Was history about to repeat itself? As I started to read, my excitement continued to rise.

Who'd have thought it? It's time to put all those jokes about shit local bands back into storage. Because the existing truth is, yes, the biggest thing to happen to British music in years is kick-starting right under our very noses, down here on the South Coast. Wave goodbye to Madchester, forget grunge and the so-called Seattle sound, 1992 is going to be remembered for Brighton Rock, a whole group of up-and-coming bands with a distinctive sound and style. Sure we've had success before, Primal Scream, the Levellers, that bloke who used to be in the Housemartins who DJs on a Saturday night, but this is different. This is a sound that IS Brighton. It's English, it's glamorous, it's cool, it's retro like those mods on their scooters, it's hard edged like Graham Greene's gangsters. The sounds of the past are being presented as the sound of the future (Very clever – get on with the gig review or you're sacked. ED).

This was just brilliant. It was so on the nail that I wondered whether anyone had actually written the piece, or whether some lazy journo had just copied out the press release he'd been given. But when the copy was this flattering, who cared? I read on.

The place where the Brighton Rocks scene centres is the 'old' Irish North Laine pub, Barney O'Blarneys. And it was here last Friday night that three of the key bands played a stupendous debut gig to a packed crowd of the cutting edge of the Brighton art scene. First up were Monkey Boy, charmingly kitsch with their psychedelic punk, one minute chanting 'Give Peace A Chance', the next spitting at the audience and asking them to 'ave a go. Then came their big rivals Frug, the Beatles to Monkey Boy's Stones, who played a majestic set of kinky Kinks-style rock. Singer Loz Green is a guaranteed star in the making, already his presence filling the room in the same way that a Morrissey or Ian Brown does. And then, bringing up the rear were the scene's Northside, the scene's joke band, there to imitate the others and make them feel good. A musical movement always seems to have a sorry group of hangers-on and Brighton Rocks is no exception thanks to Double Top. Or should that be Double Flop? An arrogant singer whose voice grates, a guitarist so stoned he was giggling at every mistake he made, and on bass guitar, Brighton's favourite Young Conservative (see photo). Maybe they were some sort of kitsch post-modern joke, you know, so shit they're brilliant. Or maybe they were just shit. Who knows? I don't, and frankly I don't care.

But enough about Double Toss. Let's give you the lowdown on Monkey Boy and Frug, the two rival bands who are going to put Brighton's music firmly on the map . . .

Ah.

'What do you think?'

I turned round to see Lauren, her hair swept back off her face and cascading down a red shirt made of crushed velvet. She looked great, and my pulse picked up in anticipation of what I was going to tell her.

'Very nice,' I said. 'Where did you get it from?'

'The shirt belongs to Rich, but I'm not talking about

that, I'm talking about my photos.' She pointed to the shots in *Rock Face*.

'Yes, fantastic. Shame about the review.'

'I know. Rich's already been on to the editor about the typing mistake.'

Typing mistake?

'It should have said his voice was great, not that it grates,' Lauren explained.

Yeah right, I thought. In Rich's dreams.

Lauren prodded my photo. 'So have you voted? Are you ready to be disappointed later on?'

'I'm not a Tory! How many times do I have to tell people . . .'

'. . . it was a set up, you didn't know what was written on the poster.' Lauren yawned. 'Whatever. So what do you think about the exhibition?'

'I think it's wonderful. Really. You've captured what people are actually like.'

Lauren smiled. 'Have you found the one of you yet?'

'There's one of me? On my own?'

'Of course there is. There's one of everyone important.'

Me? Important? Fuck, I thought, all excited. Maybe I am in with a chance, a thought that began to gel when Lauren led me by the hand, guiding me past the display of guitar heroes (Danny sandwiched between Jimi and Eric) to a quieter spot away from the main displays. There was a picture of our recording studio, looking all natural and rural in its farmyard setting. A picture of Townie, his face creased in concentration. And a shot of me, on the Palace Pier, looking out to sea.

'What do you think?'

The sky, I had to say, was stunning, full of strips of cloud lit up by the late afternoon sun. I had my hands on the railing and a look on my face that I hadn't seen before. I looked, well, thoughtful.

'That sky is fantastic,' I said.

'Yeah, well, that was God, can't take credit for that.' Lauren punched me playfully. 'What about the person in the foreground, dummy?'

'I, I don't know what to say, I've never seen myself look like that in a photo before.'

'How do you normally look in photographs?'

'The wrong way. Or I've got my eyes shut. Or I'm pulling a face. Or I'm half off the edge. This is like a *proper* photograph.' I looked at the picture again. 'Do I really look like that?'

'You do to me.' Lauren smiled. 'There's an air of thoughtfulness, of vulnerability to you. It's one of my favourites in the exhibition, actually.'

Lauren thought I was thoughtful! Just call me Will 'profound' Harding. I imagined myself as Rodin's philosopher. I think, therefore I'm in with a shout. This has got to be my chance, I thought. I've got to take it.

'Lauren, there's something I've been meaning to tell you.'

'Yeah?'

'I want to talk about . . .' Come on, Will, you can do this. I gathered myself, and went for it. 'I want to talk about love.'

Lauren's reaction was not what I was expecting.

'Oh God,' she blushed. 'Has Rich told you?'

Rich? I didn't get it. Had Lauren told Rich she fancied me?

'I thought I told him to keep it quiet.' Lauren looked out over the room. 'Hey Rich!'

Not Rich, please. I glowered at him as he strutted across. Please fuck off. But Rich, as per usual, was oblivious to anyone but himself.

'Hi there, sexy.' Lauren and Rich embraced, embraced with such vigour that Rich virtually reclaimed his crushed velvet shirt. I couldn't fucking believe it. Not only had he interrupted my chance, he'd now taken it for himself. What was this? Some kind of macho posturing, proving he could have anyone he wanted? I hated him. *I* was about to ask her out, and now I was standing there like a gooseberry, watching *him* snog Lauren.

'You wanted something?' Rich asked Lauren, when he came up for air. I might as well have been invisible.

'Yes,' Lauren pulled one of those annoyingly stupid lover's faces at Rich. I felt sick. 'Oh I can't remember, can't have been important. Get us another drink.'

'Sure. Will?'

'Hnng,' was about all I could say.

I simply couldn't believe it. *Rich and Lauren were going out.*

'. . . yeah, so we've been going out properly for a few weeks. Got it together the night after you guys played that ball,' Lauren said.

The ball? The night when I learned that Rich and Lauren weren't going out? No wonder Lauren had been so brusque with me. All the time I'd been asking her out, she had been secretly seeing Rich on the side. I'd never stood a chance.

'. . . I've always turned him down up until then, I mean, I've always found him sexy and that, making his plastercast was hardly a chore,' she laughed. 'But that's as far as it had ever gone. Until that night I never felt I really knew him. And then suddenly I wanted to know what he was like inside.'

'And what's that?' Complete? Fucking? Tosser?

'He's incredibly sensitive,' Lauren said to my surprise. 'Behind all the arrogance and bravado, there's a thoughtful, vulnerable individual. If you ever get past that, Will, you'd find out that deep down he's really, well, he's really like you actually. At the end of the day, Rich is a man who just wasn't made for these times. Not only that, but he's not afraid to express it, something almost unique in a man. He's got such a way with words. He touches me. Deeply.'

I bet he does. I've seen the plastercast.

'The sexiness is great,' Lauren continued, 'but it's the vulnerability that really won me over.' She sighed. 'What more could anyone want? I know we haven't been going out long, but I think I . . .'

'Please. Don't say it.'

'You're right. It'd be tempting fate.'

Would it? I've changed my mind. Say it, Lauren, shout the fucking thing out loud until it's all completely shafted.

'Oh!' Lauren spotted someone on the other side of the room. 'That's Magnus. He owns a gallery in London. I'm just going to go over and say hi.'

I watched Lauren cross the room in full flight, a person in the full flush of romantic and professional success. And where was I? I looked at my photo. Staring bitterly out to sea, thinking about my missed opportunities. My stomach hurt. These weren't those pretty butterflies flitting around in there, but something far more vicious. Something I was having trouble digesting.

'Hey! Where's the skirt gone?'

I felt gutted. Lauren didn't deserve this. I didn't deserve this. I'd like to have believed Rich had the sensitive side Lauren was talking about, but I reckoned, I suspected it was just a device he used to bed people.

'So, so you and Lauren are now an item?' It felt painful to say it.

'That's right,' Rich threw me my can. I didn't open it. 'Finally fucked her. For a moment there, I thought I was going to owe Loz a fiver.' He glugged his drink. 'When it comes to Rich, the chicks always give in eventually.' He smiled. 'She's not half bad in bed either. Or on the kitchen table. I don't normally like them so *headstrong*, but Lauren more than made up for it, if you know what I mean.'

'Hey,' I snapped. 'Don't talk about Lauren like that.'

Rich shook his head, like he was doing a double take. 'Excuse me? What's it to you?'

He stared at me, trying to work out what I was thinking. I've gone too far, I thought. I can't let him know I fancy her.

'What I meant was, hey! Don't talk like *that*,' I punched him on the arm, in what was meant to be a playful buddy-buddy sort of way, though I couldn't stop myself letting out a bit of anger at the same time. 'Don't talk like that, not when there's all those groupies to deal with.'

'Let me put it like this,' Rich said. 'The way Lauren is going, and she *goes* all right, I'm not going to have any energy left for groupies.'

'But I thought you liked a bit of variety. You can't have that and stay faithful.'

'Of course I can,' Rich smiled. 'It's not like oral sex is adultery.'

'It's not?'

'Of course not. Doesn't mention blow jobs in the Bible. I can have all the fellatio I fancy and still stay true to Lauren.' Rich shook his head. 'Not that I'm a religious man anyway. You know my philosophy. Don't get caught.'

'But what if someone told her?' I must have said this a little too pointedly.

'Then they'd be out of the band.'

Our eyes locked. Just try it, Rich's stare was saying. I think he expected me to back down, but I was now so worked up, there was no way I was going to. After what seemed like an age, but what must have only been seconds, he laughed and broke it off with a wink.

'I'm off to join the others,' he shrugged, walking away.

I watched him go, shut my eyes as I heard the laughter as he rejoined the group. I had to get out of there. I just didn't want to be around, around Rich being around Lauren. I was going to go for a walk, clear my head by the sea. And then I was going to go home, switch the television on and attempt to cheer myself up with the one thing I had left to rely on, watching Neil Kinnock become Britain's new Prime Minister.

17

Do you believe in love? Do you really? I'm not talking about liking the idea of love – everyone does that, in the same way that everyone thinks world peace is a great idea. I'm talking about *believing* in love, about being naively willing to go that extra mile for romance, about allowing your life to be ruined by your heart and your feelings and your instincts, whatever you may have hoped otherwise.

Because it's not all fluffy bunnies and a dozen red roses you know. God do I know that. Forget the heart-skipping and heartgiving: it's heartache and heartbreak all the way. Be prepared to take the bad with the good, the rough with the smooth. Actually, you can forget about the good and the smooth. It may be rough, but be prepared to take the bad and bad only.

Because if you're a romantic, being in love will make your whole world miserable. I can only speak from experience, but for what it's worth, I loathe being in love. It's when everything is more painful, more unsettling, more unjust. I hate that: the misery, the tears, the vomiting. And it doesn't stay within the confines of your relationship. The despair and misery of being in love is so all-consuming that it permeates throughout your entire life: you hate your job; you take missing the bus as another symbolic sign of where your life is going – or rather, where it isn't. You can't be arsed to cook in the evening, and the resulting takeaway is just revolting: greasier and lumpier and crunchingly overdone and out of date. You can't sleep like you've never been able to not sleep in your life.

Yes, as far as states of being go, being in love just can't be beaten.

Of course, you may disagree with what I've just said. You may be sitting there, snorting through your nose, mumbling words like 'drama' and 'queen' under your breath. You may dismiss me as the soppiest of sentimentalists. You may think that what I'm talking about is the stuff of suicide notes and Morrissey lyrics. Well, if you're thinking like that, all I can say is this: you've never been in love. You've never allowed yourself to fall, to really *fall*, to let yourself go without knowing what's going to happen next.

I said it wasn't going to be easy. I warned you to fasten your seat belt, that it was likely to be a bumpy ride. You know, I've changed my mind about love; it's contentment I want, it's a smooth state of affairs I'm after. Yes, I want a low-maintenance lover with a steady job who likes order and routine and everything just so, the sort of person who thinks going out on a 'school night' is a bad idea, who thinks it is better to save than to spend, who is private even in their private life, who doesn't drink because they like to be 'in control'. I might not be happy, I know that. But I wouldn't be *really* unhappy, and that's got to be a good thing.

Why did I become a romantic? Fuck knows. Next time around, Sleeping Beauty and the Frog Princess can go in the bin: my childhood's going to be spent reading about war and death and bombs and blowing people up. Is it too late to make the change? Can I nail down that capacity to be romantic, to keep it under lock and key and well away from where it might do some serious damage? I wish I could. That's one of the miseries of love – once you've fallen, you're down for the count. Getting up again just isn't a possibility.

*

The weekend after I learned that Rich had conned Lauren into believing the bastard loved her, the last place I should have been was at a wedding. If you get hay fever, you don't go out and get yourself a job at a florists. If your stomach churns when you set foot on a ship, you don't book yourself on a round-the-world cruise. I was seriously, almost deliriously lovesick, and yet despite professional medical advice, found myself watching my cousin Stephanie get married.

If I could've got out of the wedding I would have, but my mother rang me up from Papua New Guinea to remind me to go. I had to, she said, to 'represent the family'. The wedding took place at a pretty little church in some small Kent village, and it was horrible. Simply everything went right. The weather was wonderful. The bride looked radiant. My uncle read out the predictable passage from Corinthians particularly well. Even the sermon was well-judged: not too long, not too preachy and liberally peppered with jokes that hit the spot each and every sodding time. As I stood outside the church afterwards, whilst the photographs were being taken, I noticed that everyone, young or old, had been buoyed by the occasion. It had reminded them why they were going out with the person underneath the bright red wide-brimmed hat in the first place, and they were getting all luvvy accordingly.

I should've expected it really. Since election night, I couldn't move for fucking couples. Every time I blinked there was another gruesome twosome, so fucking *together*, rubbing in the fact that I was on my own. I'd switch on the television and there'd be yet another soap couple spooning and snogging for all that they were worth. I'd turn on the radio and every sodding song would be about love (Bryan 'Bloody' Adams and 'Stay' by Shakespear's Sister, I particularly loathed). And then, when I went out in the streets, I couldn't help noticing couples wherever I looked. Necking on the back seat of the bus. Hand in hand queuing up for the cinema. Strolling down the seafront sharing a single ice cream or candy floss or can of Diet Coke and laughing and giggling and sharing their horrible little private jokes. It was a cruel, vicious circle – the happier people looked, the lonelier I felt. And the lonelier I felt, the happier people looked.

The Cure, that last bastion of black cardigans, deep depression and utter unhappiness had a new album out. Fantastic, I'd thought. If Lauren doesn't want me, I'll buy that record, close all the curtains and wallow in Robert

Smith moaning on about how terrible he is feeling, how the world doesn't love him and how everyone is out to get him.

But no.

Even Robert Bastard Fucking Smith was happy. 'Friday I'm In Love' blasted out of my speakers, as the turncoat twat wore his first smile for fifteen years.

I was seriously out of sorts with the rest of the world. And it *stung*.

If only. If only when Lauren said she and Rich were partners, I'd responded, 'Business partners? Tell me about your cash-flow situation.' If only that Tory hadn't turned up with that photographer. If only Rich hadn't agreed to a drugs challenge with Frug, then I wouldn't have had to make a fool of myself in front of Lauren, pretending to have taken an E that I hadn't. If only someone had told me Lauren and Rich weren't going out when I thought they were.

The photographer was calling for me. It was time for the 'family' shot. I tried to hide inconspicuously behind my not so skinny Aunt Rachel, but was spotted and made to stand next to my Uncle Bernard instead. The photographer called me 'sonny' and told me to 'cheer up'. 'Think of something nice,' he said, to everyone's amusement bar my own. 'Imagine you've just seen some lovely Baywatch beauty behind me,' he winked as my face went crimson.

Click.

I'm so fucking stupid. How could I ever have thought I had a chance? Maybe I should ring Neil Kinnock up, ask him if he wanted to go out for a drink. He'd know what I was feeling, thinking that he'd won, only for some annoying tosser to slip in and steal what he desperately wanted. *If we look at the swingometer*, I could hear Peter Snow flap about excitedly, *we can see how these unexpected late changes have affected the final outcome. There we have Will Harding, his pathetically small arrow PUSHED back into second place, BARGED aside by Rich Young's large, thrusting arrow. And if we go into our virtual reality House of Commons we can see what this result means. There's Rich on the front bench, giving Lauren one for all he is worth . . .*

One of the world's great seducers versus a serial virgin. What chance had I had? Rich had slept with more women at once than I had in my entire life put together. He was a man of great one liners, whereas I couldn't put two words together. He was good looking and he knew it. And I, well. I knew it too.

With the Big Gig only a couple of weeks away – our headline slot at Sound City in Norwich – I couldn't move for Rich. We were rehearsing pretty much all the time – it was getting so critical even Rich was rehearsing now. And everywhere Rich went, Lauren went with him, whispering sweet nothings and biting his ear, shrieking with laughter as he squeezed her bum. Again. If that wasn't enough, Rich had moved on from moving in on Lauren to moving in with her. They were fucking living together. They were, I could hardly bear to think it, they were turning into a *couple*.

And me? I just stared out the window, trying to

ignore them, swallowing the lump in my throat, only to see yet more young lovers walking past outside.

*

'Anyone sitting here?'

I was sat, no, *slumped*, at a table to the side of the wedding dancefloor. The DJ was doing his best to whip the alcoholic audience into some sort of frenzy, playing such sordid showstoppers as 'Don't Leave Me This Way' and 'Come On Eileen'. It was only a matter of time before 'Oops Up Side Your Head' hit the turntable, complete with a row of badly mashed relatives spread-eagled on the floor. Standing in front of me was one of the bridesmaids, in a dress that looked like a meringue someone had sat on. She had soft brown hair, tied in two Princess Leia style buns.

'No,' I drew my bottle of champagne closer to me.

'It's all right,' she arranged herself and sat down with a pfft. 'I'm not going to steal your drink.' She reached inside her dress, pulled out a hip flask. 'Emergency supplies,' she explained. 'In case Stephanie got nervous.'

'So you're a bridesmaid,' I said.

'I'm the vicar actually. We agreed to swap clothes for a bet.'

'Really?'

'Joke. You *are* drunk, aren't you?'

'Little. I'm Will, by the way.'

'Kate.'

'No, Will. I've been called Cynthia before, but never Kate.'

Kate asked what I did. I told her about the band. She was impressed, in a gently mocking sort of way.

'So, are you going to be a big famous rock star?'

'Don't know. We've got this big gig in Norwich, with all the record companies coming to watch.'

'*Wow.*' Kate went a little gooey-eyed. 'You really are going to be famous.'

'Oh, I doubt it. Bass players never are. It's always the singer who gets the glory.'

And the girl. Even though it didn't mean a thing to him.

'Don't be so down on yourself. It's a group effort. You've all got your own part to play.'

'Oh yeah. Do you know what Ringo Starr's role was in the Beatles?'

'To play the drums?'

'To sit there and shut up. John Lennon didn't want four John Lennons in the band, they'd just argue and nothing would ever get done. He needed a Ringo Starr to do what he was told.'

'Maybe John Lennon was crap at the drums.' Kate smiled. 'You put yourself down too much.'

'Sorry.'

'Sorry for what? Stop being so apologetic.' She took another swig from the hip flask. Flinched. 'Never be a bridesmaid, Will. You spend the entire day in shoes too small, dressed up like something off a sweet trolley, smiling like there's no tomorrow, putting up with the bride's last minute nerves, telling her she's doing the right thing even though you think she's making the biggest mistake of her life, all because of a promise that you can't not get laid in a bridesmaid's dress, which turns out to be as big a load of waffle as the dress itself.' She drained her flask, and belched. 'Hand me your champagne bottle. *Now.*'

I handed her the champagne bottle.

'So you're having a good time then?' I asked. I might have been wrong, but I had the faintest impression she was trying it on.

'Oh fantastic.' Kate drank from my bottle, passed it back. 'Nearly as brilliant as you.'

'Me?' I took the bottle, drank from it myself.

'Yeah. I've never seen anyone look so miserable at such a happy occasion.'

'I'm not being miserable.'

'You are *so* being miserable Mr Bass Player. I'm surprised you haven't been up to the DJ, asked him if he's got anything by the Smiths.'

'They haven't. Or Joy Division.' A roar went up as the bass line to 'You're The One That I Want' ripped in. 'I'm sorry, it's just there's this someone who I really liked, I mean *really* liked. I missed my chance to ask her out, and now she's going out with this, this complete *wanker* who doesn't care about her, who I know is going to hurt her.'

'Is she happy?'

'Very. Just like the rest of the entire fucking world.' I nodded towards the dancefloor, where a carnival of congas was taking place. 'I *hate* weddings. Everyone making sickly speeches about what a great thing love is.'

'Well, if she's happy, maybe it was meant to be.'

'He's lied to her. He doesn't deserve her.'

'OK. And what are you going to do about it?'

'What can I do? She'll never go for me. I don't have what she likes.'

'What you need to do is to *do* something.' Kate said. 'The fact you didn't make a move in the first place means she's going out with this other guy. Now you're proposing to sit there and wait for the whole thing to fall apart.'

'What's the alternative? I mean, do tell me.'

'Well. Either you've got to stand up and tell this girl what you think, whether it means you spoiling her happiness or her making you miserable by turning you down. At least she'll know what you think.'

'Or?'

'Or you've got to forget about her and move on. Shag somebody else to get her out of your system.'

'Yeah?'

'Yeah.' Kate squeezed my knee. 'Look, we could both do ourselves a favour here, Will. I can fulfil the final duty a decent bridesmaid has, and you can start to get over this mystery woman.'

Even in her half-cut state, I could see Kate was attractive. And I considered it, really I did, but the more I thought about it, the more I thought about Lauren, and the more I realised that I couldn't do it.

'I'm sorry,' I said. 'This is going to sound really odd, but the thing is, if I got off with you, it would feel like I was cheating on Lauren.'

God, I thought. Does this mean I can never have sex?

'*Cheating* on her? You're not even going out.'

'I can't explain.' I sighed. I couldn't. 'Um. Sorry?'

Kate sat back and folded her arms. She watched the

dancing for a bit. 'I Will Survive' by Gloria Gaynor. Will I? I thought. I wish I was so sure.

'Oh don't worry about it,' Kate turned back to me and smiled. 'I'm glad you turned me down.'

'You think I'd be that bad?'

Kate shook her head. 'You really are in love with this Lauren, aren't you?' Then she leaned over, stared at me intently. 'You just make sure you get off your arse and do something about it, that's all I can say.' Kate eyed me up and down. 'Well, well. Who'd have thought it? An old-style romantic. And I thought they'd all died out.'

It's not going to be long, I thought, the way my life is going.

18

Kate made it sound so easy. The fact was, it was anything but. If I told Lauren how I felt, I knew exactly what would happen. She'd turn me down. Rich would kick me out of the band. And that, I felt, would be both unfair and pointless; what was the good in getting myself deliberately kicked out the band just when things were about to kick in? No, I decided on reflection, maybe I should try a different option. Maybe I should see what happened if I turned my attentions elsewhere, to see if I was capable of moving on.

So I cheated on Lauren. And it cost me my job.

The girl in question was Samka, one of my language students. I'd been teaching her English every morning for a fortnight, and a cup of coffee in one of the tackier tea houses the Lanes had to offer was her way of saying thank you. For what, I wasn't sure. As Samka prepared to go back home, her English was noticeably worse than when she had arrived.

'So have you enjoyed England?' I asked, as we sat down.

'Yes, very much.' Samka was an eighteen-year-old

Eastern European with a smile that would be fantastic once her brace had been taken off. She wore a navy blue sweatshirt with Oxford University written on the front (even though she'd never been), had pink-framed glasses and hair in two thick plaits tied with blue plastic bobbles, which, she informed me, was all the rage in whichever part of Eastern Europe she came from. She spoke with a strong foreign accent, not sexy like French or Italian, but with a thick, unrepentant monotone. 'I like England. But I think it is very sad at the moment, very like my home country. There are no work and the shops is closed and the peoples are all miserable . . .'

I noticed a couple kissing at the table behind Samka. Was there no escape?

'. . . all the peoples are miserable,' Samka continued, 'especially you. Why are you so down, Will? Do you have a pain of the heart?'

'Oh it's nothing,' I said in a voice that meant 'it's everything'.

'Because when I started you seemed so happy, and now I am leaving you seem so sad. Why is that?'

I jolted out of my Lauren-induced coma. Did Samka think I was sad because she was leaving?

'You think I? Oh no, it's not . . . I mean you're . . . and everything, but . . .'

'Hey,' Samka mocked, 'that sounds like my English.'

It wasn't that Samka couldn't be attractive. Behind those glasses and brace and bobbles, there was a very pretty Eastern European struggling to get out. And I'd nothing against Eastern Europeans. It was just that, well, I preferred people from New Zealand.

'There's this girl, see, called Lauren . . .'

And that was when it all came out. I hadn't intended to tell her, but once I started I couldn't stop. The floodgates had opened. In a way, it seemed odd that I was offloading all my emotional baggage on to a girl I hardly knew. On the other hand it made perfect sense – Samka didn't know anything about Rich or Lauren, and so wasn't going to prejudge what I was going to say. That and the fact that Samka didn't understand half of what I was saying. I'm sure that was a factor in my opening up, though perhaps it made me speak more freely than I should have. It took a good ten minutes to explain what a plastercast was.

'So what should I do?' I asked.

'I tell you story.' Samka smiled, a warm, friendly smile, and pushed her glasses back up her nose. 'I have friend at home, OK. Nice girl. Very pretty, all the boys make the sex with her. When she was fourteen, she kiss man – tall man from the village. He is not so clever, but he has big . . .' She looked down at her notebook, where she wrote all her new words. '. . . he has the big *plastercast* and she is very happy. One day he goes to the town, and does not come back. And my friend is very sad, like you . . .'

'And so what happened next?'

'That's it.'

'That's *it*?'

'Yes.' Samka shrugged. 'She remind me of you, that's all . . .'

'Well, what kind of a stupid story is that?' I wanted my money back. 'What about the bloody punchline? The message? The clue as to what I should do next?'

'Is no message,' Samka said a little sharply. 'Is life. Life has no, what you say, punchline.'

'Oh thank you very much. That's just what I needed to hear.'

I sank back and folded my arms as Samka continued her wise woman act.

'My friend is now very miserable, all the time. We used to go out dancing, to look for the men with the big plastercasts, but now she stays at home and cries. At first I feel sorry for her. I make effort, I say please smile!' Samka smiled at me. I didn't smile back. 'But she is miserable, all the time. So I have choice – to go to friend's house and sit in dark and cry, or go out with dancing friends, looking for the man with the big plastercast.'

'And how old is your friend now?'

'Twenty. For six years she cry.'

'Wow.' I was impressed.

'No wow,' Samka corrected. 'Less of point. How long will you be sad for this Lauren? How many years?'

Samka had a real knack for depressing me. I was going to feel like this for *years*? I could feel a lifetime of misery stretch out ahead of me.

Samka, though, had other ideas. 'I think Lauren is special because she is the first. If you see other girls, maybe you see what is special is not Lauren but . . .'

'But what?'

'I'm sorry. I know not English word. I blame English teacher.'

*

I couldn't work out what the word was either. The nearest I got was that it was a cross between a fireworks display and some sort of exploding flower. Or perhaps there just wasn't an English equivalent. I gave up, and offered Samka a lift back to where she was staying.

'What's this?' Samka asked, waving a tape in my direction.

'It's a tape,' I said, glancing across whilst trying not to crash the car. 'Of my band.'

'You in rock band?' Samka sounded half surprised, half impressed. 'Really?'

'Yes. Really.'

'Please, may I listen?'

The sound of 'Special' filled the car. I'd have to admit it didn't sound bad at all on a car stereo, probably because you could only hear the tinny trebly end of the sound spectrum, my bass being blocked out by the rumbles of the car engine.

'This is beautiful.'

Samka was either enjoying it, or at the very least pretending to, to jolly me up. Mind you, having seen the Eurovision Song Contest, I knew what kind of cobblers her country was capable of.

'So who writes the songs?' Samka asked.

'Danny the guitarist, he writes the music, and I write the words.'

'YOU write words?'

'Yes.'

'Oh Will, the words are beautiful, very romantic . . .'

Romantic? Really? When Rich had originally read the

223

words, he'd shrugged and gone, now what had he said? 'Brilliant. What a fucking brilliant idea of mine to get you to write the words. With my delivery, they'll work a treat.' I thought there might be a compliment for me in there somewhere, but I'd never managed to tease it out.

'You like them?' I asked, milking Samka's praise for as long as I could.

'They are *fantastic*,' Samka was all animated. 'It is big surprise for me, because you look like ordinary person, like man in bank, but inside you have heart and power and beauty.'

'That's, um . . .' I didn't know what to say, '. . . nice. Oh sorry, I've missed your turning.'

'Is OK. We can go this way.'

'Are you sure? Doesn't that go out of town?'

'That is good.' Samka pressed rewind on the tape player. 'I want to hear your song again.'

We drove on. And on. Part of me felt really chuffed that my words had connected with someone. I'd written them specifically about Lauren, but maybe, just maybe, I'd tapped into something that other people could understand as well. And then the happiness at connecting with someone else became crowded out, as images of Lauren and Rich flooded my mind. *She's not half-bad in bed*, I could hear Rich strut. *Or on the kitchen table*.

'Pull in here,' Samka pointed to a lay-by.

'Uh yeah.' I pulled in. 'Why? Are we lost?'

'I am not. You are.' Samka smiled, her brace catching the evening sun. She unclipped her seat belt. 'You have lost beautiful girl, this Lauren, and now you are lost to women.'

'That's right. They've been telling me to get lost for years.'

Samka unclipped my seat belt.

'No, you are *lost* to women. You say you will never find another girl, but cry for this Lauren. This is very sad because you write beautiful words,' she tapped the stereo. 'There are not the many men who are simple and pathetic . . .'

Simple? Pathetic?

'Sympathetic. Excuse my English. I think you like this Lauren because she plays with your plastercast.' Samka took off her glasses, undid her hair and tossed it back. She looked, *well*, she looked exactly the same as she did before, to be honest. Except without her glasses on and her hair hanging down. 'I think it very special for you, first time a woman play with your plastercast. And now you are sad because you think this exciting time is not again to be repeated. *I* think,' Samka said, 'that I should show you that other women can be special too . . .'

'Huh?'

Samka gave me a look, which I think was meant to be seductive but came across more as boss-eyed. Then she leaned across and undid the top button of my jeans.

'Woah.' I glanced around to see if there was any-one around who could see us. 'Samka, I'm not sure this is a . . .'

'Shh. Just relax.'

Relax? With my luck a police car would just happen to be passing. And how do you explain away a blow job? *Oh I'm not feeling well officer, and Samka here was resting her head against my stomach to help me feel better.* He'd have to be a particularly thick policeman to fall for that sort of cock and bullshit story. I'd end up getting arrested, and knowing my notoriety, the local press would whoop with merry delight. *SLEAZE! Teenage Tory Endorses European Integration as Private Poll Shows Sudden Surge.*

My mind was all over the place. My romantic side was saying no, this is cheap and sordid and wrong. I'd said no to Kate, surely I should say no to Samka? I didn't even fancy her. But part of me was also saying, now is your chance to get over Lauren. Stop being so prissy. She's offering you a *blow job.*

'Hold still,' Samka said, and she started to unzip my trousers with her teeth. There was a sharp and ominous-sounding metallic click, and then a pause.

'Fuck. No.'

My thoughts entirely, said my romantic side.

'Have I done something wrong?' I asked. 'Am I . . .' Had she peeked inside my pants and been disappointed?

'It's not you, Will. It's me.'

Unbelievable. We're not even going out, and yet I'm still getting dumped.

'I am catching your zip.'

'What?'

'I know not the English.' She tapped her teeth.

'Your brace is caught in my zip?' Bloody hell! Even inanimate objects were coupling up now. 'That must be painful. Here, let me . . .'

'NO! Do not touch. Is very delicate.'

OK. Well, we'll just sit here then, shall we?

'Can you see?' Samka asked. 'Is it good to hook off?'

'I don't know. If I could bend down that far, there'd have been no need for you to . . .'

'Is not funny!'

I stifled a laugh. 'I know. Let's try and take my trousers off . . .'

This was easier said than done. For wherever the zip went, Samka's head was sure to go. It reminded me of that game you get at the funfair, the one where you carefully guide a hoop along, trying not to touch the electric wire causing the thing to buzz. Similarly here, if I moved too fast, Samka screamed. I don't know what my score was by the end, but I'm fairly sure I hadn't won myself a large pink teddy bear. Just a small, red-faced, annoyed Eastern European.

'Well, that wasn't so bad,' I said, trying to sound encouraging.

'*Not so bad*? I have your trousers on my *face*.'

She had a point.

'This'll be a doddle now,' I said. 'I think I've got a spanner in the boot of the car.'

'Spanner? Samka asked. 'What is spanner?'

I found one and showed it to her.

'No spanner,' Samka said decisively, then she looked out of the windscreen and sighed. For a moment I thought she was going to cry. I was struggling for the words to comfort her when she turned back and snapped at me. 'I hate you, Will. You and your horrible words.'

'I thought you said they were romantic.'

'Oh yes. This is very romantic.' Samka shut her eyes. 'I need proper person to unhook. We must go to hospital.'

'Hospital? Are you sure that's really necess . . .'

'Yes!' There was a psychotic edge to Samka's voice that I wasn't going to argue with. 'Take me to hospital! Now!'

*

The nurse on duty was just starting to nod off when we got to Casualty. I coughed and she woke with a jolt and a yelp. She stared at us in a strange way for a few seconds, like she couldn't decide whether she was awake or asleep. Fair enough. I guess it's not every day you see a young couple, the girl with a pair of Levi's jeans hanging from her face, the bloke in his Darth Vader boxer shorts, worn second time around, inside out, to save on washing.

'So what happened to you two, then?'

'What do think happened?' I said testily.

She was doing her best to hide it, but you could tell the nurse was trying really, really hard not to laugh. It was the way her facial muscles were tightening, the way her voice was wobbling.

'I'll just get my supervisor . . .' She ran off covering her mouth. From behind the screen where she'd disappeared there was a shrieking howl of laughter, as all her suppressed giggles were released at once. That and a cry of, 'Jean! Get over here now! This one's ever better than that kid with the vacuum cleaner.'

'It's good to see we're getting so much personal attention,' I whispered to Samka, as every nurse, doctor and specialist on the South Coast came to check out our situation.

We sat down in the queue, next to a small boy with a tap on his finger. I did my best to cheer Samka up.

'Hey,' I said, 'this is going to be all right.'

'*You do not understand, do you?*' Samka was still in shrieking mode. Thank God the trousers were there to muffle her voice. 'I am not English. For me this service is not free. I must have money, which means I must ring my father.'

'Your father?'

'Yes. He will speak to doctor and ask what is problem. Doctor will tell him.' Samka shook her head forlornly. 'He will be angry. He think I his little girl.'

I thanked God he lived far enough away not to cause me any trouble. Then I had a nasty thought.

'You don't think he'd like, like ring up the language school?'

'Oh yes. When he learn that you are my English teacher, he will speak to director, want money back.'

'But, but I'm *not* your teacher. You'd finished the course when this happened.'

'He will not care.'

Well, this is just great, I thought, as the doctor called Samka in. Fucking great. Was this some sort of sign, that I shouldn't be trying to get over Lauren? I thought about how she'd be in this situation. And I knew if she saw me sitting here, she'd laugh, sure, but she'd reassure as well as rib me. But instead I was alone in a hospital, freezing cold in my boxer shorts, about to lose my job, and wondering what kind of crap fate was going to throw at me next.

19

Samka had been right about my job. The school director read me the riot act – shouted it is probably a better description – telling me I was lucky not to be charged with assault. He took the cost of Samka's dental work out of my last wage packet, leaving me with £12.67 for the last three months' work. I took that down to the amusement arcades on the Palace Pier, in the desperate hope a fruit machine might sort me out. I lost it all in less than five minutes.

I joined the massed ranks of the unemployed. John Major's government had promised that green shoots of recovery would start appearing the day after they were re-elected, but I can't say I saw any signs of them in Brighton. It wasn't a wonderful life. I spent my evenings practising with the band, the days moping around my bedroom. I'd stay in bed until two or three in the afternoon, just listening to records.

Everything I used to enjoy had changed. Not only couldn't I have Lauren, I couldn't even bring myself to masturbate these days. Linda Lusardi got hairs stuck in the back of her throat at unfortunate moments. Wendy

James from Transvision Vamp got cramp in her legs. Susannah Hoffs kept complaining my elbow was getting in the way. And Daphne from Scooby Doo had developed an unfortunate habit of farting at inopportune moments.

I thought about what Samka had said, that Lauren was special because she was my first almost-girlfriend – that I was so short of sexual experience, I thought Lauren was 'the one' because I'd nothing to compare her with. It was something I'd have to find out, I decided. And I wasn't going to let nature take its course – if I did that I might end up waiting ten years for an answer. No, I was going to have to take matters into my own hands. It just so happened that I had to go to London with Rich to be interviewed by *Melody Maker*. And while Rich wanted to spend quality time with Lauren beforehand, I knew exactly where I was going.

*

Soho is one of those places that the word juxtaposition was designed for. Posh eateries rub shoulders with the lowest, seediest side of capitalism, the sort best avoided in polite conversation. And hidden away, round the corner from the advertising agencies are the strip joints and peepshows. It's ironic, I thought as I wandered round. Both are full of employees embarrassed at such a blatant abuse of their talents.

'I'm only doing it for the money,' explained a so-called 'creative' in Michael Caine glasses. His tie looked like someone had thrown up on it. 'What I really want to be is a writer.'

'I'm only doing it for the money,' said a girl with sunglasses. Her top was tighter than Townie, and believe me, that was saying something. 'What I really want to be is an actress.'

I know the girls were only saying it, but it did my ego no harm at all. As I wandered up and down the seedy streets, I got propositioned more times in twenty minutes than I had in the rest of my life put together. I wouldn't have done it with any of them for a minute, but then that's premature ejaculation for you.

'Well, *hello.*'

I stopped outside a club called Swinging Sixties. The woman in the doorway must have been frozen, on account of having forgotten to put her trousers on that morning. Her red hair matched her basque and knee-high boots. 'Sorry, Tigger, I'm not sure you're old enough for this place.'

Not old enough? I reached into my pocket, and pulled out a proof of age card. The woman laughed at my photograph.

'What I mean is, *Tigger*, that this place might shock you. Why don't you try Betty's Bouncy Castle down the road?'

For once, I didn't want anyone telling me what I should and shouldn't see. This, I thought, could be exactly what I needed to get over Lauren. Gorgeous girls in sixties gear, grooving along to the Beatles. People re-enacting the summer of love. If this didn't sort me out, then I didn't know what would.

'Well, OK,' the woman sighed, shoving my twenty-pound note down her cleavage. 'But don't say I didn't warn you.'

I wandered down a dark set of stairs, towards a flashing green neon arrow, then along a corridor, towards a room full of voices and music. Strange, I thought, that music sounds suspiciously like Engelbert Humperdinck, not so much a sixties icon as an anti-sixties icon, the man who stopped the Beatles' best single, 'Penny Lane' / 'Strawberry Fields Forever', from getting to number one. Of all that decade's songs you could choose, why had they gone and picked that piece of granny music?

I opened the door, blinked twice and shut it again. No, it couldn't be. I opened it again.

Ugh.

It was.

Oh. My. *God*. The room was full of what could only be described as passionate pensioners, copulating codgers, an orgy of OAPs. People growing old disgracefully. Dirty old men and dirty old women slobbering and dribbling all over each other, and none of them could have been any younger than . . . *Ah*. I was beginning to work out why the club was thus called.

I slammed the door and went back upstairs. When the woman on the door saw me, she laughed.

'Blimey tigger, you don't last long do you?'

'I want my money back,' I said.

'Certainly, sir,' she smiled sarcastically. 'Do you have a receipt?'

'Of course I haven't got a receipt.' I wasn't going to

let this go. 'Look, please give me the money. I'm on the dole. That twenty quid is a lot of money. And I don't suppose you care that I've had a really rough time with relationships recently, and I know it was sad of me but I thought this place might help me get over it.'

The woman looked me up and down. As I turned to go, she stretched an arm out, put a hand round my neck, and pulled herself towards me. Before I knew what was happening, she was kissing me fully and firmly, her tongue pushing insistently against mine. I felt a hand reach down and slip into my jeans pocket, squeezing my arse.

'You don't need to come to a place like this,' the woman smiled. 'Not with a young, thin, sexy body like yours.'

Young? Thin? Sexy? I felt myself blushing.

'And certainly not if you carry on kissing like that.'

Kate the bridesmaid. Samka. Now the woman from the Swinging Sixties club. Afterwards, as I wandered through Soho in a daze, searching for a tube station, I couldn't help feeling that something important had happened. Well no, that's not true. Nothing had actually happened, but it *could* have done, yes, that was the thing. Each of these women had seen me as a possibility: someone sort of attractive, someone *fanciable*. I'm all right, I realised. I'm never going to be a Rich, but I am all right. And that, I thought, is good to know. Yes, whatever happens with Lauren, that's good to know. I'm all right.

Later, when I was searching for some change for the

tube, I discovered the women from the club had put the twenty-pound note back in my pocket.

*

The interview with *Melody Maker* was taking place in Camden, at a rather down-at-heel dive called the Good Mixer. I arrived five minutes late, which in rock terms, of course, meant I was still fifteen minutes early. I'd already drunk half my second pint by the time Rich and the journalist arrived.

'Will, this is Simon,' Rich swaggered in with the journalist. Simon was small, with thick NHS-style glasses, and the desperate look of someone who wants to be trendy, but is trying just that little bit too hard.

'You're the bass player.' Simon shook my hand.

'Keen to meet you,' Rich sneered at me. 'Fuck knows why.'

Rich's networking skills had paid off in abundance. He'd already had a photo and gig details done about our Brighton Rocks gig. Now, to coincide with Sound City, we were getting ourselves a feature, as one of the country's rising bands.

'This is my first interview,' I said, whilst Simon fiddled in his bag for a Dictaphone.

Rich kicked me. Ouch. To his surprise, and a little to mine, I stamped back.

'Mine too,' said Simon. 'I'm a bit nervous to be honest.'

'It's probably a good thing,' I said. 'New band, new journalist. We can be like your pet project.'

Rich looked at me as if to say 'I'll manage the PR...'

'Right.' Simon clicked record on his Dictaphone. 'Let's begin at the beginning, shall we? When did it all start?'

'Had the idea in the bath,' Rich leaned forward and across the table, blocking me out of the way. This was his moment, and he wasn't going to let me have a second of it. 'There was this song on the radio, a Beatles song, and it sounded so fresh I thought, Hey! We should do this all over again. So I did.'

'And when did you come in?' Simon asked me.

'I can't do it all by myself,' Rich answered for me whilst I was still thinking what to say. Bastard. 'It's more time-saving to get someone else to do the menial tasks.'

'Actually,' I interrupted, 'I write the words.'

I thought Rich was going to kick me again. Instead he scraped his heel up and down my leg. The funny thing was, though, I didn't feel intimidated by him. What with my brush with the woman from the club, I felt buoyed up by a little bit of confidence. I scraped Rich's shin back.

'Really?' Simon turned back to a grimacing Rich. 'So the words are, what was your phrase ... menial?'

'Well, no, not at all, the words are everything ...'

Sweet. I sat forwards, head on my hands, looking interested in what Rich was saying.

'So Will is better than you at writing lyrics?'

'Hrmmpth,' said Rich.

'Cool, cool,' said Simon. 'So Will, if I can ask you about your inspiration ...'

Rich's face. He'd been so excited, like a kid at

Christmas, only to have his present taken and given to someone else. Me! I looked at him and smiled.

I must have been a bit drunk, because I said, 'I have a muse. An unrequited love.'

'Well this is an interesting situation. Rich, do you have a problem singing about this love of Will's?'

Rich perked up, pleased that the conversation had turned back to him. 'As long as Will doesn't have the hots for some goat or something, it's not a problem. But as I was saying . . .'

He tried to twist the conversation round, but Simon was having none of it. He turned back to me and asked, 'And you, Will? Do you have a problem with Rich singing what you feel?'

Yes I did, I thought. I looked at Rich who mouthed the words, 'No you don't.'

'I think it's fair to say that Rich is extremely successful in getting across my basic message.'

'It says here you're playing Sound City,' Simon said, flicking through his notes. 'Any thoughts about that?'

'I'll answer this one,' Rich said. 'Norwich is going to be a very sad place. All those dreams shattered . . .'

Shattered?

'Really?' asked Simon. 'Not very confident of your chances, then?'

'. . . all those other unsigned bands we're going to blow off stage.' Rich was back in his stride now. 'The Brits are coming, Simon. Mark my words. In a couple of years' time everyone will be copying us. The charts are going to be chock-a-block with sixties-sounding guitar bands.'

'God help us,' said Simon.

'You're not a fan of our sort of music then?' I asked.

Simon smiled diplomatically. 'If you want to sound like some sort of second-rate Beatles tribute band, that's up to you. I just think that when you compare the American bands like Nirvana and Dinosaur Junior and Hole and . . .'

'If you ask me,' interrupted Rich, 'that's just America discovering punk ten years after it happened. It's every bit as retro as what we're doing.'

'Bollocks it is,' Simon pulled a face. 'Fuck's sake, my mum likes the Beatles, you know what I'm saying.'

'Well maybe your mum's got taste.'

Simon laughed. 'She's forty-two, Rich. How can she possibly have taste? The Beatles are no different to anything that happened before punk. They're completely shit.'

'And everything after punk?' I asked.

'Well OK,' Simon confessed, 'most of that is shit too. That's where magazines like the *Maker* come in, to support the Spaceman 3s, the Valentines of this world . . .'

'But these are the small bands who never sell,' Rich said. 'They never get into the charts.'

'Of course not,' Simon said. 'That'd be like selling out.'

'I see,' I said. 'So for you, a great band is one that doesn't sell any records.'

'Exactly,' said Simon.

'So what about Nirvana?' Rich asked. 'They're selling records by the bucket load.'

'Yeah, well,' Simon said. 'They're really losing it if you ask me. *Nevermind* is nowhere near as good as the stuff they were making a couple of years ago.'

'If you think we're so shit,' I said, 'why have you come to interview us?'

'Well, if we only sold to people like me,' Simon said, 'we'd end up going out of business. We need to seduce people by including the odd,' he shivered, '*commercial* band.'

'But doesn't that mean you're selling out, too?'

'No it doesn't.' Simon stopped the tape. 'Er, I'm going to the bog.'

*

As Simon headed off, Lauren appeared. My heart somersaulted, then stopped. Lauren, you could tell immediately, was not happy about something. It was the way she was striding towards us, eyeballing Rich on the way.

'Jesus,' Rich stood up, glancing at the toilet door to check where Simon was. 'What are you doing, Lauren? I'm being interviewed by the fucking *Melody Maker* here. We agreed they shouldn't know I have a girlfriend.'

'Will,' said Lauren, ignoring him and talking to me (ignoring Rich! Talking to me!). 'You'll have to finish up for us. Rich's coming outside with me.'

'Lauren. I'm doing an interview,' said Rich.

Lauren and Rich locked eyes. Just what was needed given the circumstances. A staring contest. Rich blinked first.

'Outside,' said Lauren. 'Now.'

Then without waiting for an answer, she stormed outside.

I looked at Rich, who watched Lauren leave with incredulity.

'Well?' I asked.

'Fucking women,' Rich got up. 'Nothing but grief.' He waved at me without turning round. 'Wind it up, Saucepan. I'd better go and calm the silly bitch down.'

I wasn't in the mood to let that sort of comment lie.

'She's not silly,' I said. 'She's not silly, and she's certainly not a bitch.'

Rich stopped and looked at me. 'Well, excuse me, Germaine fucking Greer. Let's have this conversation again when you finally manage to pull someone. I don't think you'll be quite so – shit, here he comes.'

Rich left, and Simon returned, double-taking to see where Rich was.

'Er, yeah, sorry, mate,' I said. 'Rich had to rush off. Bit of a crisis.'

'That's OK,' said Simon, reaching for his tape recorder. 'I think we're all but done.'

'So this piece will go in in a couple of weeks' time?' I asked.

'That's right,' said Simon, putting the tape recorder back in his bag. 'It's going to be a big issue. We're all very excited about it at the *Maker*. The cover is going to have the headline, "The Best New Band in Britain". It's the first time we've ever put a band on the front who haven't had a record out.'

Us? On the front? The best new band in Britain?

'This is great publicity for us,' I said. 'People are really going to remember who we are.'

'They certainly will,' Simon drained the dregs of his pint. 'By the time they've read my article, you're going to be recognised by every indie kid in the country . . .'

*

My head, I had to say, was spinning. I still couldn't get my head round the fact that we were going to be on the front of *Melody Maker*. We were bound to get signed after that. I was so excited about my potential rock stardom, I'd almost forgotten about Rich and Lauren. Almost.

I finished my pint, and left the pub to see Rich and Lauren having a massive stand-up row in the middle of the street. They were having a row! I didn't normally enjoy other people's discomfort, but in this case I'd make an exception. I hid in the shadows of a nearby doorway to listen in, though their body language said it all. Rich had his palms open in a Gallic what-did-I-do sort of shrug. Lauren was pacing up and down, fingers jabbing, pointing at the accused.

'For fuck's sake, Rich, what did you think you were doing?'

'Honestly, Lauren, I'm sorry. I'll get rid of it.'

'You said that before.'

'Well, I will this time. I promise.'

'You hid it in my *bag*, Rich,' Lauren waved her seventies Adidas holdall at Rich to press home the point. 'I was getting an *A-Z* out of my bag to ask a *policeman* for directions when I saw it. Do you know what could have happened to me?'

What? What had Rich hidden?

'Lauren, look, just calm down . . .' Rich said, pushing his palms towards the ground.

'No I won't fucking calm down,' Lauren pulled a hand angrily through her hair. 'That's class A stuff, Rich. If he'd seen it, I'd have been nicked.'

Of course. Rich's stash.

'OK, OK,' Rich lowered his voice, suddenly sounding all serious. 'Just keep your voice down . . .'

'No I won't keep my fucking voice down.' Lauren raised her voice in retaliation, punctuating the start of each sentence by jabbing Rich in the stomach. '*You* listen to me. *You* know what the deal was when you moved into my house. *You* promised to sort yourself out. *You* get rid of the drugs or I'll get rid of *you*.'

'Oh, now come on, Lauren,' Rich pleaded. 'Now you're just being ridiculous . . .'

And then she slapped him.

20

With that one slap, it all made sense. I wasn't just going to fall out of love with Lauren, however hard I tried to make it happen, be it through shenanigans with Eastern Europeans, visiting gruesome sex clubs or whatever. I'd got it all wrong. For I shouldn't have been focusing on how *I* felt at all. What I should have been putting all my efforts into, what I should have been concentrating on – of course – was undermining Rich.

I tell you. How I resisted shouting out, 'Fucking yes! And knee him in the bollocks too,' I'll never know. It was the first time I'd smiled for weeks, and I made up for lost time by beaming as broadly as I possibly could. My face may have been hurting from the strain, but it was not, I kept reminding myself, hurting as much as Rich's did from Lauren's left hook. Ah, happiness. My one regret was that I hadn't caught the moment on film, thus being able to freeze-frame the image and get it made into a T-shirt, a mug, a tea towel, a poster, a badge, a sticker, a baseball cap, and a matching pillow and duvet combination pack.

With that slap, that – hang on, I've just got to remind myself of it again – mmm, where was I? Oh yes. With that slap, everything changed. Beneath his cocksure sure-footedness, Rich, I realised, was no better than me. Better looking, maybe, but not better. I'd put up with his put-downs for so long, I'd begun to believe there was something in them. But not any more.

Because I'd discovered Rich's weakness. He was like a kid in a sweet shop with the shopkeeper's back turned: he couldn't resist temptation. And sure, he had this clever little philosophy about how everything was OK as long as you weren't stupid enough to get caught, but it was so long since he *had* got caught, he'd forgotten where the line was. It meant he was taking risks, and the more risks he took, the more likely he was to make a mistake.

Lauren, I was sure of it, was way down on Rich's list of priorities. He'd promised her he'd get rid of the drugs, but he was clearly up to his old tricks whenever he got the chance. Quite simply, Lauren was lower down the list than Rich's nose. I just had to make her realise it. And thus a plan of action was formed; I was going to go all out to wind Rich up. For the more agitated he got, the more he was going to want a snort of his little white friend. And the moment he slipped up, I'd have him.

*

It was by now less than a week to the Big Gig at Sound City, Norwich. All of us were practising like crazy, even Rich, everyone putting in as many after-hours hours in Danny's guitar shop as we could. Each of us was reacting to the pressure in our own different way – Townie was twitchy, and letting off steam on the dustbins out back; Danny was withdrawn, disappearing behind his fringe and noodling ever more obscure scales on the guitar. Rich, meanwhile, was irritable, irascible and increasingly agitated. He wasn't used to hard work, and, as I'd hoped, being without his powder of preference wasn't helping.

And me? How was I reacting to the thought of thirty minutes that could bring me fame and fortune and celebrity and my own chain of themed restaurants?

I was turning the screw.

'What,' Rich asked, as I crunched the song 'Special' to a halt, 'is your fucking problem?'

'Oh, it's not me with the problem,' I replied. 'It's you.'

'You think I've got a problem?' Rich asked. 'You're right. I've a problem with the person playing bass fucking guitar.'

He turned away, as if to signal the conversation was over. Ah well. I never was very good at reading body language.

'At least I play my bass guitar in tune,' I answered back.

There was a pause. Out of the corner of my eye, I noticed Rich clench his fists, unclench, then clench them again.

'Are you saying I can't sing?' he said slowly and deliberately.

'Oh good gracious, no,' I babbled along, putting on my best irritating Teenage Tory voice. 'But that top note, it's coming out flat every time.'

'Will,' Rich said, continuing to try to sound like Clint Eastwood. 'I'm a fucking great vocalist.'

'Oh absolutely,' I agreed. 'Great vocalist.' I waited for Rich to relax before continuing with relish. 'Within your range of course. That top note is *just* beyond it, hence you're having to overstretch yourself.'

'Dan,' Rich said, 'tell this twat he's talking bollocks.'

'You're not overstretching yourself,' Danny said.

'Thank you,' said Rich.

'But Will's right,' Danny agreed. 'You're having problems because of where you're breathing. By the time you hit that note, you've run out of puff.'

'Oh yeah? And how should I sing it then?'

Danny sang him the line. Note perfect.

'What is this?' Rich asked. 'Do you want to be the singer?'

'Hey,' Townie butted in. 'Cut it out you two. Just concentrate on your own parts.'

'Yeah, well maybe Will should do that as well,' Rich said. 'Then he'd stop playing so many shit notes. Let's do the song again.'

We restarted, the atmosphere crackling with tension. As we approached the top note, it was almost as if the music paused, with everyone waiting to hear what Rich was going to sing. Rich saw us all looking at him.

'Oh, for fuck's sake,' he said.

'There's going to be pressure next week,' I was enjoying this. 'You're going to have to be able to hit that note.'

'Who the fuck's in charge here?' Rich shouted, like a man not much in charge at all. 'If I want to hit that high note I'll hit that high note.'

Rich looked around expectantly for support. It didn't come.

'As it is, for the moment I'm going to go for a lower note.' He glowered at me. 'We're short of time, and I've got to think of the bigger picture.'

We carried on. Briefly. With a feeling of pleasure, I couldn't help myself from stopping Rich again.

'Oh, this had better be *fucking* good,' Rich almost hissed at me.

'It's your phrasing,' I smiled back. 'We need to get it sorted out.'

'I'm going to sort *you* out in a minute,' Rich spat at me, then turned to Danny. 'Phrasing? What the fuck is he on about?'

'It's how you say the words,' Danny explained. 'Making sure the stress is in the right place.'

Rich squared up to me. 'Are you saying I can't speak properly?'

'The first line in the chorus,' I said. 'It's all wrong.' I read the line out. '*You're special because you're different.* And this is how you're singing it. *You're special because you defer rent.*' I couldn't resist a dig. 'What is it? Do you not like landlords or something?'

'I can only be as good as the tune I was given,' Rich was on the defensive now.

'Hey, don't knock my tune,' Danny was polite, but firm.

'Dan, it's a great tune,' I backed him up. 'As Rich would find out if he sung it properly.'

'Look. Let me tell you how singing works,' Rich said.

'It's like acting. You get the lines and then reinterpret them in your own way.'

'Well, I think you should consider interpreting them differently.' I smiled about as patronisingly as I could. 'Or should that be defer-rent-ly?'

*

The practice fizzled out, but I wasn't done with Rich. Oh no. As he flounced off to Lauren's house for some tea and sympathy, I headed home. And one quick change of clothes and I was back, sat in the car, staking out Lauren's front door. It wasn't a bad door as doors go, quite a nice deep green colour, with a 'no free newspapers' note above the letterbox. Surprisingly enough, it wasn't the door I was interested in. But the someone behind it.

My knowledge of stakeouts, I'd have to say, was limited. Any knowledge I had was gleaned from a few bad cop shows and that terrible mid-eighties film starring Richard Dreyfuss and Emilio Estevez. But what I had picked up – and what was always adhered to, however bad the programme – were the two golden rules of stakeouts. The first, was that you had to have as much junk food as you could possibly cram into the car, the sort of junk food that makes a family pack of peanuts look like, well, peanuts. I must have bought enough rubbish to shore up the share price of Burger King for weeks, not to mention Coca Cola, Cadbury's and who-ever makes that disgusting 'own brand' lemonade you get in corner shops.

The second rule about stakeouts is that the action always happens when you're momentarily not looking, when you can wait no more and have nipped out for a piss or are changing the tape on the stereo or are scraping the last piece of congealed fat from the bottom of your KFC bargain bucket. In other words, those thirty seconds when you're looking the other way are crucial. I had thus set up what I considered a rather clever combination of mirrors – well, my parents' bedroom mirror lying horizontal on the back seat – to let me follow the action even when I was looking the other way.

I looked at my watch. Nine-forty. Rich, longing for a line, would be feeding Lauren a load of fabricated bollocks by now. *I might just go out for a quick pint, got a bit of music to discuss with the lads. You don't mind staying here, do you?* And Lauren, because she was nice and forgiving and believed him, would nod and say OK.

I looked at the front door. Nothing.

All right. Maybe this. Lauren looks at Rich and yawns, says, I'm really bushed, maybe I'll get an early night. And Rich, sniffing his chance, goes, oh, I'm going to be awake for hours. And Lauren says, well don't let me stop you – why don't you go and find the lads, there's bound to be someone down the pub. And Rich says, well if you're sure, and Lauren says, I'm sure, and off Rich goes.

I looked at the front door. Silence.

Um. OK. Lauren, doing her domestic bliss bit says, What do you fancy now? A mug of Ovaltine? A game of Scrabble? And Rich says, Oh yes, that sounds wonderful, but I'm a bit worried about my voice, what with all this rehearsing. And Rich says, I know I'm probably being overcautious but I'd like to have some medicine here, in case my throat swells up. I won't get to sleep otherwise. I'll be back from the all-night chemist before you know it.

There was a noise from behind the car. As I looked round to see a cat land on the boot, I saw the green door begin to open in the mirror on the back seat.

I turned round to see Rich shut it, and make his way down the street.

Bingo, you bastard. I unclipped my seat belt, opened the door and began to play follow my leader.

It was at about this point that I began to have serious doubts about my disguise. I'd felt Rich might cotton on if he saw me wandering around town after him, so I'd cunningly turned up in costume, a costume, I reckoned that would have had Templeton Peck nodding in admiration.

The look I'd gone for was the American tourist.

This consisted of my father's golf visor, my mother's sunglasses from the year before last, a bright-red checked shirt I'd got for Christmas from my colour-blind grandmother (and never worn, I hasten to add), a pair of cream trousers, and the pièce de résistance, four pillows, stuffed up my front, back, and down each leg respectively. All I had to do was say, 'Honey, isn't England *cute*,' and you'd be crossing the street to avoid me.

The pillows were both a brilliant and a terrible idea. As I sat there, wedged behind the wheel, I wondered if I was ever going to get out without setting off the alarm or the horn. But when I eventually rolled out on to the pavement, landing heavily on my arse, I was more than glad they were there to cushion my fall.

As I wobbled along after Rich, doing my best Weeble impression, I worked out that Rich was travelling towards the seafront. This was good news for me: at least I'd look less conspicuous down there. But where was he going? One thing was for sure, it wasn't the pub. The only pubs round there were the really tacky ones on the pier, and I knew Rich wouldn't be seen dead in any of them.

Rich stopped at a telephone box, on the edge of the Laines. I crunched to a halt as well, pulling out my map and holding it upside down, looking confused, and mumbling, 'Huh?' in a bad American accent to myself. Ringing someone up from a call box? I knew it, I thought. He's up to no good, Lauren. I was too far away to hear what he was saying, but near enough to see him put the phone down and just stand there for what felt like an age, but must have been only a minute. Then he looked at his watch, lit a cigarette, and headed for the sea, meandering as though he had time to kill.

Rich walked along the promenade for a while, then cut down on to the beach towards the West Pier. I can't go down there, I decided. It'd look far too obvious. So I leaned on the railings, following his progress via the zoom lens on my camera. I skipped past him to the pier, to see if anyone, was waiting for him there. And there she was.

I couldn't believe it. The girl from Mel's party.

Tasmin.

Or was it Camilla? I couldn't remember which one was which to be honest, but it was the one who'd dressed like she could have been in Abba. Let's call her

Tasmin for now. Tasmin didn't look like she was in Abba standing under the pier, but that was OK. I knew the name of her game and that was more than enough.

They made to embrace. Got you, I snapped away. I waited for them to snog, but instead Rich just pecked Tasmin on both cheeks and pulled back. Did he know he was being watched? Certainly Rich seemed to glance over his shoulders a couple of times. I carried on taking pictures anyway. Rich pulled something out of his coat pocket and handed it to her. I couldn't make out what it was, but I could guess. They stood there and talked some more before heading back up to the promenade, making for a bus shelter a little way down from where I was standing.

The shelter had two sides, one facing out to sea, the other into town. Rich and Tasmin took the sea side. I knew it might look suspicious if I sat on the other side, but at the same time I was desperately curious to know what they were talking about. Curiosity won. I wobbled over.

'. . . I can't believe we're doing this, Rich.'

'I know, it feels wrong doesn't it?'

Bugger, I thought as I sat down. Why hadn't I brought a tape recorder with me?

'Whenever I've needed something *naughty*, you've always been the one I could turn to.'

'Not any more,' Rich said. 'I've got to think of Lauren. I've got to be clean.'

Woah there. Clean?

'So what is this stuff you've given me?'

'Jesus, don't get it out now! Why do you think I gave

it to you down on the beach? It's really good shit, Jeremy brought it back from Columbia, you know what I'm saying?'

'There must be a tonne of it here. This must be worth . . .' Tasmin gave out a little gasp. 'Are you sure you want to get rid of it all?'

'That's what I promised Lauren.'

I felt numb. This was terrible. Far from gathering evidence of Rich's misdemeanours, I was garnering proof of his conversion to being a good guy. I couldn't believe it. He was actually getting rid of his drugs.

'I said I'd flush it down the loo,' Rich continued, 'but it seemed a bit of a waste to me. Might as well give them to someone who'd appreciate it . . .'

'Oh, Rich.' Tasmin sounded like all her birthdays had come at once. 'What can I do to thank you?'

'It's a kind thought, but I'm not like that. Not any more.'

Oh pur-lease.

'You *have* changed,' Tasmin said. 'No drugs, no sex.'

'Oh there's still lots of fucking. It's just with the same person.'

They laughed. I didn't.

'I'm going to have to move,' Rich said. 'I've got to find a chemist, otherwise Lauren's going to wonder what I've been doing.'

'Don't you find sex with the same person boring?' Tasmin asked, as they stood up.

'With Lauren? Are you kidding me?'

Rich's tales of sexual exploits hung heavy in the air as they walked away. I sat there, watching them go, then slipped round and sat on the other side of the shelter. Oh *fuck*. I looked out to sea, like my love life, disappearing into darkness. Oh *Lauren*. The fact that Rich had changed that much, it spoke volumes to me about how special Lauren was – so special that Rich would give up his philandering and pharmaceuticals for her. Was it possible that Rich did deserve Lauren after all? Had I been blind to his good points because I'd wanted him to fail? No, I thought, there was something about him I still didn't trust. And maybe not this time, but at some stage soon, he was going to slip up. It was only a matter of time, I told myself, it was only a matter of time.

21

The day of the Big Gig in Norwich was always going to be a defining one. It was a day when dreams about the future finally turned into reality. It was a day when Danny, Townie, Rich and I would learn exactly where we were, and where it was we were – or weren't – going.

Like I said, it was always going to be a defining day. And though it didn't disappoint in those terms, I'm not sure anyone expected things to turn out quite as they did.

As we drove up to Norwich, I don't think the importance of the day was lost on anyone. Lauren and Rich sat in the front, while Danny, Townie and I kept ourselves to ourselves in the back, brooding over what was to come. We weren't on stage for another twelve hours, but already my nerves were creating if not waves of nausea, then certainly little ripples, lapping at the shore of my stomach. Either that, or Rich's driving was getting to me more than usual.

'Will,' Danny kicked me out of my comatose state, 'are you with us?'

'Er, yeah. Absolutely,' I said.

'Yeah right,' said Danny. 'Don't take this the wrong way, mate, but you look fucking awful.'

Well how would you feel, I thought, if you'd been playing private detective night after night, with the only tangible result being a severe lack of sleep? And not only that, but you found yourself sitting inches away from the woman you loved, as she chatted and chuckled and joked with someone else.

'You always were too uptight, Saucepan,' Townie smiled nostalgically. 'Just relax. It'll be fine.'

In one way, I was glad we were playing the gig. At least it gave me the excuse to show exactly how I felt, and pass it off as nerves. More than once I'd considered jacking the whole thing in. Part of me wondered if I needed to move on, to get Rich and Lauren out of my life, not help set up a situation where I'd see even more of them. Part of me just wanted to get up and walk away. But looking at Danny and Townie sitting there, tense but excited, I knew I'd done the right thing by turning up. They'd worked just as hard as I had, and I didn't want to let them down. I'd do the gig for them, I'd decided, get them the record contract, and then decide what to do.

'I'm sorry,' I said. 'What with the gig and losing my job and my parents coming back in a few weeks, I'm a bit stressed out.'

'We noticed,' Danny said.

'I hope I haven't been too much of a pain in the arse.'

'Not to us,' said Danny. 'But you've been a bit sharp with Rich. Like at that rehearsal . . .'

'Yeah, well,' I said. 'I know he thinks he is in charge, but that doesn't mean he's right about everything.'

'Sure,' Danny agreed. 'It was just the way you went about it that was a bit off. You were spot on with what you were saying. Even Rich said so.'

Rich? Humility?

'A couple of nights ago he turns up at the shop. Wanted to go through the songs, just me and him, so we could tweak the tunes and sort out his phrasing.' He grinned. 'Just like you said. Don't tell him I told you that, though. I promised him I wouldn't.'

'Sure.' I looked at Danny, who winked at me, and Townie punched me playfully on the arm. Ow. They were nice blokes, I thought. 'So how come you two aren't as nervous as me?' I asked. 'Why do I feel like I'm the only one who's shitting bricks?'

'That's because we've got our lucky charms,' said Townie.

Lucky charms? Danny and Townie both reached into their inside pockets, and pulled out pieces of paper. Townie handed me his first. It was a kid's painting, with bright splotches of reds and greens.

'It's by Tim,' Townie said.

'Tim?'

'Our sister's youngest,' he said proudly. 'Smashing kid.'

Yeah. I'll bet.

'When I told him I was going to Norwich, he did this picture for me. Said it was for his favourite uncle, to wish him luck.'

I was tempted to ask what the picture was meant to be, but thought better of it.

'That's really nice,' I said. And it was. And it *was* nice, too, the way Townie was smiling. There was something almost, well, paternal about it.

'And what about you, Danny?' I asked. 'What's your lucky charm?'

Danny handed me a folded up, ancient-looking press clipping. It was from a very old edition of *Melody Maker* (*Melody Maker*! A shiver of excitement rippled through me as I remembered we were going to be on the cover). I couldn't help noticing the date. 23 April 1967. Twenty-five years ago to the day.

'It's a gig review. Of my mum,' Danny said.

I unfolded the cutting. There was a picture of Danny's mum, singing into a microphone, her eyes closed, her straight, black, sixties bob complementing a simple, elegant white dress. The headline was '*MARTIN'S TRIUMPH*'.

'Danny,' I said. 'She looks beautiful.'

'I found it last night in a photo album,' Danny said. 'Have you seen where the gig was?'

I looked down. Spookier still. The gig had been in Norwich.

'It's a sign,' said Danny. There was an almost serene edge of certainty to his voice. 'I just know it. History is going to repeat itself.'

I wonder if it is, I thought. As tragedy or farce?

*

'OK, give me stressed, give me worried, look into the camera like you've just realised you've left the oven on . . .'

Snap.

Soundcheck over. I was sat on the edge of the stage, swinging my legs, feeling sorry for myself. Danny and Townie had gone off for some food. Rich had disappeared to find a copy of *Melody Maker*. Which left me and some sound guy, tapping microphones and testing leads.

And Lauren.

'Well I think I've got the whole gamut of Harding expressions now.' Lauren jumped up and sat next to me. 'Every look from run-over-by-a-bus to I'm-about-to-be-sick to pass-me-that-handgun.'

'Ha,' I smiled thinly. 'Ha.'

'Chill *out*,' she shoulder barged me, the mere contact sending currents charging down my spine. 'God, first Rich. Now you.'

'Rich?'

'Yeah. He's gone all withdrawn and preoccupied. Won't tell me what it's about.' She leaned in conspiratorially. 'I think he's scared about tonight, but he won't admit it.'

'Unlike me.'

'Exactly,' Lauren said. 'You'd have to be a Martian to miss that you weren't relaxed. And even then, they could probably have a good stab at guessing it.' She looked round the hall. 'What do you think to the venue?'

'I think it stinks,' I said. And it did. It was one

of those places that never quite shifted the stench of the night before. It wasn't helped by the décor; black walls and a low, sloping ceiling. I thought the way the floor was sticky with alcohol a particularly nice touch.

'Yeah, well you've got to start somewhere,' Lauren smiled. 'Oh aren't you excited, Will? Of what might happen?'

'I don't know. I mean, that sort of thing only happens to other people. I'm the sort of person who watches, whilst others get the good stuff.'

'Maybe the others get the good stuff because all you're doing is watching.' Lauren paused, the tip of her tongue resting on her top row of teeth. 'Or do you like to watch, Will?'

I looked at her. She was sitting close enough for me to smell her perfume. 'No,' I said, sadly. 'No, I don't like to watch.'

'Well, then. You've got to get more pro-active. Make things happen. Because when you do that, anything is possible.' She smiled, jumped down. 'You've just got to keep believing in yourself, that's all.'

I watched her sling her camera over her shoulder, and walk, no, *saunter* towards the door at the back of the hall. I watched her turn, flash a smile at me, and then with a flick of her hair, she was gone. I watched her go again in my mind. I couldn't say why, but there was definitely something *final* about the way she'd left. Like, well, like I was never going to see her again.

*

I knew things were about to go horrifically wrong the moment I walked into the newsagents, and picked up a copy of *Melody Maker*. The headline the journalist had promised – '*The Best New Band in Britain*' – was there all right. But the group in question wasn't Double Top, but some other band I'd never heard of.

'Suede? Who the fuck are Suede?' I opened the magazine up, but the cover story was exactly as I feared. Pages and pages about this bloody band called Suede. How they hadn't had a record out yet, but their debut single was going to be brilliant, how they hated shoegazers, how they didn't want to sound American but wanted to play music that was very, very English. How they were audacious, androgynous, mysterious, sexy, ironic, absurd, perverse, glamorous, hilarious, honest, cocky, melodramatic, mesmerising . . .

'Oi,' the newsagent shouted at me. 'Are you going to pay for that, or just stand there and read it?'

I handed him the money and walked outside, still reading. I was *sure* the journalist had said we were on the front cover. I must have misheard him. Still. If this Suede were half as good as the article was making out, then they were the biggest thing to hit British music for years. I shivered, remembered Rich's talk about how we'd been waiting for the next link in the chain. Were Suede it? Were they the band to start the British revival, with a string of British guitar bands to follow in their wake, complete with knowing nods to the past in their music and Englishness in their lyrics, with rival bands going head-to-head in the singles charts and the whole thing culminating in some epoch-defining, Zeppelinesque gig at Knebworth? Looking at *Melody Maker*, I couldn't help thinking that maybe that first link had been found, and we were perhaps six months late.

'Having a good read?'

I stopped and saw Rich standing there, leaning against a lamp-post, gently swinging Lauren's bag in one hand.

'Rich . . . it's all . . . I don't understand.' I looked at him, almost pleadingly, to tell me I was dreaming. 'I thought it was going to be us in this issue. But it's all Suede.'

'Oh we're in it, all right. We're up to our fucking necks in it.' Rich said. There was a menacing edge to his voice, even worse than when we'd had that argument in the rehearsal. 'Haven't you found the article yet?' He snatched the paper out of my hand. 'Here, let me help you.' Rich flicked through until he found what he was looking for, then shoved it back under my nose. And I'd thought not being on the cover was bad.

RIGHT ROCKERS!

Still gutted after John Major and his tosspot Tories got back into power? So are we, and so are the majority of the world of rock. From Billy Bragg to the Manics, everyone hoped that this would be the sorry end to the sorry f***ers, but no! Us British like nothing better than giving ourselves a good kicking. Five more years of corrupt, shagging politicians who don't give a monkey's left b*****k for what the youth of this country think? Yes please!

Still. It's not doom and gloom for the entire rock world. Some pop stars are actually pleased that the Tories got back in power, and not just because they get a lower tax bill. Call it a Downing Street Of Shame, a Who's Who of Who's a T**t, but in a unique piece of public service broadcasting, we bring you a list of the right t*****s . . .

1. Phil Collins. Well there's a surprise. Old Phil is a Tory. From the Genesis of public-school days, he's always had the right side of his bread buttered, if you know what I mean. If only it was 'one more night', rather than another five sodding years.

2. Suzi Quatro. Suzi, who shares her surname with a revolting eighties soft drink, recently played at the Young Conservative Ball in Eastbourne. How young is 'young' exactly? Forty-f***ing-seven?

But it's not all old farts folks! There's a whole raft of new bands, breaking the mould, taking the Tory message to the Rock heartlands. People like . . .

3. Double Top. Hailing from Brighton, this fourpiece extol classic English values like hanging and foxhunting. They hate grunge, define a good record as one that has sold a lot of copies (Rick Astley must be brilliant then), and play music that your mum might like. If that wasn't enough, on bass guitar they boast William 'Churchill' Harding, known in the Brighton Area as the 'Teenage Tory' (see photo)

'But I'm not a Tory!' I looked at Rich despairingly. 'I voted Labour! Three times!'

'You never have understood pop music, have you?' Rich snatched the *Melody Maker* back off me, and flung it in a nearby bin. 'It's all about image. What's true doesn't matter, it's what people think is true that's important. And in this case they think you're a right wing *shit*.'

For a second I thought, is it me? Is it me who has been dragging the band down all this time?

'It's not good, I'll give you,' I said. 'But we've had bad press in Brighton and carried on. We'll just have to do the same nationally.'

'You see, that's you all over. You're so used to fucking up that you're used to dealing with it.'

'What do you mean I'm always fucking up?'

'Well,' Rich sneered. 'I'll say it slowly, shall I? What it means . . . is that you're . . . always . . . fucking . . . up.' He unzipped Lauren's bag. 'Do you know how else you've fucked up, Will?'

I shook my head. I had no idea what he was talking about, but I didn't like the look on his face.

'Perhaps this will jog your memory.'

Rich reached into Lauren's bag, and I could feel myself go cold at what he pulled out.

My plastercast.

'I . . . I don't know what you're talking about.'

'Don't piss me about, Will. I know it's yours. It's got your fucking *name* on it.' He flung it at me, winding me in the stomach. Oooph. On the bottom, it did indeed say *Will Harding, 1992*.

Rich was by now pacing up and down, rubbing his hands against his temples and hurling accusations at me. 'What the fuck do you think you're playing at? Messing around with my fucking girlfriend? You think I wouldn't find out?'

'It's, it's not like that.'

'No? Well what is it like?' Rich growled. 'Because from where I'm standing it looks like my girlfriend's been sucking your *cock*.'

I thought he was going to hit me, but instead he stood so close to my face that I could feel his breath. I noticed his nostrils were flaring.

'Well, um, yes, maybe,' I said, thinking fast. 'But this was all ages ago, er, yes! Before you two were going out. I mean, I *thought* you were going out, but you weren't. I didn't mess with your girlfriend because she wasn't your girlfriend. I just thought she was.'

I took a step back, and realised I was standing against a wall. Rich stood there eyeballing me. My heart, I could feel it, was thumping.

'Let me get this straight. You *thought* we were going out, but you messed around with her anyway?'

'It doesn't matter what I thought,' I said. 'The fact is you *weren't* going out with her.'

'But you thought I was. It's exactly the same as the article in *Melody Maker*. It doesn't matter what's the truth, it's what you *think* that's the truth that counts.'

Is he going to hit me now? I thought. But Rich paced away again, muttering to himself, before striding back towards me.

'You know, it explains a lot,' Rich said. 'It explains why you've been so *fucking* weird since Lauren and I've been going out. It explains why Lauren wouldn't fucking fuck me for so long. And it explains why she finally fucking did.'

'What do you mean?'

'She wouldn't fuck me. Said she didn't trust me to hang around. Then when you wrote that song, 'Special', she went completely gaga. No wonder she related to it so much, because you wrote it about her, didn't you?'

'Yeah. But what's that got to do with . . .' And then I worked it out. 'You told her you wrote it, didn't you? You told her you wrote it so she'd sleep with you.'

'I'll tell you what she said,' Rich sneered. ' "The man who wrote this song is the man I fall in love with." Of course I told her I wrote it. I wanted to fuck her.' He smiled for the first time in the entire conversation. 'And I did.'

I couldn't take this in. Rich had used my words? The *bastard*. I felt so hyped up, so angry that I could barely think straight, except to realise that it was all Rich's fault.

'You used me,' I said, shoving Rich hard away. 'You used me, and then you lied to Lauren.'

'Hey, she did all right out of it,' Rich sneered, stood right back up to me. 'She ended up with my full twelve inches rather than your pathetic little *prick*.'

'Well, size isn't everything.' I gripped the plastercast tightly, and swung it at Rich, winding him in the stomach.

'*Ach scheiße!*' Rich swore in fluent anger. He doubled up, then grabbed my arm by the wrist, digging his nails in until I dropped the plastercast, which broke in two as it hit the floor. He pushed me back against the wall, snatched up the base of the plastercast and lunged at me.

'*Oooph!*' I could feel it jab into my ribs. I lashed out at Rich, but Rich knew what he was doing. He was punching and jabbing powerfully and precisely, and I had the frightening memory that Rich had been a boxing champion at school.

'That's for messing around with Lauren,' Rich wheezed.

At the mention of Lauren, I finally landed a decent punch across Rich's nose. Crack. Rich took a step back and dabbed at his nostril. There was blood on the end of his fingers.

Yes, I glowered. You deserve that.

'You're going to be sorry for that,' Rich half screamed, half whispered. 'Oh you're going to be fucking sorry.' But he was acting more wary now. I raised my fists in readiness, and he paused, unsure what to do next.

'If you come near me again,' I said, 'you're the one who's going to be sorry.'

Out of the corner of my eye, I noticed something small and blue and flashing in the distance. And then a siren.

'Shit, Rich.' I said, pointing. 'Behind you.'

'Yeah,' Rich snorted. 'Like I'm going to fall for that.'

I tried to make a run for it, but Rich shoved me back against the wall.

'You're going nowhere,' he growled, and lunged at me again. Rich's punches were different now; they were desperate. He didn't care if I hit him, just as long as he hit me back. Somehow I found the breath to speak and started shouting at him that the police were coming, that we had to stop this, but he wasn't listening. He wasn't going to be got through to. Not until the car had screeched to a halt behind us, and the police had leaped out of it and hauled him to the ground.

22

Learning that somebody loves you is an epiphany every bit as special as the moment you fall in love; as the subsequent recognition that you are in love. It's the final part in that wonderful trinity of romantic beginnings; the moment when everything comes together, when to your heart's soaring delight, you learn your love is reciprocated, when the word unrequited blissfully becomes two letters too long. There's nothing like learning that you have moved someone as deeply as they have moved you. It's a moment that grounds your emotions, makes them *real*, the moment when you no longer say, *I*'m in love. For there is no 'I' anymore. You're a 'we' now, and your life will never be the same again.

To be deprived of that moment, to have it stolen by someone like Rich – well, I hope it never happens to you, that's all I can say. It's just *shattering*. To be told, and then punched, and then bundled in the back of a police car, and then taken to the station and shoved in a cell for the night – I wouldn't wish it on anyone. Thank God Rich wasn't in the same room as me. I think I might have brained him.

Oh yes. Rich. I can tell you where his interests lay in all this. 'I've got a fucking gig!' he screamed from the cell next to me. 'I demand my brief!'; 'I can explain everything!'; 'I want to see the chief constable now!'; 'I was going to be famous tonight!'. And as the thin strip of light that served as a window slowly slipped from blue to black, and his hopes of fame faded the same way, Rich's increasingly hysterical attention turned to me. 'You twat, Saucepan!'; 'You've ruined my whole fucking career!'; 'I was going to save British music!'; 'Do you know what you've *done*, Harding? You've killed British music! I really hope you can fucking live with yourself!'.

I'd like to say that I felt guilty for what had happened. I'd like to tell you that I felt desperately sorry for Danny and Townie, felt gutted that all the hard work we'd put in, all the dreams we'd had, had turned to dust. I'd like to tell you that I looked out wistfully into the Norwich night, thinking about what might have been. But the truth is, Danny and Townie and the gig didn't even cross my mind. All I thought about was Lauren, and what she'd said.

The man who wrote this song is the man I fall in love with.

Lauren was in love with me. I may not be as good-looking as Rich or as confident, or as well endowed, but I could connect with her in a way Rich never could. That was what she had gone for. And that was what Rich had used to get her for himself.

I didn't sleep. My mind had too many conflicting thoughts racing through my head: a heady mix of love for Lauren, mingled with hatred for Rich, merged with fury at myself for being so fucking English about the whole thing, for standing aside while Rich had taken what wasn't rightfully his. I couldn't believe what Rich had done. And at the same time I could. It was him all over.

I remembered something Lauren had said. 'Maybe the others get the good stuff because all you're doing is watching.' And she was right. And as dawn finally followed night, I remembered what else she'd said. 'You've got to get more pro-active. Make things happen. Because when you do that, anything is possible.' She was right again. I loved Lauren. Lauren, I knew now, could fall in love with me. I just had to find a way of making it happen.

I remembered the last thing Lauren had said to me. 'You've just got to keep believing in yourself, that's all.' And even though I was stuck in a cell in a police station in Norwich, having thrown away probably the best chance I'd ever get for stardom, I sort of did. I felt like *me*, if that doesn't sound too strange. I'd stood up to Rich, I'd stuck up for what I believed in, and I felt good about it. For perhaps the first time in my life, I realised, I quite liked being me.

*

At eight-thirty, a police sergeant appeared, and led me into an interview room. My lack of sleep made it feel surreal to say the least, like I was in a TV drama. I'd seen *The Bill* and such bollocks so many times, it felt like I'd wandered on to a set. The police sergeant, who was greying, and getting on a bit, returned with a younger colleague who, I couldn't help thinking, looked both less experienced, and less intelligent. He confirmed my suspicions by doing nothing smarter than nod during the course of the interview.

'Right then, Mr Harding,' the police sergeant spoke with a soft Norfolk burr. 'Let me explain something to you. We don't like people fighting on our streets in broad daylight. In fact we will not tolerate it, do you understand? I hope you've got a decent explanation for what was going on.'

It was at this point that the full reality of the situation hit me. I was in a police station! I could go to prison! Suddenly I felt really, really scared. I took a deep breath and told him, as best I could, what had gone on and how the situation had arisen. I told him everything, about the band, about Lauren, and about the plastercast, which I noticed, was sitting on the table in a plastic bag labelled 'evidence'.

'I see.' The sergeant's look was ever so slightly suspicious. 'Mr Jung has decided not to press charges against you,' he continued, 'and I would advise you to do the same. I would hope that your night in the cells will serve as a deterrent against such behaviour in the future.'

'Mr Jung?' I was confused. 'I take it you mean Mr Young?'

'Oh, is that how you pronounce it?' The police sergeant asked. 'You're obviously better at German than I am.'

'German?'

The sergeant laughed. 'Well, I hardly think Friedrich is an English name.'

'Hang on,' I said. 'The person I had the fight with is called Rich Young. Richard Young.'

'Well, that's not what he told us.' The sergeant showed me the form. And there in Rich's writing was his name. His real name. Friedrich Jung.

'But, but . . .' It didn't make sense. Rich was as English as they came. He went on and on about English music, about how it was his duty to revolutionise English music, about how important it was to get as many English references into my lyrics as possible. Then I remembered. When I'd hit him, he'd sworn in German.

'Unbelievable,' I murmured.

It was breathtaking. Rich was a total fraud. A fraud with a good record collection, but still a fraud. He'd seen English music as ripe for the picking and reckoned he was the man ready to exploit it. Rich was a twisting, turning chameleon, happy to hoodwink and cajole, pleased to appropriate whatever it took to get what he wanted. And the lengths he was prepared to go to . . . Rich had rejected his own nationality, his own legacy of pop music (Nicole, Nena, Opus) and had decided pretending to be English stood him in far better stead for fame and success. The more I thought about it, the more it fitted. It was no different to him using my words to woo Lauren. Bastard. I hated him all over again.

'Am I free to go?' I asked.

'Not quite,' the police sergeant said. 'I want to question you about another matter if I may. When we searched Mr Jung, we found this in his bag.'

He produced another plastic bag, containing a further little bag containing . . .

'Cocaine,' I said.

'We found it inside this card.' The police sergeant passed it across to me. On the front was a picture of a horseshoe, and the words 'Good Luck'. Inside was scrawled the following message:

Rich,

Hope you're as good as the gear you gave me the other night. Thought you might like a last minute lift before you go on stage. Think of it as the thin line between success and failure!

Tasmin xxx

Oh. I tried very hard not to smile. How un*fortunate*.

'Are you going to charge him?' I asked politely.

'Oh yes. Mr Jung has something of a history with regards to narcotics. This isn't his first offence.'

'Really?' This was getting better and better.

'Would you be able to shed any light on the source of Mr Jung's supply? We can fine him for possession, but if we catch the dealer and bang him up, my DC's going to be delirious.'

'Will it affect what happens to Rich?' I asked.

'Not really. If he'd told us himself, then we would have been more lenient, reduced his bail.'

'So Rich's going to get out?' I sounded deflated.

'Presuming someone comes up with the money.'

Shit. I had to find a way to keep Rich in the nick. I had to . . .

'Of course!' It hit me. 'When I emptied my pockets, there was a camera film in there wasn't there?'

'Let me see,' the police sergeant said, glancing down at a piece of paper. 'Yes, yes there was.'

'Get it developed,' I said. 'I think I can sort your crime statistics out a treat . . .'

*

'. . . well, well, well.' The police sergeant flicked through my photos an hour later. 'This is all very interesting. Where did you say these photos were taken? Brighton?'

'That's right.'

'And that is certainly Mr Jung. And who is the other person?'

'It must be one of the other people he sells his drugs to.'

Got you, I thought. That's the last time you stitch me up, Rich Friedrich Young Jung.

'Well I don't think Mr Jung's going to be going anywhere for a while,' the police sergeant said. 'What with possession and now this evidence of dealing, I don't really think bail could be recommended in this instance.'

'He might do a runner,' I added helpfully.

'We'll have to bring charges against him within the next forty-eight hours,' the police sergeant nodded. 'Then he'll be remanded in custody until his court appearance. That time will be taken off his jail sentence.'

Fantastic.

'Hey, she's the girl that came in earlier,' the second policeman broke his silence, pointing at a photo I'd taken of Lauren.

'Lauren? What happened?' I asked.

'She started shouting. One of the lads wrote it down.

Here we are.' He flicked through his notebook. ' "Possession of drugs? The lying little shit. You can tell him I
never want to see him again." '

Was this for real? Lauren and Rich were finished?
Was this, finally, my chance?

'I'm still going to caution you, Mr Harding,' the
police sergeant put his notebook away and looked at
me sternly. I gulped. 'This incident is going to go down
on your criminal record. If you do something like this
again, you won't be treated so leniently. Do you understand?'

'Oh yes,' I gushed. 'Absolutely. Thank you, yes, thank
you . . .'

'All right,' the sergeant nodded towards the door.
'Get out of here.'

'Sure. Right.' As I got to the door I paused. 'Oh, one
last thing. I almost forgot. You did search Rich thor-
oughly didn't you?'

'How do you mean?' the sergeant asked.

I smiled. 'I remember this one time in the pub, when
he was boasting about being able to evade arrest by
secreting his drugs. Apparently, he's got quite a knack for
it. You have to really *probe* to find them.'

'I see,' said the police sergeant. 'Think we might have
missed something?'

'It's probably nothing. But, you know, it might be
worth another try.'

The police sergeant nodded. 'I'll get one of the lads
on to it right away.'

The sun was shining as I stepped out of the station.

I may have been mistaken but I'm sure I heard the succulent sound of a rubber glove being thwacked.

*

'What do you mean she's gone?'

'What I said,' said Lauren's next-door-neighbour. 'She's just . . . *gone.*'

I couldn't believe what I was hearing. I'd got out of the police station, caught the first train to London, then dashed across London on the Underground, and got another train back to Brighton. As the taxi I'd caught from the station sped away, I looked at her neighbour in disbelief. He was tall with messy hair, and had a frustratingly spaced expression on his face. He seemed a little freaked by my stress.

'She knocked on the door, yeah, couldn't have been more than an hour ago. Looked a bit out of it if you ask me. Gave me her key.' Her neighbour fiddled in his pocket, pulled out the key and waved it at me. He put it back in his pocket. 'Said she was going away.'

'Do you know where she was going?'

He shook his head.

'She had her bags packed, though, like she was off for a while. She said she was going to say a quick farewell to Brighton and then go.'

'Did she take her car?' I asked.

The neighbour looked down the street.

'Well it's not here . . .'

Fuck. I had to catch her before she left Brighton, before it was too late. Where the hell was she going? I was out of breath by the time I reached the end of her street, then wheezed my way back towards the centre, feet thumping on the pavement. Saying goodbye to Brighton? I really didn't like the sound of that – it didn't have the ring of someone going on holiday for a few weeks. What if she had been so hurt by Rich that she wanted to get Brighton out of her system? For good?

I lunged along the pavement, wondering where the hell Lauren might go. The beach? The North Laine? Barney O'Blarneys? The beach, I reckoned, was as good a bet as any. Lauren loved the beach. I bashed into tourists here there and everywhere, but could see no sign of her. I ran round the pier. Nothing. I stopped, I could feel myself hyperventilating, and was catching my breath by one of those telescopes when I had an idea. I reached into my pocket for twenty pence, and started to scour the beach.

Lauren.

She was halfway between the two piers, skimming stones into the sea. I couldn't really say from this distance, but her body language implied she was crying. The shutter clicked shut, and my view went black. Time to go. My body, which was groaning to the point of refusal, moaned again. I thought madly of jumping off the pier into the sea, but was saved by one last remaining rational thought, which pointed out that drowning wasn't so romantic. I ran round and down towards the beach as fast as I could.

But not fast enough. I bounded along the stones, crunching crisply underfoot, but by the time I'd got there she'd gone.

''Scuse me!' I shouted at a child who was paddling near where Lauren had been. 'Did you see where that lady went, the one who was here just now? Please?'

There must have been something desperate in the way I said it, because the girl looked like she thought I was about to kill her. She pointed towards the promenade, then ran away screaming.

'Oh, please no.' Could she have gone the way I'd just come? I ran back up to the promenade, but there was no sign of her. Shit.

'Did you see a girl here just now?' I asked a granny at a bus stop. 'With a camera bag? Long black hair?'

'What? You'll have to speak up a bit, dear, I'm a little . . .'

'DID YOU SEE A GIRL HERE JUST NOW? CAMERA BAG? LONG BLACK HAIR?'

'Yes, yes that does sound familiar . . .' The granny thought about this.

'PLEASE!' I was finding it fucking hard not to scream. 'It's really important.'

'She went to buy a postcard.' The granny pointed to a stall just down the road. 'She seemed ever so upset.'

I lunged on, picked out every uneven paving stone on the way to the stall. But the only people there were a couple of bloody tourists.

'Excuse me,' I said, 'sorry to butt in, but . . .'

'Hey, I think we were next.'

'I'm sure you were. But this is an emergency.'

'An emergency?' The tourist looked confused. 'How can buying a postcard be an emergency?'

'Listen, mate,' I turned to the seller. 'Did you just

sell a card to a girl just now? Camera bag? Long black hair?'

'Yeah, just a minute ago. Seemed in a bit of a hurry.' The postcard seller was wearing a baseball cap, which he pushed up with his thumb. 'Asked her how long she was staying in Brighton for. She said about five minutes. Said she was going to write her postcard, have a cup of coffee at her favourite pub . . .'

'. . . Barney O'Blarneys,' we said together.

'You know it?' The seller asked.

How was I ever going to make it? Lauren had a five minute start on me. And a car. And I was so tired, I couldn't even will myself to run. All I could do was jog for a bit, then walk, then jog a bit more, through the Pavilion Gardens, and on until at last I saw the pub. I swung in, to see a barmaid clearing away a cup of coffee.

'Lauren?' I looked round, with depressing familiarity. Nothing. 'Let me guess. I just missed her.'

'Just a moment ago,' the barmaid said, as I collapsed in a heap, trying to catch my breath. 'Had a cup of coffee, wrote a postcard. She looked a bit weird, a bit strung out. Is she all right?'

'No time to explain,' I said. 'Did she say where she was going?'

'Out of town. I asked her if she wanted me to post the postcard for her, but she said, no, she could drop it off on her way.'

Drop it off? On the way out of town? I wondered who she knew who lived on the way out of town. And then I realised.

Me.

23

Will,

    By the time you read this, I'll be gone, but I couldn't leave without saying goodbye. I've just got to escape from Brighton for a bit, go away and get my head together. Maybe I'll come back, maybe I won't, but wherever I end up, I won't forget you. Like the song says, you're special cos you're different . . .

    Lauren xxx

I'd missed her. I'd missed her by seconds, but it might as well have been hours. For nobody ever remembers who comes second in life. And at least if I'd missed her by hours, I wouldn't have had to face the sight of her driving off into the distance.

Fuck.

I had nearly killed myself. I was so focused on catching Lauren that I'd run into the road, causing a bus to crunch on its brakes and slither to a halt just inches from my face. It didn't hit me, though the horn almost shattered my eardrums. I noticed the number and the destination, and realised it would be heading past my house. *It wasn't there to kill me, it was there to save my life.*

And the man swearing at me from behind the windscreen wasn't Death disguised by driver's hat and moustache, but my Guardian Angel.

Does exercise always addle the mind like this?

'You, sir, are sent from heaven,' I said as I climbed aboard.

'You, fuckface, owe me seventy pee.'

'I'll give you a pound if you put your foot on it.'

'I'll give you a smack if you don't fucking sit down.'

He lurched the bus forwards. Normally I'd have thought it was deliberate, a ploy to throw me off balance, but today I knew the bus driver was on my side. We crashed along, ignoring such minor inconveniences as zebra crossings or picking up passengers.

We reached my house. My heart soared. Lauren's car was sitting there in the drive. I'd made it.

But then the bastard bus driver let her out.

'In you come, darling,' he leered. 'I'll sit up your rear anytime you like.'

I couldn't believe it was happening. But it was. Lauren waved, not at me, but at the lecherous leech behind the wheel, who said, 'Phwor. I'll remember you for later.' As final sightings went, it couldn't have been more tarnished. I shouted at the driver to open the door, but by the time he did it was too late, and as I ran down the street I had a sad, sinking feeling of inevitability, I wasn't going to make it. And I didn't. I stared at the space where her car had been, then turned away, trudged back to see what the postcard said.

*

It was so cruel. So unfair. I went to bed with my clothes on, shut the curtains and went to sleep. When I woke up, I felt hollow. It was like someone had died. I thought about staying in bed, and two months earlier I probably would have done. But instead I forced myself to get up, and found something to do. You've got to keep believing in yourself, Lauren had said, and she was right. I remembered something else Lauren had said, something she'd suggested to me on the beach at New Year. 'I think you should resolve to do something adventurous. You know, like travel somewhere exciting.' And I thought, Yeah, that's exactly what I should do.

I was gutted about Lauren but at the same time, I wanted to prove to myself that I could get on with things. And Lauren, I thought, would have been proud too. The fact that I was doing something she had suggested felt good as well. In some small way, Lauren was there with me. I rewrote my CV and applied for every job I could find in the local paper, so I could start saving up the cash. I went to the library and got out travel guides for all the most faraway places I could find. I bought a world map, and started plotting possible routes with drawing pins and pieces of string.

Three days later, someone started knocking on the door. I ignored it. The knocking didn't stop. On and on it went. Please go away, I thought. And then I heard a familiar voice shouting through the letterbox.

Danny.

'Will, I know you're in there. Come and answer the door. I'm not leaving until you do.'

The *gig*. Shit. His big chance and I'd buggered it.

'Are you going to hit me?' I shouted bravely through the woodwork.

'Are you going to hit me?' Danny shouted back.

I looked through the window. Danny smiled at me apologetically.

'Why would I want to hit you?' I asked, opening the door on the chain.

'I've, well, um . . .' Danny's left hand was scratching at his jeans.

'What?'

Danny spat it out. 'I've got a record contract.'

It went something like this, Danny explained, once I'd let him in. When me and Rich had disappeared, everyone assumed we'd gone off drinking or something. But the nearer the gig got, the more worried they'd become. And when we still didn't show, Lauren had rung the police, to see if they knew anything, and found out we were in the cells. She'd pleaded for us to be let out, but the guy on the desk was having none of it. We were in for the night, and that was that. So they'd gone to the promoter and told him the gig was off.

'He must have been furious,' I said.

'You bet,' said Danny, stirring his tea. 'So furious he started waving contracts at us, threatening to sue us for thousands.'

'So what did you do?'

'It was Lauren's idea. She said I should go on stage, do it acoustic, sing some of our stuff, some of my mum's songs. I didn't even know she knew about my mum.'

'Yeah, she's got some of her records,' I explained.

'Right. Well, I said no one's going to be interested in that, but she persuaded me, said my mum was cool. So I did. I've never been so nervous in all my life, Will, just me and an acoustic guitar out there. So I go on stage, and the place is packed. I apologise for the change of programme and start playing.'

'And?'

'Well, some of the audience were pissed off. There were a couple of *Socialist Worker* types there, waiting for you after that article in *Melody Maker*. They left, but most of the others stayed and seemed to like it. Then at the end, this bloke comes up, looks like a complete loon, mad professor hair, old leather jacket, bizarre pair of glasses. Anyway, he said he knew my mum, that he used to be a promoter in the sixties, put my mum on a few times. Was a really big fan.

'We get talking. He works for a record company now, the one my mum used to be on. Says they've got all these unreleased recordings, bits of her just singing on her own, things like that. This was like, wow. So I said I'd really like to hear them. But he said what *he'd* really like is to hear my mum singing, with me playing along on guitar. And then he offered me a deal.'

'Danny,' I said. 'That's brilliant.'

'You don't mind?' Danny asked. 'I was worried you'd be cross with me.'

'I think it's fantastic,' I said. 'I mean, it was your music that made the band. And it's not as if there's much of a band left anyway. Oh, I'm really chuffed for you.'

And I was. I felt a tinge of sadness that I wasn't involved, but I couldn't have any complaints. He was a natural. He deserved it.

'It's going to be weird,' Danny said. 'You know, hearing all these new songs and that. I'm going down to the studio tomorrow, to hear them. Steve, that's the bloke's name, he says there's even a couple of songs there about me.'

'I think your mum would be really pleased,' I said.

'Yeah?'

'Yeah,' I said. 'How did Townie take it?'

'He was all right about it, actually. Did you know he's joined Frug?'

'Frug?'

'Yeah, first thing he did when he got back to Brighton was to twat their drummer. I think Loz let him in before he got smacked as well.'

I smiled. 'Maybe Frug have got a hit on their hands after all.'

'So what happened to you?' Danny asked. 'Why did you and Rich fall out?'

'Friedrich,' I corrected.

I told him about Rich being German.

'That's mental. Are you serious?' Danny laughed. 'Is that why you argued?'

'Oh no, I only found out about that afterwards.'

I told him about the song.

'Oh fuck, Will. She fancied you? The *bastard*.'

I showed him the postcard, which I was keeping in my back pocket at all times.

'Nice handwriting,' Danny said.

It was. A sophisticated, arty sort of swirl, not some sad girlie scrawl with little circles instead of dots over the 'i's'. Like Lauren, I thought. Like Lauren.

'I've no idea where she's gone, Dan. She could be anywhere. And I've racked my brains, but I can't think of any way of getting a message to her, to tell her what I feel about her.'

Danny took a swig of his tea. 'Masturbate,' he said.

'I tried last night, to cheer myself up,' I said. 'But I couldn't do it. Not even with Wendy James and Miki from Lush *and* Winona Ryder . . .'

Danny smiled. 'You misheard me. I didn't say masturbate.'

'What did you say, then?'

'The person who's going to solve your problem.'

'And who's that?'

'Mister Bates.'

*

Eleven o'clock, three weeks later. The gentle strains of the love theme from Franco Zeffirelli's 'Romeo and Juliet'. The dulcet tones of a broadcasting legend . . .

'We get a lot of sad stories on Our Tune, tales that . . . make you wonder sometimes if it's worth continuing with life. Stories of hope destroyed, dreams unfulfilled, tales of love unrequited . . . Today's Our Tune combines all three in what I hope . . . will be a message that others will learn and live from.

It concerns a guy called Will, from Brighton. Will, I hope you're listening mate, and hanging on in there. Just writing in to me, I hope . . . has helped you come to terms with what has happened to you over the past few months. By sharing your difficulties with me, and with the millions of listeners of Radio One, I like to think that . . . somehow, you'll be able . . . to find a way to pick up the pieces of your shattered life.

Will, I think he would be the first to admit, has not been the luckiest person when it comes to matters of the heart. His love life has been . . . stillborn for many years now. I guess that some of us have it . . . and some us don't. And if, like Will . . . you're one of those people who don't, then when you do find someone you really care about . . . it makes it that much harder when things fall tragically apart.

Will is a musician, if we can call a bass player such a thing, and last year formed a band with a mate called Rich. It was through Rich that Will met Lauren, a photographer, who was working with the band. When Will met Lauren, he knew immediately that she was someone special. They got on, they talked, they laughed, they had a lot in common. It wasn't long before she . . . no, I can't say that on national radio. Let's say she created a symbol of their love for each other.

So Will did what any young romantic fool would do. He wrote Lauren a love song, to explain just how much she meant to him. It was, well, a beautiful piece of work, and it wasn't long before Lauren fell in love with the person who wrote it. Unfortunately for Will, she was under the impression that the words had been written by Rich. His rival had taken his lyrics *of love to steal the girl that should rightfully have been with him.*

Torn between his love for Lauren and his hopes for the band, Will watched, unable to do anything but see Rich and Lauren's love blossom right under his very nose. It was hard for him to take, but he was glad to see Lauren so happy and didn't want anything to upset that. He tried to turn away, to find a new girl who could capture his heart. But this only confirmed to Will what he already knew. That . . . he was in love with Lauren and nothing was going to change that.

Now Rich was not a man to be trusted, and Lauren . . . taken in by his lies, learned the hard lessons of broken promises. They split up, their relationship no more. Which at last gave Will the opportunity to ask Lauren out.

It would be nice for this story to have a happy ending, for Will and Lauren to be united as they surely deserve to be. But before Will could find Lauren, she made the decision to move on with her life and leave Brighton behind. There is, tragically, no way for Will to get in touch with her, to tell her the truth about those lyrics and about his feelings. For her, Will remains an opportunity she never knew she had. And as for Will, all he can do is to listen to this song, to remind him of what could and what should have been . . .'

So sad. Like the thousands of lorry drivers who had pulled over into lay-bys up and down the country, I had a tear in my eye. I knew the second the needle went down on my chosen song, 'I Want You' by the Beatles, I was liable to burst into floods. Simon Bates must have seen this coming because the record that he played, *my* tune, *our* tune, was not 'I Want You' by the Beatles at all. It was Bryan Adams. 'Everything I Do (Goes On And On For Fucking Ever)'.

That dried the tears up pretty sharpish. Humiliating myself in front of the entire nation for Lauren was one thing. The thought of them thinking I was a Bryan Adams fan was quite another. Apart from anything else, Lauren absolutely hated the song, with its sickly sweet tune and sixteen never-ending weeks at number one. 'Anyone who likes that record,' she'd once said to me, 'must have been romantically neutered at birth.'

I picked up the phone and rang the BBC, demanding to be put through to Simon Bates's studio. They put me through to his assistant.

'This is Will Harding,' I said, 'Today's Our Tune.'

'Oh, Will,' the woman sobbed. 'Such a romantic story, I'm so sorry for you.'

'You've got to take that record off,' I said. 'That's not my tune. I fucking hate that song. I asked for "I Want You". By the Beatles.'

'The Beatles?' The woman sniffed. 'Listen, love, we can't have the listeners deciding the records on this show. We have got a playlist to keep to. Sometimes, we have to edit the choices . . .'

'You mean replace the Beatles with Bryan bloody Adams?'

'. . . make sure that the records fit in with the demographics of our target audience. We're trying to appeal to a younger audience. I don't mean to be rude but the Beatles are not very Fabulous One FM . . .'

*

Lauren didn't ring. I sat by the phone all day, waiting for that call, but it didn't come. My last chance, a long shot but still a chance, a possibility, had failed. *I'd* failed. I sat in the sitting room, not moving from the armchair, as day turned to dusk turned to night. I couldn't think of any other way of working out where she was. Bates was right. Some of us had it, and some of us certainly didn't.

It was about nine o'clock when I flicked on the television, to try and take my mind off things. The news had just started on BBC1, the top story was about some rave in the West Country.

'. . . Police today broke up attempts to hold a huge illegal rave on Chipping Sodbury Common, northeast of Bristol. A huge police presence ensured that travellers and rave-goers could not congregate on the site as intended. However, the convoy, consisting of hundreds of vehicles, failed to disperse, and has been tracked by police all day, growing in size. Police attempted to move it north of Bristol . . .'

The news cut to a map of South Wales and the west of England, complete with arrows showing where the convoy had gone and where it was heading. The words 'illegal rave' and Malvern Hills were mentioned. This is public service broadcasting at its best, I thought.

The only thing they haven't done is say if there are any roadworks to avoid.

The news cut to a report, a mixture of police and locals denouncing the ravers and travellers, and pictures of the convoy, a bizarre mix of clapped-out camper vans, buses, ambulances and army vehicles. There was a shot of a particularly psychedelic-looking bus, full of people waving and smiling at the camera.

And then I saw her. Second from the back, grinning. Looking directly at the camera. Looking directly at me.

Lauren.

21

I drove through the night, arriving at the Malvern Hills at about dawn. From there, finding the rave couldn't have been easier. I just wound my window down, and followed the drumbeat. I came across it on Castlemorton Common, shrouded under a thin layer of morning mist. Silhouettes of marquees, buses, trucks, cars, here there and everywhere as far as the eye could see. And the noise! A dozen thumping drumbeats merging into one, a score of pumping bass lines, snatches of screams and shouts and whistles and keyboards. There were police vans too, a blue ring of steel around the common, and I went white as one of them pulled me over. But all he did was give me advice on where was the best place to park. Unbelievable. I dumped the car and headed on towards the action.

I'd never experienced anything like it. I mean, it was early in the morning, *really* early in the morning, and yet everyone was lively and full of magic beans. The music was pumping away, beats banging in all directions, the sound of the city stuck in the middle of the countryside. The atmosphere, too, was surreal, so much smiling and friendliness. I didn't know a soul, yet strangers kept saying hello, asking how I was. Smells kept on wafting over then disappearing: dope, dew, lavender ... I couldn't move for people offering me drugs; E, speed, Vicks VapoRub, whatever your tipple, you could get it.

A naked child, about five or six with dreadlocks, ran past screaming at the top of his voice, followed a few seconds later by another. Travellers' kids, I thought, looking at the ornately painted buses to my left. There was a police car to my right, full of officers, jammed in by the crowd. A guy with a green mohican was sitting on the bonnet, handing out LSD. People were clapping, waving at the policemen, who just sat there and laughed. There was nothing they could do. It was anarchy, but a gentle, good-humoured one at that.

'THIS IS THE RUSH HOUR! COMING UP FROM THE UNDERGROUND! MAKE SOME NOISE!'

I wandered towards one of the sound systems, a large truck with its tarpaulin side pulled up, displaying a stack of speakers, a DJ and a guy with a microphone jumping up and down. In front was a mass of people, cheering, screaming, blowing whistles, hands pushing the air like they were trying to hold the sky up. Many were wearing sunglasses and T-shirts with drug-abused logos. The T for Texaco had become T for Techno. The F for Fila was replaced with an E for Ecstasy. Smarties had become Smart 'Es. Hoover had become Groover.

'WE'RE ALL IN THE SAME STATE! WE'RE ALL IN THE SAME STATE!'

I'd never seen dance music live before, I'd always

dismissed it as the pressing of a button on a computer. As I stood there and watched the guys on stage, I noticed the skill that was involved. The bloke on the turntables was constantly flipping records, spinning them, splicing them together, adding a snatch of lyrics, a splash of *Sesame Street*, then a bit of dialogue from some seventies cop film. He pumped the beat up and up and up, then suddenly would flood the speakers with long, high keyboard chords, the sound of a choir, at which everyone would cheer and wave their hands in the air frantically. Must be to do with the drugs, I thought, but if it was, that guy knew how to manipulate them.

'COME ON!' yelled the guy with the mike. 'PHIL COLLINS IN THE HOUSE EVERYBODY!'

Phil Collins? The hero of middle-class, middle-aged, middle-of-the-road rock fans everywhere? The man who lit a thousand fag lighters? The Tory-voting, sick-bucket singer, holding centre stage at the biggest illegal rave ever?

Now I've heard everything, I thought.

The version of 'In The Air Tonight' wasn't one I'd come across before. The delicate drums of the original version had been ripped out, replaced with the most driving of beats. And Phil's voice was different too, higher and faster than normal, like he'd just swallowed a shitload of helium. Either that or, and I'll admit my imagination ran riot at this point, he was singing whilst having his bollocks crushed in a mangle. The way the crowd were smiling, maybe they'd had the same thought as well.

I watched the MC head off for a fag break. This was it. No more waiting for things to happen. It was time to make them happen myself. I ran on stage and grabbed my moment.

'Hi!' I shouted into the microphone. 'If I could have your attention for a moment. My name's Will, and I was, er, wondering if you can help me. I'm looking for someone called Lauren. I don't know if anyone can help.'

'Yeah!' The crowd shouted back, blowing their whistles.

'You can? Brilliant!' I felt buoyed by their support, which I needed considering what I was about to say next. 'You see, she's really special, and I want to tell her that I love her.' I felt my face flush ever so slightly red. 'OK, I guess I'd better try and describe her for you. She's tall, quite thin with long black hair, very good-looking, probably has a camera with her.' I looked across at the DJ who was staring at me in bemusement. 'Er, has anyone seen someone resembling that description?'

'Yeah!' The crowd waved back.

'You have? What, today?'

'Yeah!'

'Fantastic,' I said. 'And where did you see her?'

Everyone started waving towards the sky.

'Oh I see, very funny,' I said.

At that point the MC returned, snatching the microphone out of my hand. 'DJ LANKY LEAVING THE HOUSE!' he shouted, pointing at me.

Everyone cheered, and I waved back.

'What do you think this is?' the MC asked, his hand over the mike. 'The Radio One fucking Roadshow?'

'Sorry,' I smiled, trying to sound cool. 'Hey, summer of love right?'

'Yeah right. Pull that stunt again and I'll knock your fucking lights out.'

I searched on, oblivious to the prat I was making of myself at several other sound stages, one in a marquee called Circus Warp, complete with sculptures and murals of weird, disfigured figures. Another one called DiY. The only one I didn't gatecrash was based round this big army-style van, whose logo was a circle with the number twenty-three in it. There was no DJ in sight, just a load of speakers belting out cold, clipped, almost Germanic beats. The crowd seemed too hard for Lauren, and while I didn't mind making an arse of myself, I drew the line at getting beaten up.

There was no sign of Lauren anywhere. It was difficult to be logical, the sun was, by now, beating down, and all the music, the people, were making me more than disorientated. I felt like I was going round in circles, ever decreasing ones, mirroring my chances of finding her. My excitement at seeing her on the television was slowly deflating, as exhaustion started to edge out enthusiasm.

I was gasping. I hadn't eaten or drunk anything for hours. I found a traveller's caravan doling out cups of tea, and a nice bloke selling home-made chocolate brownies, full of funny-tasting chewy bits. I ate one and felt better almost immediately. I found a tree, and sat down in the shade to try and think for a minute. Rich, I decided, had been wrong in his attempts to reinvent rock's wheel. Dance was the big thing we'd been looking for, and whether I liked it or not, this was where it was at. It had what rock had had in the sixties, the spirit of rebellion, and the innate ability to get up parents' noses. Ripping off a few Beatles records made the next generation up feel comfortable, not threatened. And that was not what music was meant to be about.

Brighton Rocks, washed away by the raves.

I pulled Lauren's folded postcard from out of my back pocket. *Don't know where I'm going, but wherever it is, I'll never forget you . . .* I flipped it over, looked at the picture of the Brighton seafront. And then, there in the sky, something I hadn't noticed before. Two birds, silhouetted. I found myself thinking of the Willow Legend, the Chinese tale forever emblazoned on those blue-and-white earthenware plates. The two young lovers, unable to be together in this world, immortalised by the gods as a pair of doves.

That was me and Lauren, I blinked and sighed.

I stood up, walking in a daze in the direction clearest of bodies. And then it happened. There in front of me was Lauren. She was standing to the side of a sound stage, talking to someone, and though there was a crowd of people dancing between us, allowing me only the briefest glimpses, I knew. I just *knew* it was her. It was something about the way the sun reflected off her hair. And the way her shoulder blades angled out of her pale blue T-shirt. And when I saw a hand push a clump of hair behind her ear, I was certain it was her.

My stomach flipped. Butterflies but different once again. Fuck, I thought, what was I going to say? I'd been crashing around for hours, but hadn't spent a second figuring out what I'd actually do if I saw her. Be calm, I thought, as I walked forwards slowly. Just tell her you love her. That's all you have to do. Tell her you love her.

I repeated it to myself as I made my way through the crowd, practising and focusing, focusing and practising, so much so that it wasn't until I was ten metres away that my mind registered who she was talking to.

Shit. I stopped. Stared.

The person Lauren was talking to was Rich.

'Will?'

'*Saucepan?*' Rich's disbelief spread into a sinister grin. 'Well, well, well, what a small fucking world it is.'

I looked at Lauren. She was about as surprised to see me as I was at seeing Rich. My throat felt dry. This couldn't be happening. Rich had beaten me to it.

'We were just talking about you,' Rich slapped his arm around me, dug his fingernails into my arm. There was a hint of undisguised malice in his voice. 'See, this nice policeman in Norwich seemed to be under the impression that I'm some sort of drug dealer. And why did he think this? Because someone set me up, didn't they, Will?' He squeezed my arm a little harder. 'Perhaps you'd like to explain to my girlfriend here what really happened.'

Rich's fingernails were hurting me, but when he said girlfriend my stomach lurched. With the sun beating down and the music banging from every direction, for a moment I thought I might faint. I looked from Rich to Lauren, and the contrast from cold to warm couldn't have been greater. There was something about the way she looked, something in her eyes that snapped me out of it, snapped me into action. Fuck it, I thought. Here goes nothing.

'Entshuldigen sie, bitte,' I said. I blanked Rich, fixed my attention on Lauren. I gulped. 'Lauren, I've come here to tell you something. You see, you were on the TV news last night, and when I saw you, I knew I had to get in the car and drive down here and find you.' Lauren was staring right at me, like she was listening hard and taking it all in, but I couldn't read what she was thinking at all. 'I've spent the whole night looking for you. And the reason I've been looking for you is because I have to tell you how I feel about you. I, I . . .'

'. . . told you so.' Rich interrupted. 'Saucepan here has a crush on you, which is why he set me up with the drugs thing. What he saw was me getting rid of the drugs, as I promised you, and then twisted it to try and *stitch me up.*'

My heart was racing. I looked at Lauren, almost pleading for support. And she nodded. A brief, small one, like it was all she could manage with all the tension, but a nod all the same.

'Rich,' she said firmly. 'Let go of Will. Let him speak.'

Rich and Lauren stared at each other. It was like in that pub in Camden, when Lauren had found out about the drugs. And like then, Rich blinked first. 'Why not?' he said finally. He let go, shoving me in the process. 'Let the lovesick schoolboy make a complete cock of himself.'

Lauren, I could sense, was being irritated by Rich. 'Go on,' she said to me. She reached across and touched my arm. It electrified me.

'I love you,' I said. 'I know that Rich told you he wrote the song "Special", but he lied to you. I wrote the words. They're about how I feel about you.'

Lauren's face flushed red. She stared at me, at Rich, and then away towards the music. She was playing with her hair, pushing clumps behind her ear, pulling and twisting strands. Fuck, I thought. What the fuck is she thinking?

Rich slapped me on the back, started clapping sarcastically. 'Oh that's a good one. That's a really fucking good one. I've heard some bullshit in my time, but I tell you. That one is up there.'

He was trying to wind me up, I knew. And he was succeeding.

'It's *true*,' I snapped. Lauren looked round at me. She was biting her bottom lip so hard it had gone white. I tried to smile at her, calm her like she had me a moment before. 'That was why we had the fight in Norwich. I found out that he'd stolen my words.'

'As I've told you many times,' Rich talked over the top of me. 'I wrote the song after that night we went out for a Chinese. Remember what the fortune cookie said? *In the cost of living, love is priceless.* Hence the line in the song, *If I had a fortune cookie, I could make you rich.*'

'It's kooky, not cookie. It's *If I had a fortune, kooky, I could make you rich.*' I might have been imagining it, but Lauren's pupils seemed to dilate when I said this. 'Because you're kooky, you know, er, different, um, well kooky. And I think that's cool.'

Lauren was twisting a strand of hair around her

finger. She opened her mouth to speak, but nothing came out. She looked at Rich. Rich was speechless too.

'Tell me,' she turned back to face me. 'Tell me about the rest of the song.'

I took a deep breath, then spoke as fast as my heart was racing. *I want to tell you, tell you how I feel, I don't want a model, I'd rather someone real.* Well, that's about when we were in Marks and Spencer with that mannequin. *I want somebody year in, year out to be there, to be with me at midnight with moonlight in her hair.* Do you remember when I bumped into you on New Year's Eve, on the beach? *You drive my heartbeat faster, make me feel good about my flaws, Cast things in a way that I've never seen before.* That was when we went back to your flat and you, well, you know. *I want so much to tell you, and if I can I Will, I Will.* I wanted to tell you but I didn't because I thought you were going out with Rich and I didn't think you'd want me. *And if I can I Will, I Will.* It's repeated at the end not because I'd run out of words, but because it's me. You know, I *Will.*'

I paused for breath, and looked at Lauren. 'I love you,' I said. She blinked, like she might cry. She knows, I thought. She knows I'm telling the truth.

Lauren turned to Rich. Quietly, firmly, she asked, 'Are you lying to me?'

Rich gave an exasperated laugh. And then another. When he spoke, there was an edge of desperation to his voice. 'First that policeman, now you. Is there no one who can't see through Saucepan and his pack of lies? This is exactly what he wants, Lauren. He's jealous of us.

He can't get a girl for himself, so he wants to drag everyone else down to his level. Do you know how long he's been pulling stunts like this? Like, like . . .' he was struggling now, stumbling over his words, '. . . um, well, slipping notes with girl's telephone numbers into my coat pocket, hoping you'd find them . . .'

'Huh? I never did that,' I pleaded at Lauren.

'Of *course* you didn't,' Rich regained a little of his composure, shoved his fabrications into overdrive. 'Just like you didn't stick your revolting porn mags into my bag. Or point drug dealers and groupies in my direction. Or claim you wrote the lyrics I sweated blood over. Or stitch me up to the police. Or the time that you . . .'

'Lauren,' I butted in. 'Did Rich tell you he's German?'

'You see?' Rich laughed, but it wasn't a confident-sounding chuckle. 'The guy can't help himself from making stuff up. *German?* What planet are you coming from?'

'This one,' I replied, and turned to Lauren. 'The police sergeant told me. His real name is Friedrich Jung. All the English stuff is just a front, he doesn't believe any of it at all. There's no such person as Rich Young. Except in this guy's imagination.'

'Well that's just ridiculous,' Rich shook his head. 'You couldn't get more English than me. I've virtually got the Beatles in my bloodstream.'

Lauren looked at Rich, then looked at me. I could see she didn't know what to believe. I needed to do something, and do something fast. And so I did. It wasn't big, it wasn't clever, but it worked.

I stamped on Rich's foot.

'*Ach, scheiße!*' He screamed. '*Verdammt scheiße! Du bist* . . .' He stopped himself, but it was too late.

Lauren had her hand over her mouth. 'Oh my God. You lied.'

'Now look, Lauren,' Rich said desperately. 'I can explain everything . . .'

Lauren shook her head. 'You know, the more I think about it, the more it makes sense that Will wrote those words.' She looked at me. My stomach tightened. 'Yes, yes of course he did. How could you have? You're not like that at all.'

Rich barked in disbelief. 'All right so I'm German. So fucking what? I still wrote you those lyrics.'

'No you didn't,' I said.

'Yes I did,' Rich replied.

'No you didn't,' Lauren said. 'Will did. I believe Will.'

There was a pause, as Rich gathered himself. 'Well fuck you,' he said eventually. 'If you're really that much of a sucker, then all you deserve is a cock as small as Saucepan's . . .'

I could feel anger building up inside me, anger mixed with excitement, at the sense that I had the situation within my grasp. Lauren, I thought, had the briefest hint of a smile, but also looked like she might burst into tears. Rich raced on, his speech laced with bitterness and frustration.

'. . . yeah that's right, I used you, Lauren. I mean, come on, why would someone as good-looking as me go out with you? I only slept with you because I felt sorry for you. I thought it might do your ego some good if you thought you could get off with me, but instead you've decided to sink back down the evolutionary scale to sad fucks, fucks like virgin features here. And I know why you're doing it. It's because if he hasn't slept with anyone else, he won't know how *shit* you really are in bed . . .'

I thought Lauren would slap Rich. I thought, if she doesn't, I'm going to punch him. But instead, Lauren looked at me and sniggered. And I realised that she couldn't care less what Rich said. Her laughter completely threw Rich. His face just crumpled. He looked utterly, utterly wretched.

This, I knew, this *was* my chance.

'Come on, you,' I said, taking Lauren's hand. 'I want to dance.'

A sense of calm washed over me. As I led Lauren into the forest of people, feeling our way through the hands and the whistles, working our way towards the centre, it just felt *right*. I glanced back once at Rich, who was just stuck standing there, staring at us.

'*Auf wiedersehen*,' I waved, as the crowds swallowed him up.

I turned back to Lauren. I stood there and watched, watched her dance to the music, and in each move that she made I felt a rush of elation that she was here, here with me.

I danced back, badly of course, but I didn't care. Lauren spun round, her back to me, her body curving and swerving, reaching for the sky. As I followed her arms up, I saw a butterfly flicker past, its wings glistening like gold in the sunshine. In my stomach, I felt a wonderful sense of calm. My butterflies had finally fluttered away. As the music pumped up to its crescendo, crashing out into large spacey chords, Lauren twisted slowly round until she was facing me. She kissed me once on the lips – softly, firmly – then grinned and carried on moving. I smiled back, and danced.